REWRIT

JEAN C. JOACHIM

Moonlight Books

Happy Reading!

Best wishes,

Jean C. Joachim

Dedication

To my friend, the late Mary Johnson Schultz.
Your joyous reconnection with your birth family inspired this
story.

Acknowledgment

Thank you to my editor, Laura Garland, and my line editor, Nan Sipe and my proofreader, Renee Waring. A special "thank you" to Vicki Locey, and Roz Lee whose encouragement keeps me on track. Thank you to the Joachim men, Larry, David & Steve, and the newest member of our family, Pam, for keeping me grounded and believing in me.

Rewrite the Stars
(Pine Grove Novel #6)
Jean C. Joachim
Chapter One

VOICES SPOKE IN HIS head as he stared at the decrepit old general store.

"No, Flint. Don't!" came a lilting teenager voice.

"Swim, Cassie!"

Flint swore he could still hear the creak of the old Cedar Lake dock under his weight as he ran to the end and jumped, showing off for his girl.

Then the sound of the splash as he hit the water. Laughter, squeals, and kisses from the prettiest girl in Pine Grove as he wrapped his arms around her waist.

And she'd applauded and giggled at every goofy thing he did. Damn. She was fine. Blonde hair like spun gold in the sun, a smile that could melt the meanest mood. And a body from the gods.

They'd dry off and pad over to Cassie's grandmother's store. Vanilla Cokes and homemade brownies topped with ice cream awaited.

But that was sixteen years ago. He shook his head, scattering the memories, returning him to the present. Hot summer sun beat down on the back of his neck. He rubbed the sweat away before shoving the key in the ancient padlock on the abandoned general store.

He opened then removed the lock. The old knob creaked when he turned it.

Dust particles, disturbed by the draft from the open door, danced and glittered in the sunlight. Flint stepped in.

"It needs work. But the bones are good. The floor? Refinishing." He turned his gaze to the shelves. "They're sturdy. Just need dusting."

He spoke aloud, though there was no one there.

"Ten years unoccupied and still standing. It's a friggin' miracle."

Flint spied a grimy red kickball in the corner. He bent down and picked it up.

"Cassie, I'm gonna give you one more chance. Your last chance to fix this place up."

Flint ran a finger through the dust on the counter. He sneezed then yanked a handkerchief out of his back pocket.

"Yeah, you're a big Broadway star. I probably won't get to see you, but I can't take Gram's place down without trying to reach you. I'll be at the stage door on Saturday. Like every other guy who's got the hots for you. It's your last chance."

Flint tucked the ball under his arm and left the building. He connected the padlock and walked to his truck. After tossing the ball in the back, he got behind the wheel. He started the motor then sat for a moment and stared at the old building. Happy memories of working there with Cassie flitted through his brain.

He could hear Gram Meacham. "Don't eat the candy. That's to sell. If you work hard, I'll give you some of your favorite. Okay?"

As the engine warmed up, he smiled. He'd loved the old lady. Never having a grandmother himself, he'd latched on to her as if she were his own. She'd doted on him, offering him brownies and the world's best blueberry muffins. His mouth watered as he recalled them, still warm from the oven. Even the Cozy Café didn't have muffins as good as Gram Meacham's.

The sound of the fire alarm broke through his reverie. Being a volunteer fireman, he had to go. Flint threw his truck in gear and headed for the firehouse.

Would Cassie give a damn about the old place? Probably not. But he had to try, had to give his old friend a chance to redeem it, and herself. She'd left Pine Grove at sixteen, never to return, never to communicate with him again.

Of course, he'd never told her how deeply he'd fallen for her. Waste of time, he'd told himself a thousand times. And for the last sixteen years, his heart had remained constant. He'd even been engaged three times but never made it to "I do." He sighed. Maybe this was his last chance, too.

When he got to the station, Gavin Dailey started the fire engine. "Let's go!"

Flint grabbed a coat and hat from a hook inside and jumped on the truck. His mind turned away from the tempting image of Cassie Wells and focused on the present.

"The Marshall's." Gavin put the vehicle in gear and stepped on the gas. Then he switched on the flashing lights and the siren.

Work at Flint's printing company would have to wait. He raised his gaze, saw smoke billowing into the air. It looked bigger than he'd hoped. A nice little gas grill fire that had gotten out of hand would've been a piece of cake. But gray smoke rose into the air, blanketing half the house. He steeled himself for a fight.

In the distance, another fire engine screamed. He said a brief prayer and prepared himself to face what awaited—a fire too big for one truck.

CASSANDRA WELLS SAT at the dressing table in her small room backstage at the Power Theatre. She blotted the oil on her face with a small sponge then sighed. Tonight would be the last performance of "Shooting Star," a romantic suspense musical. She couldn't complain. The show had busted box office records for four years. While she'd sweated her ass off show after show as a musical theatre performer—not a dramatic actress—she didn't miss the grueling day-after-day dancing of a long-running show. Or pampering her voice for months on end and then singing the same songs night after night.

For sixteen years, she ate, drank, and slept performing. Rising late, quick breakfast, then heading to the theatre until lunch had been her routine. She hadn't seen a movie or finished a book since this show opened. She'd been nominated for an Academy Award for a movie she did five years ago, won a Tony for this play, and had been offered this role in the movie version. Great success didn't happen to people who goofed off or had a life.

She recalled her mother wondering aloud how her daughter managed to keep a relationship going with the sexy British film star Basil Evans-White.

"I can't believe you actually got engaged. Have you two ever been in the same city for more than a weekend?"

"Not spending too much time together keeps us from getting bored."

Caroline Wells snorted. "And keeps it sexy, too, I'll bet."

"Mother!"

Cassie had turned away to hide her blush, but once again her mother was spot-on. Having your mother know you so well alternated between great and downright annoying.

Staring into the mirror, her eyes zeroed in on the dark circles carefully hidden beneath heavy theatrical makeup. No one could see them, but Cassie knew they were there. Her shoulders slumped under the weight of her life, as if she carried an anvil on her back.

The door flew open, bouncing off the wall with a bang, and her quiet moment evaporated as her fiancé, mother, brother, and his wife burst in. Eating up every square inch of space in the small dressing room, they bumped against each other. With the air sucked up by her entourage, Cassie could barely breathe.

"Darling, the first act went great. I have the contract here from Al, but other scripts are pouring in. I guess the word is out this run is over. I haven't had a chance to go through them all, but there are several promising musicals with big directors. You'll have your pick!" Grinning, her mother eased her elegant bones into the only other chair, next to her daughter.

"Mom. Let's finish this first."

"Really, darling. You don't want to sit on these offers. They could go to someone else."

Cassie tried to smile.

"Mom's right," her brother, Brian, said.

Another voice joined theirs. "Sweetheart, there must be something opening in London. We could be there together," Basil Evans-White, her fiancé added.

Cassie tuned them out, reducing their strident voices to background buzz. She stared into her eyes in the mirror. *Who is this woman?* She had no answer. Straightening her shoulders, she pushed the exhaustion out of her body. There would be plenty of time to collapse after the final curtain. In the meantime, she had to suck it up for the millionth time and finish the show.

"Please! Everyone. I need a moment. Do you mind?" Cassie motioned with her hand.

One by one, the others filed out. Last to leave, Basil blew a kiss and closed the door. Cassie let out a sigh. She stretched her arms above her head, took a deep breath, and let it out slowly. Reciting the first speech of the second act brought her back to the present. Pushing to her feet, Cassie exercised while she recited her lines.

Grabbing a bottle of water, she downed it before the telltale knock indicating the start of the second act drew her attention. Blowing out a breath, she opened and closed her mouth, loosening her jaw muscles, pushed her arms out in front of her, shook them out, and responded, "Coming!"

She picked her way through backstage ropes and paraphernalia to stand in the wings, awaiting her cue. When she stepped out onto the stage, the audience burst into applause. The adulation energized Cassie. Like a drug to an addict, the approval of the audience was what she lived for. She morphed into her character and delivered her lines with gusto.

She couldn't believe it. Three standing ovations! Tired beyond belief, she simply wanted it to be over so she could crawl into bed. But the audience had other ideas. They stood until the curtain rose three times. The last time was only for Cassie and Braden Carpenter, her co-star. They clasped hands and bowed again and again in front of the people hungry for more. An intern popped up on the stage to deliver a bouquet of red roses to Cassie. Her co-star disappeared into the wings, leaving her to take her last bow alone.

Finally, the curtain went down and stayed down.

"Oh, thank God," she muttered.

Braden leaned over and kissed her. "Great run, Cassie."

"Thanks." She hugged him then made a beeline for her dressing room. Her entourage had returned, packing the tiny space, awaiting her arrival. She was hugged, kissed, criticized, congratulated, and told what to do next by everyone in the room as she pushed her way through.

Finally seated at her dressing table, she picked up a towelette and wiped it over her cheek. Her mother, Caroline Wells, also her agent, yapped on and on about the next movie or the next show, or whatever. Cassie didn't listen. The buzzing gave her a headache. She simply couldn't concentrate on the torrent of words flying around the

room. Snatches of conversations found their way into her consciousness. Caroline talking to Brian, and then Basil chimed in.

Cassie closed her eyes for a moment, rubbed her temples, then
scrubbed her face with the damp cloth. She had to get away.

"Not so hard, darling! You'll ruin your perfect skin," Caroline
said, reaching for her daughter's wrist. Cassie pulled away. Shooting
daggers with her eyes at her mother, Cassie finished cleaning the
stage makeup off then pushed to her feet.

"Out! Everyone! I have to change."

"Even me?" Basil raised his eyebrows.

"Yes."

"But, sweetheart—"

"Out! All of you." She ushered them through the door then
shut it. As if they'd all push their way in again, she leaned her back
against it and closed her eyes. Alone, finally. But it wouldn't last. She
stripped off her costume, hung it carefully on the rack, and pulled on
black leggings and a big, white, silk shirt.

"Wear black leggings, dear. They'll make your legs look slimmer,"
her mother had advised.

After stuffing her feet into ballet slippers, she paused long
enough to apply a touch of blush to her cheeks and lipstick. It was
too warm outside to wear her long sweater. So she yanked it from the
rack and stuffed it into her dance bag.

Squaring her shoulders, Cassie pasted a smile on her face. One
more hurdle before she could collapse—the fans waiting outside. She
headed there, telling herself this was the last time. She ran past her
family and shoved the back door open. People clustered around the
entrance applauded and cheered. She stood on a small metal plat-
form a few feet above.

Something flew toward her. She ducked but not in time. A big,
rubber ball bounced up and knocked her shoulder. She dropped the
bag and grabbed the ball. Damn! Studying it, she opened then closed

her mouth. Memories of kickball games on late summers' eves flitted through her brain.

"Can I have your autograph?" A man interrupted her thoughts.

"Of course." Cassie tucked the ball under her arm and scrawled her name. Then she looked up, her gaze shooting across the crowd to a man standing thirty feet away.

"Oh my God. Really? Is it you?" She pushed her way through the admiring throng.

The man stared back.

"Flint McKay? Is it really you?" Cassie stopped just shy of touching him.

A grin spread across his face. "Cassie Wells. Good to see you."

"You haven't changed."

"You have. You look great." He squeezed her shoulder.

The crowd swarmed over her again.

"Don't leave," she shouted over several heads.

"I won't." Flint moved to the side and leaned a shoulder against the building. Her gaze traveled the length of his lean, rangy form.

"Take this," she shouted, hurling the ball.

He caught it. She signed every autograph. When the people left, Cassie stood in front of him. "What are you doing here?"

His eyebrows shot up. "I need to talk to you."

"Really? Why now?"

Voices from her entourage, coming from the stage door, caught up with them. Cassie hooked her arm through Flint's.

"This is Flint McKay. He's an old friend. We're going to grab a burger. I'll see you later," she said, urging him forward. He followed her lead. "Hurry," she whispered, "before they catch up."

They scurried down the alley, disappeared around a corner, and got lost in the crowd on Eighth Avenue.

"I know a little place where no one famous ever goes."

"Sounds good."

They crossed the avenue and descended the stairs of Tuck's Hide-away, below ground level. Flint opened the door for her. She picked a small table in a dark corner and eased into a chair. Sitting next to her, he took her hand for a moment then dropped it.

A waiter plopped two menus on the table. "Be right back."

Cassie faced Flint. "Okay. Now, why are you here?"

FLINT CLEARED HIS THROAT. He'd spent the entire ride on the bus choosing his words, going over and over what he had to say. But when confronted by her beauty, especially those clear-blue eyes staring into his, his mind went blank.

Her radiant smile lit up the dim atmosphere of the restaurant. She took his breath away, as she had when he was a teenager. But they lived worlds apart. He had no idea what her life was like now, except for the few snippets he'd found online on gossip websites.

His gaze dropped to the bright, shiny diamond twinkling in the flickering light of the little candle on their table. He swallowed. Right. Cassandra Wells was engaged to Basil Evans-Something, wild-ly successful British actor. So, what the hell was she doing here with him? Or what was he, Flint McKay, Mr. Nobody, doing here with a star of Broadway and movies?

"Well?" She tipped her chin up, her gaze darted to the window and back. She drummed her fingers on the table.

"It's about Gram's general store."

"What?" Her eyes widened.

"Gram's general store." Once the words were out, he realized how feeble they sounded. After her grandmother had died, the town had notified Cassie—or said they did. She never responded, so the store was put up for auction. Flint had bought it for a pittance, which was good because it wasn't even worth what he'd paid.

Suddenly, he realized it wasn't that Cassie had been too busy with her career to get in touch with the town of Pine Grove about the store. She hadn't given a flying fuck. Humiliation washed over him. What was he doing here?

Convinced she had an emotional connection to the old shop, he'd gone out of his way to keep the place decent enough to remain standing, holding on to it until she got around to returning to claim her property.

One look at her face, and it became apparent she simply didn't care and had no idea what he was talking about. The desire to escape overwhelmed him. He pushed to his feet.

"This was a mistake. I'm sorry. Sorry to waste your time."

She tugged on his sleeve. "Where the hell do you think you're going?"

"Home." He leaned over and kissed the top of her head. "Take care. Good luck. Again, sorry to bother you."

"Sit down!" Fire flashed in her eyes.

He stopped.

"Sit down! Damn it! You're not leaving until you tell me what you came here to say."

"This was a mistake."

"I ditched my mother, my brother, and my fiancé to be with you. You're not brushing me off. Don't be an asshole. Sit down."

When the waiter returned, Cassie faced him. "I'll have a vodka tonic and a cheeseburger."

Flint took his seat. "Same."

"Thanks," the man said, collecting the menus.

"Now. Where were we? Gram's store? What about Gram's store?"

The waiter delivered their drinks. Cassie took a big sip.

Flint took a deep breath. Truth time. Total truth.

"When the town didn't hear from you, they put the place up for auction. I bought it for pennies on the dollar."

"So you want me to reimburse you? How much?" She rummaged in her handbag. Flint's hand stopped hers.

"No." If she had shot an arrow directly into his heart, it wouldn't hurt as much as her words. Fuck. This wasn't about money. Not by a long shot.

"Then what do you want? The suspense is killing me."

He reached into the breast pocket of his suit jacket and slapped a photo on the table. Anger bubbled up in his chest, tightening his muscles. "I want to know if you want the place. If you do, it needs work. Serious work. I'll help you get it in shape. If you don't want it, I'll let the town demolish it, like they want to. We have to either fix it or let it go."

"Demolish? Like destroy?"

He nodded.

"Oh no. No. I don't think so."

"This is your last chance. Words aren't enough."

"Money?" She raised her gaze to lock with his.

"Among other things."

"How much?"

"I have no idea."

"So you come here to present...nothing? You don't have the facts. Come back when you do." She pushed to her feet. The waiter appeared, putting her plate down. "Can you bag it to go?"

"Sure." He leaned over to pick up the plate.

"She's only kidding. Aren't you, dear?" Flint shot her a steely stare. "She'll eat it here." He grabbed her forearm in a firm grip. "Sit down, sweetheart." The last word dripped sarcasm.

Cassie obeyed.

The waiter put Flint's food in front of him. "Anything else?"

"Another round?" Cassie raised cool eyes to Flint.

"Sure. I'm not driving."

WHILE FLINT TOOK A big bite of his burger, Cassie picked up the photo. She held it close to the candle to see. Her stomach clenched at the sight of the boarded-up old store. A stinging at the backs of her eyes warned her of tears. Nope. Not gonna cry.

"What happened?" She studied the picture.

"Time happened. It's been ten years since Gram passed and sixteen since you were last there."

"I know."

"Buildings deteriorate if no one lives in 'em."

"I guess." The shabbiness of the structure, visible in the dim light, shocked her. She hadn't thought about the place in years. Brian, her brother, had told her to forget about it. But he hadn't been the one to spend every summer there with her biological grandmother, working in the store, or swimming in Cedar Lake with her Pine Grove friends.

Brian was Caroline and Parker Wells' biological child. By the time they got around to wanting a second one, five years later, they were set on a girl. So they adopted Cassandra. Her mother had died in childbirth, and she never knew who her father was. Cassie's biological grandmother, Frances Meacham, had begged for visitation rights. Caroline and Parker agreed to send her to Pine Grove every summer to live with Frances.

Those summers, working in the general store, had been magical and a respite from dancing and singing lessons and acting classes. Caroline had groomed her daughter from age three to become a stunning actress, and Cassie hadn't disappointed.

At sixteen, she got her first break—a movie role. With her career launched, she left Pine Grove, never to return. On lonely nights in her small hotel room, Cassie would close her eyes and relive those beautiful days of kickball games, nickel candy, homemade ice cream, and skinny-dipping with her first love, Flint McKay.

"What do you want from me? Money? I'll contribute to the renovation." She dug into her handbag.

"You're not listening."

She stopped. "Then what?"

"I want you to come to Pine Grove. See the place. Then decide, if you want it, whether to sell it or let it be demolished."

"Really? You might as well ask me to fly to the moon."

"Why is this such a big fucking deal? You're here in New York. Pine Grove is two hours away."

"Typical of somebody who doesn't know this business. I have a schedule."

"You've finished the play. You want me to believe you can't take off a day or two?"

"Bingo."

Flint shifted in his seat and cast his gaze to his plate.

"My mother's my manager. She's got me booked until I'm sixty."

"It's your life, Cassie. You call the shots."

Cassie gave a snort. "That's what you think. And, by the way, nobody calls me that anymore."

Flint cocked an eyebrow. "Well, pardon me, Ms. Wells."

They sat, eating in silence. Flint finished first. He reached in his pocket, pulled two twenties from his wallet, and rose to his feet.

"Good to see you, Cassie. Good luck." He dropped the bills on the table and headed for the door.

"I've got this."

"Nope. You can't even control your own life. You sure as hell can't control mine."

Before she could reply, he pushed out the door and climbed the steps. Spying the kickball, she raced after him, hollering down the street.

"The kickball!"

He faced her. "Keep it! A souvenir."

He'd left her speechless. She watched until he turned the corner. Cassie went back to her table, but her appetite had gone south. Her mother would be proud knowing she only ate a quarter of her burger. *Gotta keep your weight down.* Caroline's words echoed in Cassie's head. She added ten bucks to the tip and headed for the street.

It was late. Her footsteps echoed on the damp pavement as a light rain fell. Her hair frizzed, and her spirits drooped. No one who passed by recognized her. Grateful, she kept her gaze straight ahead. Even blinking rapidly couldn't stem the tide of tears pouring down her face.

Exhaustion gripped her. Her back and shoulders ached. Her hotel suite was only two blocks away. She picked up her pace, anxious to get in bed and lose herself in dreamless sleep.

She huddled in a corner of the elevator as it climbed to the top floor.

"Say, aren't you...?" a man started. But the woman with him tugged on his sleeve and shook her head. "Oh. Sorry," he mumbled.

Thank God. No, she wasn't Cassandra Wells, star of stage and screen. She was little Cassie Wells, clerk at Meacham's General Store and lover to a fireman.

Chapter Two

F lint walked to the bus station. Numb, he didn't feel the rain. He had been sharing a table with the famous Cassandra Wells in a hole-in-the-wall restaurant. Him, Flint McKay, Mr. Nobody from Pine Grove. He could hardly breathe.

Yet when she opened her mouth, she became Cassie again. Feelings he'd stuffed so far down inside he didn't even know they still existed surfaced. Like a geyser, they shot up through him, taking over his mind and body.

Sassy little Cassie Wells was as smart-mouthed and beautiful as ever. Sentences starting with "Remember the time..." had buzzed through his brain, but he'd ignored them. He didn't traipse all the way to New York to talk about old times. He'd had a purpose, a mission, even if he didn't remember what it was. Oh, yes, the general store.

He snorted. What a chump he'd been. He'd actually expected Cassie to give enough of a shit about the place to come home with him on the bus. He stopped. Home. Yeah, it was still his home, but it had been her home, too. At least for a little while.

She had a life, which was more than he could say for himself. Busy with the printshop and rescuing people, he hadn't been able to unlock his heart in sixteen years. He'd tried. He'd been engaged three times, and each time he'd crapped out.

Sure, he'd become the town joke.

"I hear it's gonna rain and Flint McKay is getting engaged, again."

"I understand Homer's is giving Flint McKay a discount on bachelor parties."

Ha-ha. So funny. Not! Ashamed to recall, he'd even left one lady at the altar. Flint McKay's heart had stopped working where women were concerned. And now Cassie was engaged—to a guy Flint could never compete with. So any chance with her was kaput, finished, over, nonexistent.

He hadn't expected to feel anything when he saw her. In fact, he'd convinced himself she wouldn't even recognize him, let alone sneak out to have dinner with him. Sure. He shook his head. One thing he promised, he'd never lie to himself. Nope, he'd been so tongue-tied because he still loved her.

Damn. He stopped. No way, he couldn't love her. It was emotional suicide to have feelings for the famous Cassandra Wells. He refused. He simply would not love her. Entering the bus station, he made up his mind to forget about her. What about the general store? He'd figure it out when he got home, when he wasn't under the spell cast by Cassie Wells.

He took a window seat on the bus to Pine Grove and closed his eyes. Memories of hot, languid days cooled by the large ceiling fan in the store came to mind. His mouth watered as the image of Swirls, caramel candy with vanilla filling, danced through his head. He shifted in his seat, looked out the window, then tried again to sleep.

This time another mental image grabbed his attention. Their last summer together had been the hottest on every level. Record-breaking heat waves drove them to the lake.

"I dare you," Flint shouted from the water.

"Oh? Right. You first." Cassie stood in her two-piece bathing suit, feet shoulder width apart, hands on hips.

"You will then?"

She'd nodded.

Flint had vaulted himself out of the lake in two seconds. He stripped off his trunks, faced her, took a bow, then jumped into the water.

He surfaced, brushing his hair back from his forehead. "Now you."

She'd hesitated.

"Aw, come on. You gonna chicken out now?"

"I have a lot more to show. I have to take off two pieces."

"Yeah. Exactly the way I like it." He'd sniggered.

She stuck out her tongue then did a little striptease. He smiled at the memory. Her body was incredible. From what he'd seen at dinner, it hadn't changed. After she took off her bottoms, she'd turned away from him to unfasten her top, slapped her butt, whipped around, and jumped in, swimming to the float.

He'd laughed and joined her. She grasped the ladder for support and kissed him until he didn't know if it was night or day. It had been the first day they'd ever made love. Cassie had been a virgin. Flint had had a quickie or two in the backseat of his car a couple of times but didn't know shit about making love. During the summer, they learned together. He'd hoped the summer would last forever. In the third week of August, Cassie's mother got the call. Caroline drove up and whisked her daughter away.

It had been the last time he'd seen her, except in his dreams.

CASSIE FELL ON HER bed, fully clothed. Exhaustion sapped her energy. Too tired to get undressed, she simply lay there. Then came a knock. Dragging herself upright, she slunk to the door. A steady stream of people poured through.

"It's about time! Where have you been?" Caroline shot a look at her daughter.

"Mom, please."

"I have some papers for you to sign." Brian whipped out a pen.

"I'm leaving some scripts here for you." Caroline put a small stack of papers on the bureau.

"I'm leaving for London on Thursday." Basil sidled up next to her and snaked an arm around her waist. "How about getting rid of these people?" he whispered.

"If you figure out how, let me know."

The phone rang. Caroline answered. "For you, Cassie."

"What a surprise. A call for me on *my* room phone." She grabbed it from her mother.

"Cassie, darling."

"Uncle Denny?"

"Guilty as charged."

"How wonderful to hear from you."

"I thought you might want to escape. I'm leaving for the West Coast, but my suite at The Pierre is paid up for the next week. Why don't you come over here and escape all the vermin who are after you?"

"That's not a nice way to talk about your sister."

"I love Caroline, but she's ferocious. So? Are you coming?"

"I'll be there in an hour."

"Splendid. I'll tell George to alert the concierge. Take care, darling. Wonderful performance."

"Thank you. Love you."

"Love you, too. Sweetie."

She hung up the phone. "Could I have a little privacy here?"

The people in the room smirked and made salacious comments. Basil grinned and closed the door after the throng had left.

"Go pack."

"Where am I going?"

"To Uncle Denny's suite at The Pierre."

"You're kidding?"

"I never kid about The Pierre. Scoot. Meet you in the lobby in forty-five minutes."

He kissed her then left.

Cassie whirled around the room like a tornado, gathering up her belongings and slamming them into her suitcases. No time to call for a bellboy. She lugged the heavy luggage herself. *Maybe that's where the word luggage came from?* Chuckling at her witticism, she hauled ass down to the lobby. Basil waited.

"Hurry up. We've got a table reserved for seven o'clock." Caroline fastened her vise-like grip on her daughter's arm. Cassie twisted her way free.

"Nope. See you, Mom." She headed for the door. Following her, Basil juggled her bags and his to the street.

"What do you mean?" Caroline dogged their steps.

"Taxi?" Cassie waved. A yellow cab pulled up. The driver jumped out and loaded their things in the trunk. Basil held the door.

"Let go, Mom."

"Not until you tell me where you're going." Caroline squeezed harder.

Cassie did a defensive move, chopping her hand sideways to her mother's wrist.

"Ow!" She grabbed her arm.

"Sorry. Bye, Mom. See you...whenever." Cassie slid across the seat, Basil followed, shutting the door. He leaned forward and whispered the destination to the cabbie. Cassie sat back, watching her mother stomp her foot and swear.

"Your mother is furious."

"She'll get over it."

"You're so independent." Basil took her hand in both of his.

"Me? You're joking, right? I'm the least independent person I know. Yes, Mom, No, Mom. Whatever you say. Do another rehearsal? Of course. Read another script? Why not?"

"She runs your career like a well-oiled machine."

"Machine being the operative word. I'm tired, Basil. I've done it all. Broadway. Movies. I'm running on empty."

"So take a few weeks off and then start something fabulous. Can you do a show in London? We could be together." He put his arm around her and drew her closer.

"No. No more shows. No movies. I need to rest."

"Not do another show? The famous Cassandra Wells?"

"I was thinking of another kind of production." She kissed his cheek.

"I hope it includes me," he whispered.

"Couldn't do it without you."

The taxi pulled up in front of The Pierre. The doorman opened the car door. The driver retrieved the bags from the trunk.

"Checking in, ma'am?" the concierge asked.

"No. Going to Denny Hardin's suite. We're his guests."

"Right this way. I'll send your luggage up."

They got the key at the front desk and took the elevator to the Deluxe Grand Suite. Basil opened the door.

"Why do I feel like I should carry you over the threshold?"

Cassie grinned, toed off her shoes, and sank her toes into the two-inch-thick light-gray carpet. She padded across the cavernous living room to the six-foot windows.

"Basil, the view! Oh, the view." She plopped down on the window seat.

"A drink, darling?"

She nodded.

"Vodka tonic?"

"Heaven." She sighed.

While he tended the bar, she gazed out over the abundant lights of Manhattan dazzling and brilliant. A cool glass pressed against her fingers. She gripped it and tipped her chin up. Basil kissed her then closed his free hand around her breast.

"Can you read my mind, Cassandra?" His voice soft and coaxing gave her chills.

"Like a book, darling. Like a book." She put the glass down and rose to be enveloped in his arms.

CASSIE STRETCHED AND opened her eyes. The unfamiliar room was cold and pitch black. A grunt from a warm, naked body next to her reminded her Basil had spent the night. Rolling onto her side, she backed toward him. Pushing up against his warm skin chased the chill from her bones. He rolled over and slung an arm over her, mumbling something unintelligible.

Barely able to stay awake long enough to make love, Cassie had fallen into a deep sleep as soon as Basil had finished. Blinking, she glanced at the clock. It was two in the morning. Sighing, she pulled the blankets tighter around her. Where the hell was the cold air coming from?

No one opened hotel windows, and it was July. Ah, the air conditioner? The huge bedroom temperature was cold enough to keep meat. Cassie slid across the king-sized bed and grabbed Basil's shirt from the chair. She fastened the buttons and rolled up the sleeves before padding to the window to turn down the air.

Basil was six foot one and Cassie only five foot three. The shirt hung to her knees. Opening the closet, she spied a blanket and pulled it down. Yawning, she continued into the living room and switched on a lamp.

She plucked the card denoting hotel services from the coffee table and headed for the window seat. The night was dark. The bright lights of apartments were fewer than when she'd arrived, but there were enough to make the city glow.

Hunger gripped her belly. She'd not finished the burger she'd had with Flint. Glancing down, she smiled to see 24-hour in-room dining. Perfect! She found a menu and picked up the phone.

She ordered a shrimp cocktail, another burger with fries, a Coke, and chocolate lava cake for dessert. When she hung up, her mouth watered. Spreading the blanket out, she snuggled it around her on the sofa and curled up.

Although there were magazines galore, her thoughts turned to her life, instead. While her mother pushed her to continue her career at breakneck speed, Cassie questioned the plans. In the quiet of the night, she could ponder her future without interruption.

A discreet knock on the door roused her. She fished a ten-dollar bill from her wallet and answered.

"Dining room, miss?"

"No. The coffee table. Please."

"Of course."

The waiter wheeled in the cart and set up the silverware. She tipped him and eyed the food. Her choices reflected her decision. She no longer cared what she ate because she didn't intend to stay so skinny. Her performing days were over—at least for now. She needed a life, a real life, like other people had. And Basil was the man to give it to her.

Although she hadn't known him long, their chemistry had been off the charts. Never having more than two days together had proved tortuous. So, he'd proposed, mostly to ease her nerves and reassure her he'd be there for her whenever she could find a spare day or two.

They'd sink deep into discussions of the theatre and movies, of directors and producers. They had so much in common, love was taken for granted. Now, the time to take their relationship to the next level had arrived.

Pleased with her decision, Cassie pushed out concerns about how to tell her mother and dreamed of her future with her handsome husband in a roomy country house. Should they have one in England or the States? Why not both? Maybe even the yellow-and-white Victorian she'd dreamt about in her youth in Pine Grove. She and Basil had enough money to live wherever they wanted.

After finishing the shrimp, she licked her fingers and took a big bite of the burger. Warmth grew inside her. Of course, Basil would agree with her plans. A new happiness gripped her, and she refused to question it. After finishing the dessert, Cassie's stomach protested. Bloated and a bit sick, she took an antacid and crawled into bed.

She snuggled up to a sleeping Basil and closed her eyes. The smile never left her lips. How lucky was she? A skyrocketing career with accolades wherever she turned and now the ideal man to build a life with. Gratitude flowed in her veins. She fell asleep, enveloped in the warmth of her lover's body and the luxurious cotton sheets and elegant wool blankets of The Pierre.

Chapter Three

Cassie slept until ten. When she awoke, the bed was empty. Frowning, she yanked the covers down and swung her legs over the side. Still wearing Basil's shirt, she pushed to her feet.

"Well, it's about time." Wearing only a bathrobe and a grin, he lounged in the doorway. "That looks better on you than it does on me."

She laughed.

He approached her. "But it would look even better on the floor." Resting his hands on her shoulders, he bent to kiss her then cupped her cheek. "Hungry?"

"Well, not really."

"I saw those dishes. What time did you get up?"

"About two."

"And ate a full meal? Didn't you eat when you went out with the Neanderthal?"

"Flint? He's a nice guy."

Basil made a face. "Any man who takes you away from me is a dog. I've ordered breakfast. Coffee is here. I'm starving."

She padded behind him to the bathroom. The chrome fixtures glittered so brightly, she almost needed sunglasses. The room was huge. *Big enough for two*. She brushed her teeth and washed her face. Staring into the mirror, she saw Cassie Wells and wondered where Cassandra Wells had gone.

"Here, darling." Basil stood in the doorway, holding a cup of coffee.

"Thank you." She took a sip. "Heaven! Perfect. Just the way I like it."

"I'm good for things outside the bedroom, too." He snickered.

Wasn't he simply adorable, and weren't they the perfect couple? Still sporting his shirt, Cassie sashayed into the living room and plopped down on the sofa, taking care not to spill the java.

"What ever shall we do today, stuck in this magnificent hotel?" He wiggled his eyebrows.

Cassie frowned. "Rain?"

"That leaves no option but to watch dirty movies in the bedroom and make love all day."

Before she could respond, there was a knock. Basil tightened the belt on his dressing gown and headed for the door.

The waiter wheeled in a full breakfast and placed it on the square table in the dining room. She sighed. Yes, the suite had its own dining room. He opened the covered dishes to reveal scrambled eggs, bacon, hash browns, and buttered rye toast. He added small pots of jam, a carafe of freshly-squeezed orange juice, and a bowl of fruit salad.

The feast had everything, including another pot of coffee, one of tea, and small pitchers of cream. Basil slipped him a twenty and held his hand out to Cassie. They took their places and ate hearty.

When they'd finished and she was on her third cup of coffee, she cleared her throat.

"Basil, we have to talk."

"Darling. It sounds so serious." His brow furrowed.

"It is. And it isn't."

"Well, which is it?"

"It's about my future plans."

"You mean our future plans."

"Well, yes. Of course."

"Did you find out if any of the scripts your mother's looking at would be opening in London?" He sat back on the sofa, holding his beverage.

"Not exactly."

He cocked an eyebrow.

"I'm not sure I want to do a show in London."

"Why not? We could be together. You know I'm doing *The Inheritance* there. I've signed for six months, depending on ticket sales."

"I know. And it's wonderful for you. But I thought we might pursue something else."

"What?"

She licked her bottom lip and averted her gaze. Why was this so hard? "Marriage?"

"What about it?"

"We've been engaged for a few months. I thought, maybe, we could get married?" She chewed on a nail.

"Get married? Marvelous idea! In London. Between shows." He took her face in his hands and kissed her.

"Between shows?"

"Maybe we could even involve the audience. A one-time thing. A surprise! Even better." Basil rose to his feet and paced the length of the room. "Think of it. We'll have co-opted every other show."

"Get married in the theatre with the audience there, like guests?"

A smile curled his elegant lips. "Perfect, darling. The publicity will be killer."

Cassie pushed to her feet. "I don't want a public wedding."

"It will be huge, fabulous. Everyone will be talking about it for years to come! Come on, darling." Basil nuzzled her neck.

She pushed him away. "No!"

"Why not?"

"I want a private wedding. I want to wear a white dress, carry a bouquet, and be given away by my father."

"That's so, so...conventional."

"It's what I want. What I've dreamt of all my life."

He sighed. "Well, if that's what you want, darling, then that's what it will be."

Cassie smiled up at him. "Thank you."

"And you'll try to find something in London?"

"Uh, well. For my next production, I had something totally different in mind."

"Different?" He rubbed his hands together.

"Yes. I thought we could produce...um...we could produce..." She raised her eyebrows. "Children?"

He stopped moving, turned his head, and stared straight into her eyes. "Children?" His voice was so low she barely heard him.

"Yep. Kids. Uh, two? Two would be enough."

"Two?" This time his eyebrows shot up. "Two spoiled, screaming, stinky little brats?"

Her mouth opened, but no sound came out. Basil pushed to his feet. He strode over to the bar then picked up and put down three different bottles before settling on whiskey. As he poured a stiff drink and took a gulp, she pressed her lips together.

"Whatever made you think I want children?" He turned, glass in hand, to face her.

"Most people want children."

"I don't. Never have. Never will. I want to act. And I want you by my side, as my lover, my leading lady. My wife. Period."

"No children?"

He shook his head. "Is that too much to ask? To want you as my wife? My one and only? Maybe to act together in a play?"

Pressure squeezed her heart.

"I'm willing to compromise on having a private wedding. I'd think you could compromise on having children."

"One?"

He shook his head. "None." He took another swig.

Cassie pushed to her feet, but a wave of dizziness blurred her vision, and she grabbed hold on the coffee table then went crashing back to the sofa. "You can't mean it," she mumbled.

"Oh yes. Absolutely. I do mean it. Darling, I want you. Isn't it enough?"

"No."

Silence.

"Just one child? I could compromise on two. One, sweet-smelling, smart, easy, talented child?"

He drained his glass.

"Is this our first fight?"

"Could be." He headed for the bedroom.

"Where are you going?" She turned.

"Away from you."

"No compromise?"

"No. No kids. Period. Make your choice. Me or children." He stopped in the archway.

Cassie bit her lip. Her eyes filled.

"Damn you! Don't you dare use tears on me. They'll have no effect. I love you, Cassie, but only you. No offspring."

"I don't understand." She reached for the box of tissues on the end table.

"I don't understand why you want the little buggers. Aren't I enough? Don't you want to spend your life taking care of me?"

"You? You can take care of yourself."

"But life would be so much better if you took care of me. And I, you."

"Oh, I see. You're willing to take care of me but not your own children."

"I'm not going to have my own children. Or any other kind, either."

Pain seared through her. "But it's my dream. Marry you. Have a couple of kids. A house..."

"White picket fence?" He laughed. "Oh no. Leave me out of the picture. A flat in London and one in Paris. A suite here at The Pierre, always ready for us—is more my style."

"That takes a lot of money."

"We have a lot of money."

"But it's such a waste. Two flats and a suite?"

"That's how stars live, darling."

"Not me."

"You have a flat somewhere, don't you?"

She shook her head. "I travel too much. I live in hotels, other people's apartments. Never my own."

"Hell! Let's get you one. First thing tomorrow." He leaned a shoulder against the wall.

"I want to live with you. Be married. Be a wife. A mother. I want to have it all. I've had my success in the theatre and movies. In a few years, I'll be too old for leading roles anyway."

"Then you can travel with me. I'll never be too old."

"Everyone's too old eventually, Basil." She shrugged.

He laughed. "By then, I probably won't even remember my own name. So who cares? Come with me. Marry me. Travel the world. Just you and me. Forever." He held out his hand.

Cassie faced him. Staring into his eyes, she didn't see anything. The love light she'd sworn had been there since the start had faded. A hungry look replaced his gentle smile. Who was this man? An empty feeling swept through her. Was he like a papier mâché figure, hollow inside?

She ignored his gesture. "I can't. I can't give up my dream. My children. Because you want me to."

He sighed, averted his eyes, dropped his hand, then made eye contact. "You never said children were part of the bargain."

"I assumed you'd want them. Every man wants kids, right?"

"Wrong. Not this one."

"You never told me." A tightness gathered in her chest.

"You never asked."

"But we...I'd thought. I mean we had, have so much. Together." She bit her lip.

"I guess we didn't know each other as well as we thought."

"You're really serious?"

He nodded.

"You won't budge?" She wiped away perspiration on her lip.

"Would you want me to? Bloody hell, would you want me to father children I'd despise?" His voice grew loud.

She rose, resting one knee on the sofa. "Of course not."

"So there you have it. The irresistible force meets the immoveable object."

"Don't say that." She shivered as the air conditioner cooled the room.

"But it's true. It's called an impasse." He gave a curt nod and disappeared into the bedroom.

Cassie collapsed in sobs on the sofa. Her body heaved as pain stung her to the core. She calmed down, hoping Basil would appear in the doorway, apologize, beg her forgiveness, and change his mind. But he didn't return. He always responded to her tears. He'd come to her, hold her, whisper soothing words. And the disagreement would be over. Then there would be fantastic makeup sex.

Not this time. An ache in her chest brought home the one thing she couldn't face—the truth. Her choice was give up kids or give up Basil. Neither appealed. He'd been so perfect, so funny, charming, bright, and witty. And an accomplished actor. He understood everything she went through, except the musicals. Basil couldn't dance worth spit.

Where was he? Why wasn't he by her side? The sound of the shower grabbed her attention. Oh okay. He was in the bathroom. When he came out, he'd comfort her, tell her he was wrong, make love to her, and everything would be okay.

But the thumping in her chest disagreed. *Not this time*, her heart said. Her pulse pounded in her ears, and her chest tightened.

He meant it. He's not coming. It's over.

Her brain refused to play along with her fantasy. Basil would change, bend to her every whim. Having kids wasn't a whim, she argued with herself. She shook her head. Nope. No way would she win this one.

The sound of the shower stopped abruptly. Hope grew in her heart. The door opened, but he didn't come. She waited. And waited. Twenty minutes later, he rounded the corner.

"Darling. I don't know how to say this." He stood tall, handsome, and fully dressed in the doorway.

She raised her hand. "Then don't."

He shifted his weight from foot to foot. "You know I must."

She sighed, pulled herself up to a sitting position, and, with exaggerated motions, wiped her face again. Maybe he'd notice she'd been crying and comfort her. The minute she did it, shame filled her. She hated manipulative people, and here she was, using tears to control him. She lowered her gaze.

"I know you're sad. So am I. I thought I'd found the perfect mate. But nothing in life is perfect."

"But I love you?"

"I love you, too. I'm sorry, darling. We're simply not meant to be."

Images she'd conjured in her head during fleeting quiet moments of Basil cradling their baby, of him playing ball with their son and dancing with their young daughter shattered like a glass thrown against the wall. Bits and pieces fell away in slow motion, dragging a gaping wound behind with each piece.

Pain shot through her head. A rip-roaring headache threatened behind her eyes.

In three easy strides, Basil was beside her. "I'm so sorry, darling. So very sorry. My heart is broken, too. I'll always love you. Really. Truly."

"A near-miss," she mumbled, turning swollen eyes to his.

"Exactly. The perfect way to look at it." He smiled.

But it hadn't been a near-miss. It had been a bull's-eye. Their relationship had gotten her through the strenuous, the tedious, the stressful days of endless rehearsals, costume fittings, blocking, and every other tiny piece needed to make a fabulous theatre performance.

Basil had been there to soothe her spirit, rub her feet, and convince her nasty, jealous people were simply wrong. What they thought didn't matter. Now, she'd be alone.

Reading her mind, he continued, "You have your mother and Brian."

"My mother is a bloodsucker."

"She's only got your best interests at heart."

"No, she doesn't." Cassie pushed to her feet and poured a cup of cold coffee.

"Of course she does. She's your mother."

Cassie added cream. "Hah!"

Basil joined her. When he took her in his arms, she stiffened.

"Don't be like that. We'll always be great friends."

"I don't want to be friends with you. I want to be your wife."

"I know, I know."

She twisted off the mammoth, glittering engagement ring he'd given her then stepped back, put the ring in his palm, and bent his fingers around it. "Here. Take it."

He stared at his hand for a moment then lifted his gaze to hers. His eyes wetted. He no longer appeared to be doing a scene from a play. The sadness, the regret became real.

He slid his hand into his jacket pocket and deposited the ring. "I-I, um…" Quickly, he brushed his lips against hers. "I have to go." And then he was at the door, turning. "Goodbye, darling. Take care. Remember, I'll always love you."

And in a flash, he was gone.

DEAFENED BY SILENCE, Cassie trembled. She didn't know what to do, where to turn. Glancing at the window, still wet with rain, she moved about the room, aimlessly. Tension gathered between her shoulders. A Charlie horse grabbed her calf, bunching up the muscle into painful knots. She fell to the floor, clutching her leg and screaming. But no one came.

In a few minutes, her massaging loosened the flesh. She pushed to her feet and hobbled to her bed. As she crawled in, she noticed she still wore Basil's shirt, which brought a fresh round of tears. She cried herself to sleep and slept the day away.

When she awoke, darkness blanketed the city. She stared at the lights, but instead of bringing warmth, their twinkle chilled. Her phone buzzed. It was call number fourteen from her mother. She didn't want to talk to Caroline, though she'd rehearsed different scenarios in her head.

"Give up the theatre and movies? Are you crazy?"

"Anyone can have babies. Not everyone can win a Tony."

"Of course Basil left you. How could you be so stupid? You'll never find anyone like him."

She didn't want to talk, yet she didn't want to be alone.

She switched on the news. Oh my God! There he was, Basil, like a deer caught in the headlights in the lobby of The Pierre. Cassie straightened. The footage was from the afternoon.

"Mr. Evans-White, where is Cassandra Wells?"

"I don't know," Basil mumbled, pushing through the crowd of reporters.

Thank you, Basil.

Someone stuck a microphone in Basil's face. "Cassandra Wells is missing. Do you know her whereabouts?"

Basil shook his head and took another step toward the front door.

"Rumor has it she's in this hotel. Can you confirm or deny it?"

"I can't." Basil pushed again, getting closer to freedom.

"I have it on good authority she's hiding in one of the suites. Why would she be hiding? Did you hit her, Mr. Evans-White?"

His face contorted in fury, Basil turned to face the reporter. "How dare you? That's slander! I'd never hit her. If the woman wants a little privacy, why don't you all just bugger off?"

Basil shoved the reporter in the shoulder and ran for the door. Poor Basil! She sighed. Thank God the press didn't know the couple had parted ways. She shuddered at the thought of how they'd eat it up. The questions, phone calls. And it was nobody's business.

"It's the price you pay for success in this business," her mother had said thousands of times.

In the past, she'd managed to deal with the nosiness of the world, but this time, she'd protect her privacy from prying people who want to make a buck on her life. Fuck them! She clenched her jaw. This time she'd keep her life to herself.

Cassie fell back against the pillows. Damn. Trapped! Reporters lurking in the lobby. Someone tipped them off. Maybe even her own mother. Anything to flush Cassie out. Now the vultures would be camped out there for days, wondering why she'd disappeared. Didn't anyone ever think maybe she simply wanted peace and quiet? No, there had to be a sinister motive.

Cassie picked up her phone and dialed her mother.

"I'm fine, Mom. Stop calling the police or the press or whoever you called. I'm taking a break, okay?"

"Where are you?"

"Hiding. Basil and I broke up." Her voice trembled.

"What happened?"

"Nothing. I can't talk about it now."

"Probably a good thing. I mean, you're never in the same city for more than a weekend."

Death of my dreams. Thanks, Mom.

Silence.

"Cassandra? You still there?"

"Yeah. I don't think it's a good thing. I'm upset, Mom. Don't you even care?"

"Your first heartbreak. You'll get over it."

"It's not my first."

"Really?" She pictured her mother's eyebrows shooting up.

"First happened at sixteen." She reached for the box of tissues.

"Ancient history. Get over it. Basil was a good man, but you've got a skyrocketing career. How many women can say the same? You're a star!"

"I'm alone, Mom."

"Men will flock to your door."

"I don't think so. I thought Basil understood me." Cassie plopped down on the sofa.

"How could he? He barely knew you. Drown your sorrows in a new show. Maybe the movie version of the show?"

"Maybe a month's vacation? Maybe Hawaii? South of France?"

"Okay, sweetheart, I understand how you want to get away. Hide out for a day or two, but these scripts—"

Cassie clamped her mouth shut then turned her phone off. Opening her laptop, she decided making a run for it looked good. Where could she go to ditch the reporters? She scanned travel sites, but none had the answer. Ah, yes. Bora Bora! She grabbed her purse, fishing around for her wallet. Thumbing through her credit cards, a business card fell out. It landed faceup on the bed.

McKay Press

Fine printing, low prices

Flint McKay, president

845-226-1700

That's it! No one would ever find her in Pine Grove, would they? They might actually think to send someone to Bora Bora but never to the tiny town in upstate New York. It was perfect. Besides, she had unfinished business there. She had to make a decision about her grandmother's general store. Flint had been kind enough to save it from the town's demolition team. The least she could do was take it off his hands and decide its fate.

She turned on her phone and dialed.

FLINT CLOSED HIS PROJECT file. While he'd never buy a mansion on the profits from McKay Press, he and his brother lived comfortably in Pine Grove. His parents had sold the business and their house to their sons when they moved to Arizona.

Flint and Marty renovated the place and took a business loan from the bank to upgrade their equipment and expand. Flint had put Marty in charge of new accounts while he took care of tried-and-true customers and maintained the machinery. The partnership worked. The brothers, separated by five years, stayed out of each other's way. In their spare time, they joined the volunteer fire corps.

"So? Did Miss High-and-Mighty tell you what to do with the store or tell you to fuck off?" The slow drawl of his younger brother, Marty, annoyed him.

"Don't call her that. She was nice, real nice."

"I bet. So why'd you come home pissed?"

"Shut up, Marty."

"Yeah, yeah, Flint. When pigs can fly, when the worm turns, and when hell freezes over, you'll get a call from Miss Cassandra Wells."

Seeing Cassie had jolted Flint. Could she be more stunning than she'd been at sixteen? Hell yeah. She'd exuded an energy from her expression, the way she'd moved, and those eyes. Damn those eyes. They were the clearest blue, like the Caribbean Sea. Her hair still had a reddish glint, too. Being in her presence had turned him on. Until she sloughed off the importance of the store. As heartless as she was beautiful. He shuddered to think she'd turned her back on her past.

The phone interrupted his thoughts.

"McKay Press. Flint McKay speaking."

"Hey, Flint."

"Oh, hi, Grey." Damn, if there was anyone he didn't want to talk to, it was Grey Andrews.

"Rumor has it you had dinner with Cassie Wells."

"There is truth to the rumor."

"Great. So? When is she coming to take care of the store?"

"Well, we didn't exactly work out a date yet." Flint glanced at the sky, asking for forgiveness for one of the biggest lies of his life.

"Why not?"

"You know, performers. Schedules. Stuff." Sweat broke out on his forehead.

"Oh. Okay. I hope she's coming soon. Town council's getting antsy. Keep me in the loop."

"Sure thing, Grey." Flint put down his phone and wiped his palm over his face.

"You're digging the hole deeper," Marty said, lounging against the doorjamb of Flint's office.

"I know, I know."

"Not ready to give up on her, are you?"

"I just saw her this week. Crap. Give the woman some time. She's real busy. It's not like she's sitting on her butt all day eating candy. She'll come around. You'll see." Hmm, second biggest lie of his life.

"Is that what she told you?"

"Never mind what she told me."

Marty shot his brother a sly grin. "Yeah, right. Like there's anything between you and her anymore."

"None of your business. Don't you have calls to return or something?"

"I'm going, I'm going." Marty held up his palm. "Hell, you can lie to me all you want, Flint. But don't lie to yourself."

With those words, Marty slipped away. Flint stared out the window. There were Chipping Sparrows at the bird feeder. Marty was right. Lying to others was bad enough, but lying to yourself was worse. He sighed and turned his focus to the computer.

His cell rang. "McKay Press. Flint McKay speaking."

"Flint?" A small voice barely audible whispered his name.

"Cassie?"

Well, shit. Pigs can fly, worms have turned, and hell has frozen over!

Chapter Four

At the sound of his voice, tears threatened. There'd always been something soothing about Flint McKay's deep voice. And with age, it'd only grown more so. If you could put sound to a warm hug, it would be Flint's bass timbre.

"Hello? Hello?" His voice rose.

"Yeah, Flint. It's me." She cleared her throat. What stage actress who was worth a damn couldn't project her voice to the back of the theatre? What the hell was she doing sounding like a little lost kitten? Speak up, woman. He was not the enemy.

"Oh, Cassie. Great. Good to hear from you. Are you okay?"

"More or less."

"According to the papers, people are looking for you."

"They are." Her tone grew tentative. She wished he didn't know yet. He might decide not to help her.

"I take it, you don't want to be found?"

"Right."

"What can I do for you?"

"I'm calling about Gram's store." Now she'd turned into a liar on top of her other faults.

"Really?"

"Uh-huh."

"That's great news. I heard from Grey Andrews this morning."

"Who's that?"

"Never mind. When are you coming out here?"

"Well, you see, there's a little problem."

"Oh?" Could she actually hear his eyebrows rise?

"Uh, yeah. Seems I'm trapped here."

"Where's here?"

"At The Pierre. My uncle offered me his suite while he's not using it. I came here to crash after leaving the show. And Basil joined me. Then we broke up. And now the media is camped out in the lobby. Basil made the local news. Did you see it?"

"I did."

"He lied for me. But it's over between us. I don't want to have to run the gauntlet of reporters and camera men. I don't look great." She bit her lip, exerting all the self-control she had.

"I thought you did."

"Yeah, well, I was wearing makeup. Without it, I look like a rag. And then they'll ask about Basil and my plans for the future. And they'll hound me. I don't want to talk about anything to anyone." She broke. One sob turned into two which became a waterfall.

"Cassie? Cassie!" Flint hollered into the phone. But she'd put it down on the table. She reached for a box of tissues. After two deep breaths, she calmed down.

"Cassie! Are you there? Are you all right?"

"I'm here." Her voice shook. "My mother wants me to sign a movie contract then a show or vice versa. I don't remember. She wants me to keep working. My life is slipping away. I'm going too fast. I need to stop."

"So this isn't about Gram's store, is it?"

She cringed at the disappointment in his voice. "It is and it isn't. I can't lie to you. I need to escape, and I have no place to go."

"You have money, don't you? Fly to Europe. Hide out in Paris."

She sighed. "They'll find me there. They'll find me anywhere I go on a plane or train. I'm famous. I'm out of hiding places."

"Except Pine Grove?"

"How'd you guess?"

Silence. She chewed a nail. Was he going to turn his back on her, too?

"What about your brother?"

How could Flint desert her? He was all she had. "He told me this morning he and his wife are retiring to a farm in Connecticut. Brian wants to raise chickens and have kids."

"Nothing wrong with that."

"I'll have to find a new business manager."

"Brian was your business manager?"

"Who else would be trustworthy?"

He snorted. "I suppose."

"You never liked Brian." She stiffened.

"I never said I didn't."

"I could tell." Unable to sit still, she pushed to her feet and went to the window.

"He always acted superior because you were adopted, and he wasn't. I didn't like it."

"He's grown up. After I made it, he wanted in, and he's taken good care of me."

"Glad to hear it. So, what do you want from me?"

"A rescue." She held her breath, closed her eyes, and crossed her fingers.

"A what?"

"Rescue?"

"You want me to drive into the city, steal you away, and bring you here?"

"Yep." She raised her gaze to the ceiling and uttered a silent prayer.

"After dark?"

"Or not. Whatever works." She paced in front of the windows.

"And you'll be sneaking out the back door stuffed into a laundry cart?"

"Well, I hadn't thought about it. I suppose if I have to." She shifted her weight.

Flint roared with laughter.

Her face heated. "What's so funny?"

"Sounds like a movie plot. A bad movie plot."

"Flint McKay, are you making fun of me?" Her chest tightened.

"Sorry, sorry. I don't mean to, but you must admit it's a bit cloak and dagger."

"Okay. Maybe I'm being dramatic. I have no way to get there except a public bus."

"You want me to come and get you? Done. Just tell me when and where to meet you."

"Really?" Her eyes filled. "You'd do that for me? After all these years?"

"Sure. And you can stay with us. Marty and I have my folks' house. We've got a nice guest room. It's all yours."

"Oh my God. I don't know what to say?" Tears spilled over and ran down her cheeks.

"Hell, I'm a volunteer fireman now, Cassie. Rescuing people is something I do. So when and where?"

"I can be packed up and ready to go by tomorrow morning."

"I'll pick you up at eleven. Text me where you are, and I'll be there."

"Wonderful." She hopped up and down. Victory!

"You'll be traveling by truck."

"Truck? Perfect. No one will ever suspect Cassandra Wells making a getaway in a truck." She laughed.

He chuckled. "Right. Till tomorrow, then."

"Tomorrow. Oh, and thank you, Flint. Thank you from the bottom of my heart." She grinned.

"No problem. And when you're here, we'll talk about Gram's store?"

"Of course. Of course. We will. Yes. Thank you again."

They said goodbye and ended the call. Cassie padded into the bathroom and ran a tub. She needed to soak. Thank God for Flint McKay. Now she'd have time, peace, and quiet to figure out where she was going and how the hell she'd get there. A healthy dose of the bubble bath provided by the hotel perfumed the steamy air. She stripped down and eased into the hot water.

Closing her eyes, she pictured Flint McKay at eighteen. Perhaps he wasn't as sophisticated as Basil, but he had been so handsome and built like a Marine. She sighed. He hadn't changed much, still sounded the same. She couldn't believe Basil didn't want children. She'd thought all men wanted kids. Thinking back, Flint had been good with little kids. He'd even rescued one at the lake.

Was he still in love with her? He'd been her first lover. Naïve, inexperienced, but enthusiastic and oh-so energetic. She wondered if he'd changed. And would she find out?

"Shame on you, Cassie." She slapped her thigh. "The sheets are barely cold from Basil and you're already wondering about Flint." Easing back into the water, she shut her eyes and conjured up memories.

"A friend. What I need now is a friend. That's Flint." She spoke aloud, reassuring herself. "And maybe I wasn't so in love with Basil after all?"

Perhaps she'd believed marrying Basil was the quick and easy way to have a new life. She'd certainly fantasized about an elegant English country house, a perfect baby, and an adoring, handsome, famous husband more than once, and somewhere along the way, it had become her dream—one even her mother would accept.

Had she cried over the loss of his love or hurt pride in the quick way he'd turned her hopes to ashes? Fame had inured her to rejection...hadn't it? Who would turn away from such a woman? Basil had. Because he had plans of his own and wouldn't bend to her wishes.

Humiliated, she had to admit to herself Basil had presented an easy means to an end, a direct route to her desired new lifestyle. But here she stood, left with nothing but a cold, empty heart where she'd thought love had been.

Was a normal life out of reach? Would she ever be a mother? She'd have to forge a new path...by herself. *If I can become a star, then I can do anything. It's my dream. And I won't let anything stand in my way.*

FLINT RAN HIS FINGERS through his hair. Holy shit, Cassie Wells was coming to Pine Grove. No, wait...Cassandra Wells. He pocketed his phone and went to find his brother. Marty was in the kitchen, fussing over a pot of spaghetti sauce.

"Eat your words."

"Huh? What burr got under your saddle?"

"Cassie Wells is coming."

"What?"

"You heard me. She's coming. I'm picking her up tomorrow morning."

"You're shittin' me." Marty put the wooden spoon on the counter.

"I am not. She's coming." Flint leaned against the wall.

"How the hell did you do that?"

Flint shook his head. "I have no idea. Oh, by the way. She's dumped the Brit she was engaged to. She's single. And she's coming here."

"Where's she stayin'?"

"With us." Flint headed for the kitchen door. Taking a walk always settled his mind and provided a way to avoid his brother's probing questions.

Flint knew exactly what Marty would ask, and he had no intention of replying. Not because he didn't want to but because he didn't have any answers. Was he expecting to take up with Cassie where they'd left off so many years ago? Hell no. He wasn't the same person, and he doubted she was, either.

Would Marty ask if Cassie was the reason Flint had been engaged three times yet never went through with any of the weddings? Probably. Flint didn't know himself, though he'd always suspected it had something to do with her.

His legs picked up the pace. He needed to move, to sweat, to stop thinking about Cassie—especially in the way he was thinking. Images of her naked body kissed by moonlight. Splashing in the water at midnight or sneaking, dripping wet, to the car because she forgot her towel. And in the car? His face heated. Damn, she was hot, even at such a tender age.

His heavy breathing had steamed up the backseat windows every time. A grin and a chuckle escaped his throat as he rounded the bend, heading for Java the Hut, and a tall glass of iced coffee. He couldn't rightly call it making love, could he? More like fumbling in the dark until something happened. Flesh bumping up against flesh, mouth-to-mouth, and other places. He shook his head. He'd been lucky she never traded him in for a more experienced model.

Now, he knew exactly what he was doing in the bedroom and could show her the time of her life. He coughed. But it wasn't on the schedule. She'd be here only until it was safe to return to her life and Gram's store was in shape to sell. Period. There'd be no love happening with Cassandra Wells, physical or otherwise. Not if he could help it. Yeah, right.

What was the phrase about pigs flying? Flint stopped at the drive-through window and ordered his drink.

"I'll bring it outside when it's ready, Flint." Winnie Briggs chewed gum while she rang up his purchase.

He plunked down at a small wooden table outside the front of the joint.

"Howdy. How you doin'?" Winnie put his coffee down. He slipped a dollar bill in her apron pocket and shot her a grin. She'd had a son, but he died in a tractor accident right after high school. Flint always wondered if she ever got over the loss. She'd been working at the coffeehouse ever since he could remember. *It must be tough to be old and have to work for peanuts.* She smiled then headed inside. Winnie must be almost seventy-five. Flint shook his head, downed a gulp of coffee, then pushed to his feet.

He strolled down the narrow sidewalk toward their property. A good two-mile journey in the warm August day didn't stop him. Life in this sleepy little town was about to get interesting—not that he had any quarrel with Pine Grove. This was his hometown and he loved it, even though he cursed it for being backward and not having a Chinese restaurant. Soon it would have a movie star in residence. Could Pine Grove handle it? Could he?

CASSIE PACKED HER BELONGINGS, ordered dinner and tomorrow's breakfast from room service, and turned on the television. One of her movies was playing. She quickly changed the channel. A baseball game popped up. She leaned against the five pillows on the bed and watched.

When the game ended, she shut off the television, curled up on the window seat, and stared out at the city. Her thoughts turned to Basil. Why hadn't she known he didn't want children? He'd been so attentive whenever they were together, seeing to her every need. But not her need for a family. Instead, he expected her to select her projects based on his location. She sighed. Following Basil Evans-White around the world like a puppy dog wasn't her style. Still, it hurt not to have his love...or whatever it was of his she'd had.

Tomorrow morning, she'd sneak out the service door, jump into Flint's truck, and speed off to Pine Grove. Could she be anonymous there? She hoped so. Damn, time to get her shit together and take charge of her life. Her mother had been running things, making it easy for Cassie to focus on her acting, singing, and dancing. But she was thirty. Time to grow up and head in the direction she wanted, not her mother, her producer, director, or brother.

As her gaze bounced from high-rise to high-rise, she thought out loud. "Other people do it. They have lives. They make their own decisions. They live with the results. Everybody does it, except me. It's time. Chips fall where they may."

As much as the idea of being an ordinary citizen perplexed and weighed on her, it excited her, too. Oh, to have an ice cream cone whenever she wanted without having to worry about putting on a pound! What joy! Not an ice cream cone—no, go all the way—a hot fudge sundae! Her mouth watered at the prospect.

Food arrived. She made quick work of the burger, fries, Coke and chocolate chip cookie. After putting the dishes in the hall, Cassie washed up and donned an old T-shirt of her father's. She slipped into bed and doused the light. Closing her eyes, visions of mint chocolate chip, cookies and cream, and butter pecan ice cream danced through her brain. Licking her lips, she fell asleep, and slept, dreamlessly, through the night.

Sunlight poked her in the eye at eight. She yawned and stretched. After a quick shower, she cuddled into a thick terry cloth robe and padded to the living room. A quiet knock called her to the door. Room service delivered breakfast right on time.

"Miss," the young waiter said, wheeling the cart into the room. He set out the dishes on the coffee table in front of the television.

"Is this everything, miss?"

Cassie eyed the spread. Fruit salad, a giant pot of coffee with a creamer and sugar jar. A basket of fresh croissants. He lifted the metal dome to reveal a platter of fried eggs, bacon, and home fries, then replaced it to keep the food hot. An elegant, small china bowl filled with butterscotch pudding rounded out the feast.

"Looks like it. Thanks." She pulled a ten-dollar bill from her pocket and offered it to the young man. He thanked her and left. The waiter had poured her coffee. She added heavy cream, which she'd ordered instead of her usual skim milk. Then a teaspoon of sugar, and the beverage was perfect. Sitting back, she sipped then uncovered the croissant.

"Real butter!" Feeling bold, she buttered the delicacy then took the dome from her main meal. Perched cross-legged on the sofa, she watched the morning news while she ate.

A spokeswoman from Celebs R Us came on.

"Well, well, looks like the engagement is off for Basil Evans-White and Cassandra Wells. Our spies spotted Mr. Evans-White having breakfast with the very single Catarina Hernandez in the tony restaurant, Seconds. We wonder who Ms. Wells is dining with this morning."

Cassie threw a croissant at the screen. "Miss Wells is dining alone today, if it's any of your damn business!"

FLINT BROKE FOUR EGGS into the pan. Breakfast was his meal. Marty handled dinner, and they each took care of their own lunches. He checked the bacon in the oven and poured himself a second cup of coffee.

Although the scale didn't show him down any pounds, there was more spring in his step. He'd whistled at the mirror while shaving before realizing a man couldn't whistle a tune and shave at the same time. He chuckled and rubbed his jaw.

"Eggs again?" Marty eyed the contents of the frying pan.

"What am I? A short-order cook?"

"Can't we ever have pancakes or waffles? Something, anything, besides fried eggs?"

"Quit your bitchin' or you can make your own breakfast."

Marty opened the cabinet. "Look. I bought pancake mix. Just add one or two things, stir it up, and bam! Pancakes!"

"And I suppose then you're gonna want 'em with blueberries or chocolate chips?"

"Now that you mention it..."

"Well, shit, man. Do it yourself." Flint shoveled the eggs onto two plates, breaking the yolks in the process.

"You don't have to get all bent out of shape about it." Marty took out utensils.

Forgetting what he was doing, Flint reached for the pan with the bacon without a potholder. A howl of pain and a quickly dropped pan caught Marty's attention.

"I've told you a thousand times, use a potholder!" Marty opened the freezer, grabbed two ice cubes, and thrust them into his brother's hand. "Did you spill the bacon grease?"

"Nope. Just permanently scarred my hand. Nothing to worry about."

"Now who's bitchin'?"

"I've got a reason. You don't need one."

Marty laughed.

"Bacon's ready." Flint moved toward the stove.

"I'll get it," Marty said, pushing his brother aside and picking up a thick potholder.

Silence ruled during breakfast. Flint welcomed it. Last thing he wanted was questions about Cassie Wells. He knew Marty would zero in on exactly what Flint didn't want to talk about. His brother had a knack for it. Flint didn't know her after all these years. Life would have molded her to who she was now like it had him. Nothing like being kicked in the teeth a few times to get your guard up.

Cassie had been a sweet girl, shy and helpful. They'd laughed their way through summer after summer, working at the general store, cooling off in the lake on scorching days, and finding joy in exploring each other's bodies.

Had he been in love? Hell, he'd been eighteen when she took off. He hadn't known his ass from his elbow, let alone what real love felt like. Marty disagreed.

"As stupid as it sounds, you're still in love with her. It's been sixteen years. You'd better snap out of it, bro, or you're gonna be a bachelor at sixty."

The last thing Flint needed this morning was another diatribe from his brother on the evil of falling for Cassie Wells. He knew the drill without his brother butting in. She'd been the gold standard, and no one else measured up. He'd better get over it so he could find a real girl and have a life. *Yeah, sure. There go those flying pigs again.*

Marty buttered his toast. "When are you picking up Miss High-and-Mighty?"

"Don't call her that."

"Why not?"

"Because I said so." Flint finished his food.

"Well, pardon me. Are you getting high-and-mighty now, too?"

"Marty, you need to learn when to shut the fuck up."

Marty laughed. "S'pose you're right. So when are you goin'?"

"Gotta be there at eleven."

Marty nodded and took a bite of bread.

"I know, I know. I'm leavin'." Flint rinsed off his plate and put it in the dishwasher.

"Take it easy now."

"I'll be fine."

"I know. Just sayin'."

Flint grabbed his truck keys from the front hall table then glanced in the mirror, finger-combed his dark hair, and headed for the driveway. As he steered for the highway, he glanced at the selection of CD's available for the trip. Too many about lost love and broken hearts. Not a good idea to go down that road.

Instead, he left the radio off and let his mind wander. He owned every movie she'd made and seen every show on Broadway, a couple more than once. Marty had ridiculed him for being a lovesick puppy. Could Flint help it if he had good taste in movies?

He chuckled. Maybe Marty was right. Cassie had played a variety of roles, but what was she like underneath all the glitz and glamour? Who was Cassie Wells? He had no clue but guessed he'd be finding out real soon—for better or worse.

Chapter Five

C assie peered in the mirror. Without makeup, she looked horrendous. She smiled. Perfect. Fishing through her things, she pulled out a scarf. Resting it over her blonde locks, she tied the silk fabric under her chin.

Checking her watch, she had fifteen more minutes before she had to be at the back door. Cassie closed her suitcase and headed for the hall. She lingered by the elevator then sent a text to Flint.

Cassie: *On my way.*

She got a reply.

Flint: *Standing by the fire hydrant.*

The door opened on the first floor. A glance to the left revealed two reporters lounging on chairs in the lobby, cameras tucked under their arms. With her head down but her eyes cast up, she turned right, heading for the back of the hotel. There it was, EXIT, in big red letters. She grinned and pushed on the handle, but it wouldn't budge.

She tried again and again. *It's locked? Can't be? It's a fire exit. Isn't it supposed to be open all the time? At least from the inside?* She texted.

Cassie: *Door's locked!*

Flint: *Fire door?*

Cassie: *Yes.*

Flint: *Violation.*

"Excuse me, miss. Are you going somewhere?"

Uh-oh. A big, burly man with a mustache folded his arms over his impressive chest.

"Out. Isn't this an exit."

"Not for you. What are you doing here? Are you a guest? You don't look like a guest. Whose suitcase is this? Did you steal it?"

Fear spiked through Cassie. This guy would haul her off to jail in a minute. She took a deep breath, puffed up her chest, squared her shoulders, and brought her gaze right to his. Steeling herself, she got into character. "Officer. This is a fire door. It's locked."

"Yeah, to keep thieves like you in."

"I'm not a thief. I'm a guest. Locking a fire door is a violation. You could kill people if there is a fire. You cannot lock this door. Open it immediately, or I am reporting you to the police." Cassie made a show of pulling out her cell and dialing.

"No, no. Wait a minute. You can't." He reached for her phone. She pulled it to her chest and pivoted away from him.

"Oh, can't I? Maybe I should call the media first. Tell them how I avoided a huge tragedy at The Pierre by getting this fire door unlocked. Open it now!"

Sweat beaded on the man's face. "Okay, okay. You swear this's your suitcase?"

"Yes, of course. The door. Now!"

He pulled a large key chain from his belt, fumbled a little, then got the right key. He unlocked the door, pushed it open, and held it for her. Cassie squeezed through the tight space.

Where is he? Sweat pooled between her breasts. *So this is what a bank robber feels like waiting for the getaway car?*

The guard narrowed his eyes, his bulk filling the doorway.

A bright-red truck screeched to a halt in front of her. Flint leaped out, grabbed her luggage, and tossed it in the well as if it weighed nothing. He opened the passenger door and helped her inside. By now, her scarf had fallen down.

"Say, wait a minute. Aren't you Cassandra Wells?" The man stepped toward the vehicle.

"Everybody thinks so. My husband thinks it's hilarious. Bye." Cassie slid her butt across the seat while Flint slammed the door shut.

"No, no. You *are* Cassandra Wells." The man rubbed his chin.

"Ta-ta," she said, waving as Flint hit the accelerator. She leaned closer to him. "A red truck? Why didn't you tell me your truck was red?"

"You didn't ask."

"A red truck." She shook her head.

"Good for business. An advertisement on wheels. How'd you get by the Goliath?"

"Acting."

"Well done." Appreciation gleamed in his brown eyes.

"Next stop, Pine Grove?" She ripped the scarf off the rest of the way.

"Yep." Flint turned right onto the ramp to the Henry Hudson Parkway.

Cassie sat back. "Thank you for doing this."

"No problem."

She sighed. "I'm tired. Disappearing is perfect."

"You will be recognized in town."

"Did you tell anyone I was coming?" She faced him.

"Only Marty."

"Good."

"Things have changed in Pine Grove. We have a few new places to eat, some new shops..."

"Is Homer's still there?"

He nodded.

"And the Thrift Shop."

"Yep."

She smiled. "I'll buy you a bacon burger at Homer's."

He laughed. "With fries?"

"With the works."

"Deal."

She rested her head on the seat back and, within a minute, was fast asleep.

FLINT CONCENTRATED on the road. The faint scent of lily of the valley drifted his way, stealing his attention. He grabbed her scarf lying carelessly on the seat and put it to his face. A deep inhale confirmed his guess.

How the hell was he going to stay away from her if she was living in his house? He pushed thoughts of colliding with her on the way from the shower or bumping against her fine chest by accident in the kitchen out of his mind.

He had business shit to take care of and a brother to watch over. He didn't need her messing up his life, turning it upside down, backwards, and inside out. No sirree. Cassie Wells was the last thing on his agenda. But here she was, soft, pretty, and vulnerable, asleep in his truck. He couldn't tell if it was his heart thumpin' or his dick. Wait a minute. Yeah. It was his dick.

He reminded himself she'd be taking one giant headache off his plate—that damn general store. She could do whatever she wanted with the place. Burn it down for all he cared. But it had to be hers and either taken down or fixed up—her decision, not his. Lord knew the damn shop would be a huge time suck—time he didn't have. She had time, unless she flitted off to do a movie or a play. He prayed she wouldn't, dumping the place on him again.

He had to get one thing straight in his head. She wasn't coming to be with him. He was only a small town, unsophisticated country guy to a big star like Cassie Wells. He got it. Who knew what man she'd end up with next? Maybe a Duke or an Earl? Or a sheik. Were there still sheiks, or had they been washed away with the tide of time?

He laughed. Cassie Wells sure as hell wasn't taking orders from any sheik. She'd intimidated the big security bozo at the hotel. He was twice her size, but she had him shaking like a leaf in a spring storm. Cassie was one helluva woman.

The asphalt and concrete of the city melted away, replaced by the messy beauty of ragweed, leafy oaks, and slim, towering pines. Flint opened his window all the way. September heat rivaled his air-conditioning. He switched it off and let the moist, warm air remind him summer lingered. Crap, there were only two weeks left and he hadn't even gone skinny-dipping in Cedar Lake yet.

He'd taken Rhonda Smith to a movie a couple of times, hoping to soften her to the idea of joining him, naked, in the cool waters of his favorite lake. She had a body that didn't quit, and he drooled at the prospect of getting her bare on the dock.

"You're horny. Can't commit, either. Three engagements but no marriage. Who needs it?" She'd shrugged him off after finishing her popcorn and soda.

Flint had to admit she had a point. Seemed settling down wasn't in his blood, or was it his timing? Couldn't be the girls. They'd been fine, and Alice, damn, women didn't come any sweeter than her. So what was his problem? He frowned. Even his mother had stopped making excuses for him and simply shrugged and walked away the last time he left a woman at the altar.

It was not like he'd meant to humiliate anyone. Flint simply figured it would be better for her if he didn't marry her. What woman wanted a man who didn't want to be there? Who didn't want to live the rest of his life with her? Wasn't it the honorable thing—to walk away? He'd saved her from a lifetime of torture, trying to get him to love her when he knew it would never happen.

But the girls of Pine Grove didn't exactly agree. Ever since, he couldn't get a woman to go on a third date with him. After the first two, some busybody would wise her up to his past, and she'd run from him as if he had the plague.

He glanced at Cassie. Breaking up with the British actor was the third, no, wait, maybe the fourth or fifth guy she'd run out on. Maybe Flint and Cassie had running in common? They couldn't seem to stick with a relationship.

His father got it. He'd overheard his parents talking one night.

"He's stuck."

"What do you mean, stuck?" she'd asked.

"Stuck on the girl. The fancy one."

"You mean Cassie? He was eighteen, Marcus."

"I know, I know. But a good woman, the right woman, sticks with you. If you're eighteen or eighty. I knew you were the one. And I was only seventeen."

"But you were a mature seventeen."

"Guess it's hereditary."

"He can't be waiting for her. He'll be waiting forever."

"Guess that's the breaks. Flint's still got it for her. He's seen all her movies. Goes to the city to see her on stage. What do you think?"

"I think he's his father's son," she said, laughing.

His memories were interrupted when Cassie opened her eyes and stretched her arms out.

"We there yet?"

"Almost. Another forty minutes."

She nodded and dozed off again. He wanted to brush away a stray curl bobbing along with the bouncing of the truck but resisted the urge.

"Both hands on the wheel," he muttered to himself as he signaled for a right turn.

THE CHANGING RHYTHM of the truck as it slowed roused Cassie. She yawned and cracked open weary eyes. She inhaled deeply of the unforgettable scent of freshly mowed grass, reminding her of happy days gone by.

"We here?" She blinked and turned her head, searching for a familiar landmark.

Flint laughed. "Yeah. We're here. Do you remember Pine Grove at all?"

"Not much. Homer's. The lake. What's it called?"

"Cedar Lake."

"Right. And Gram's place. Small house. Two bedrooms, kind of like a trailer?"

"That's been sold and torn down."

"Really?" A stab of sadness shot through her. Even without Gram, Cassie figured the small house would hold memories of meals—large and intimate—and of games and movies. She remembered the tiny back porch where she'd hung out on peaceful evenings. Of course, without Gram, the house wouldn't be the same. Still, it was a totem to carefree summers and her sweet relationship with her grandmother.

Flint reached over to give her hand a brief squeeze. "I know. But you still have the store."

"Right."

She'd spent more time in the store than the house anyway. "How bad is it?"

"Not so bad."

She cast a sideways glance at him. "Liar."

At a stop sign, he hit the brakes hard and faced her. "What do you want me to say? It's in mint condition? You can walk in, dust off the counter, and sell it for a million bucks?"

"You don't have to get hostile." She sat up straight.

"I've been waiting for you to take an interest in the damn place for ten years, Cassie. Don't expect much. It's a wreck. But it can be salvaged."

She wrapped her arms around her chest and stared out the window. *Coming here was a mistake.* "I shoulda let you tear it down."

"Wait until you see it. You might feel different."

She narrowed her eyes. "Right."

He pulled over to the curb and slammed the truck into park. "Look. If you're so pissed off about being here, I can turn around and drive you right back to the hotel." His eyes darkened to almost black, his face clouded over. She reached out and folded her fingers over his biceps.

"I'm sorry. I don't mean to be a brat. I'm wondering out loud, you know?"

"If you'd been at Gram's funeral, you'd know all about this."

"I couldn't. I was in London, doing a show."

"Figures." He fixed his gaze on the road and pulled out.

"I appreciate you buying the place and keeping it from being destroyed."

"I didn't do much."

"I promise to take care of it. Whatever that means." She bit her lip.

"Are you going to take it down?" His brow wrinkled. Did he care what happened to it? Why?

"Don't know. I gotta see it first."

"If you want to restore it and, maybe, sell it, I'll help you."

"Don't you work?" She gazed at his profile, still so handsome.

"I own a printing company. My time's my own."

"Nice. I can count on you?"

"Yeah. I guess." He shrugged.

"Don't blow me away with your enthusiasm." She raised her eyebrows.

He laughed. "Okay, okay. I'll help."

"Good. I don't think I could face doing it alone." She turned her gaze to the window.

"Gram meant so much to you?" His brows rose, and he glanced at her.

She nodded. The fresh-cut-grass smell brought memories of other more delicious ones, like the aromas of cinnamon in the large jar of red candy and of molasses cookies baking. Her stomach protested its emptiness.

"Homer's is right around the corner. Maybe we'd better stop for lunch before taking you home."

"Okay by me." When did she last eat anyway?

He slowed as he pulled into the restaurant parking lot. They walked in together. The smell of frying meat and onions got her stomach churning. She needed food. World's best hamburger smothered in sautéed onions was right here at Homer's. It had been her favorite meal along with sweet potato fries. Her mouth watered.

"Do they still have burgers and fried onions?"

"Yep. Still their signature meal."

"And sweet fries?"

He nodded and opened the door. Homer greeted Flint.

"Oh my God. Look who we have here!" he bellowed so all could hear. "It's the famous Cassandra Wells, a Pine Grove girl from way back."

The heat of embarrassment crept up her face, but Cassie smiled.

WITH A FULL STOMACH, she climbed into the truck.

"We live on Windham Street."

"We? You live with a girl?"

"With my brother, Marty."

"Oh, yes, yes. Sorry. I forgot." She remembered a staid white house with ugly, lime-green shutters. This house was painted navy blue with ivory trim and shutters. "This is your house?"

"Marty and I bought it from my parents. We modernized it." He fished her luggage out of the truck and followed her up the front steps. Shouldering the heavy load, he trudged toward the rear of the house. "You're back here."

"And you're...where?"

"Upstairs."

She nodded. Flint kept a safe distance. Probably a good idea. Why start something now, when she had no idea where she'd be heading in two weeks?

"Good." She followed him down the hallway and into a charming room with white eyelet curtains and a dark-purple shaggy area rug. "Did you do this?"

"Nah. My mom."

"I see." She ran her palm along the hand-made lavender-and-purple quilt, the softness of the fabric caressing her skin. "It's pretty."

"The guest room." He put her largest suitcase on top of an old oak trunk at the foot of the bed. "Bathroom's right here." He opened a door. "You good?"

She slid her hand across the smooth top of the white dresser then took a book from her purse and dropped it on one of the nightstands next to the double bed. "This is perfect." She nibbled on her lower lip. *Would living in his house be perfect?*

"Tomorrow's Saturday so let's get an early start. How about right after breakfast?"

"Works for me."

"Breakfast is at eight. Marty makes dinner. We eat at six."

"Thanks."

Flint hesitated at the door to her room. She sauntered closer. "Where's Marty?"

"Working."

"Oh, of course. He was a kid when I left. Guess I'll see him tonight."

Flint laughed. "He's still a kid sometimes. How long you plan to stay?"

"At least until I finish the store. If that's okay with you?"

"Oh right. Yes. Yes." He hesitated. Did he lean a little closer then pull away, or was it her imagination? Had he wanted to kiss her but changed his mind? She raised her gaze to his. Surprised at the lust and longing there, she stepped back. Hell no, she didn't expect it. Not after so many years apart.

"If you need anything, just holler. Unpack. Rest. I'll see you at dinner." He opened the door.

"Flint, I..."

He stopped. "What?"

"Forget it." She jammed her hands in her pockets.

"No, come on. You wanted to say something?" He closed his fingers around her arms.

"Nope. Really. No." She shook her head.

This time he leaned down and brushed her lips with his. He dropped his hands and turned to go. Halfway through the door he faced her. "If you're expecting me to apologize, I'm not."

"Oh. Well, good then." She nodded and touched her lower lip with her fingertip.

And he was gone.

Cassie unpacked then flopped backwards down on the bed. Turning on her side, she stared out the window. Moist early September air hung over her. A butterfly lit outside her window. Orange and black wings slowed as the insect crawled closer. The second she shifted, it fluttered and effortlessly bounced up and out of sight. A breeze stirred maple leaves tired of being still. The song of a chickadee floated into the room.

The bird flitted by and landed on the screen, curling its tiny claws into the mesh. Cocking its head, he gave the familiar call again then zoomed off to a branch on a large maple.

Chickadees had been her favorite bird when she lived in Pine Grove. She hadn't seen one since. The tiny creature brought tears to her eyes. How much of everyday life had she missed living so fast, every moment sucked up with responsibilities, rehearsals, workouts, lessons, and performances. How much had she lived preparing for the future, always anticipating the next play or movie?

Although the trees were a whole lot taller, there were familiar smells, houses she remembered, and the sound of quiet she'd loved. Pine Grove hadn't changed much. She smiled, toed off her shoes, and slipped under the bedspread. Scrunching the pillow under her head and propped up on her arm, she watched puffy clouds drift by slowly, like giant cotton balls. She loved the colors of the sky, even the gray of a rainy day when angry clouds rained their frustrations on her. But sunset was her favorite time. With Gram, she'd watch the sun go down and the sky throw its light show, turning pink then orange, melting into teal blue.

Cassie sighed, forcing her heavy lids to stay open until her body demanded rest. Tomorrow would be another chance to watch birds and butterflies and smell the sweetness of grass.

Chapter Six

Flint yawned and scratched his chest as he ambled down the stairs to breakfast.

"It's about time." Marty stood pouring water into the coffee machine.

"What makes you so grumpy today?" Flint stopped in the doorway.

"You comin' to breakfast like that?" Marty gestured to the boxers his brother wore.

"Like what?"

"Don't we have company?"

"Oh shit!" Eyes wide, Flint took the stairs two at a time. He'd forgotten about Cassie. In his room, he rummaged through a messy drawer and pulled out a wrinkled but clean T-shirt. Grabbing his jeans from a chair, he stuffed his legs in them and ran the zipper up then hit the stairs.

"Better."

"Bathrobe? Didn't think you owned one." Flint got three mugs down from the cabinet.

"Dad left it behind."

"Figures."

"What the hell does that mean?" Marty faced his brother.

"Nothing."

"Coffee's ready. Pour your own, asshole."

"It's a little early."

"You've got attitude already, and it isn't even seven." Marty retied the sash on the moth-eaten checked robe.

"That robe's pathetic." Flint leaned against the counter and eyed his brother.

"You're pathetic. You're in love with the girl asleep in the guest room and you're too chicken to tell her. Now that's pathetic." Marty added milk and sugar.

"Shut the fuck up. I am not." Flint folded his arms across his chest.

Marty laughed. "Are we going to go there? De Nile isn't just a river in Egypt, is it?"

"I swear if you don't shut up, I'm going to..."

The sound of the guest room door opening drew their attention. A moment later, Cassie lounged against the archway.

"Geez, guys. What's going on?" Rubbing her eyes, she padded into the kitchen. She wore an ivory silk short gown, with satin spaghetti straps, which left nothing to the imagination. Flint swallowed hard.

"Morning, Cassie. Nice to have you staying with us." Marty moved toward the counter. "Coffee?"

"Thanks."

Flint cocked an eyebrow at her. "Don't you have a bathrobe or something?"

She gave him a drowsy stare. "Or something?"

Geez. Seemed she didn't get his meaning, so he flapped his hand at the sexy nightie that outlined every dip and curve of her body. "That's giving Marty ideas."

Marty burst out laughing. "Me? You're the one with ideas. And you don't need a revealing nightgown to get 'em, either."

"Shut up, Marty," Flint rumbled.

"Oh this? Okay. Sure. Be right back."

Flint punched his brother in the arm. "If you don't shut up, it'll be the nuts next time."

"I speak the truth. Can't punch it out of me."

"Wanna bet?"

"Boys, boys. Come on. What's for breakfast?" Cassie had added a silky, matching robe—but the dang thing revealed almost as much as it covered up.

"Just eggs and toast this morning. Flint was supposed to do breakfast, but he got up too late, and I have an appointment in New York. Hey, bro, can you handle the toast?"

"I'll do the toast." Cassie nudged Flint out of the way. "Where's the bread?"

Marty pointed. While setting the table, Flint watched her work. Marty scrambled eggs.

"Flint, how many pieces do you want?"

"Two'll do."

"Marty?"

"Same."

"You boys are easy."

Cassie burned the first ones then struggled to spread cold butter on the next two.

Flint muffled a laugh behind his hand then approached her. "Need help?"

She snatched the piece of bread from his hand. "I can do toast, Flint. What do you think I am? An idiot?"

He backed off and smiled. "No way, no. Go ahead."

"Eggs are ready." Marty shoveled eggs onto three plates and put them on the table.

"Juice?" Flint opened the fridge and took out a bottle of juice then filled three glasses and set one at each place setting.

"Sure." Cassie finished buttering the last piece of toast, piled them on a plate, and joined the men.

The three ate in silence for a while.

Marty turned his gaze on his brother. "Going to the office to-day?"

"Thought I'd take Cassie over to the store first."

"Why don't you get a bomb and be done with it?" Marty's brow furrowed.

Cassie looked up. "It's that bad?"

"You can still salvage the place. But it's going to take a lot of work. And money."

Cassie frowned as she tore a piece of toast in half.

Flint patted her hand. "We'll do it. You'll see."

When they were dressed, the trio parted company.

"It's kinda a long walk from here. We need the truck to get stuff to the store anyway."

Cassie climbed up into the vehicle, and Flint got behind the wheel.

"What stuff?"

"Cleaning stuff. Maybe a sander. Some paint."

He started the engine. "By the way, here." He reached into his breast pocket and produced a key. "It's for the house." He fished another key out of his pants pocket. "And this one is for the store."

"Thanks. I appreciate you doing this for me. I need this. Need to stop for a while. Breathe a little. You know?"

"Actually, I don't know. When I need to slow down, I go fishing for a couple of days. I have no idea what your life is like."

"I never stop. First, it's a show. When it closes, then it's a movie. Then another movie. Then a benefit. Dance rehearsals, singing lessons. I'm always running from one thing to another. If you slow down in this business, people think you're done."

Flint raised his eyebrows. "Really?"

She nodded.

"That's tough. Why do you do it?"

She laughed. "I really don't know anymore. At one time, it was all I wanted. But not now." She shrugged.

Flint pulled into a parking space on the street in front of the store.

"Brace yourself." He helped Cassie out of the cab.

"Why?"

"It might be a bit of a shock."

She nodded. He took her hand and walked her around to the front. There were two-by-fours nailed over the windows. The formerly-white paint on the front was nicked in some places and peeling in others. The bright-red front door had faded to a washed-out watermelon shade. She gasped, her hand flying to cover her mouth.

"We've boarded up the windows so kids wouldn't throw rocks and break the glass. But the light isn't completely blocked."

Flint put the key in the lock and twisted it. When he opened the door, the hinges creaked like in a Halloween movie. Dust belched forth onto the sidewalk. Flint waved it away, clearing the air.

"Marty was supposed to turn the electricity on yesterday."

She held her breath for a moment. He reached in and flicked the switch. Light flooded the store. She hesitated in the doorway. Maybe she didn't want to see the inside.

"Come on, honey. It's not so bad." He offered his hand.

SWEAT TRICKLED BETWEEN her breasts and broke out on her upper lip. What was she afraid of? Boldly, she pushed his hand aside and stepped over the threshold. There! She was inside and hadn't been struck by lightning.

The breeze from the open door scattered dust into the air. Bright sunlight poked through cracks in the boarded-up windows, lighting up the specks like tiny stars. The air shimmered amidst dirty walls, broken chairs, and empty candy jars.

When the glittering pinpoints settled on the floor, Cassie saw the remnants of a once robust, thriving shop, bursting with a cornucopia of items for sale. From tiny things, like needles and thread to large bags of charcoal or gravel, Cassie remembered Gram's Pine Grove General Store had carried a little bit of everything.

Cassie scuffed across the dirty floor to the counter. Five large, wide-mouthed empty jars waited to be filled with nickel candy. She turned to face the now-empty stack of small shelves that had held calico print fabric for quilts.

"Gram, will you teach me how to quilt?"

"You finish school with good grades, and it's just what we'll do next year."

But next summer never came. Cassie's mother whisked her away to become Cassandra Wells, actress extraordinaire.

Stepping behind the counter, she spied an old calculator. Gram had used it to add up things, check her math, or figure the cost of the fabric she sold by the yard. The old cash register, bought secondhand and out-of-date when her grandmother had acquired it, still commanded a rigid presence, lording it over the displays.

"So much is the same and yet so much has changed."

Flint nodded. "I'll get the cleaning supplies."

When he went out, the screen door banged shut, like it always did.

"I've got to get the darn door fixed," Gram said at least twice a day.

Choking on dust, Cassie coughed until her face reddened. She went to open the back door. She needed air. Leaning against the doorjamb, she looked out over the unruly yard. Weeds had taken command and grown high in the years they went unchecked. Was there even any grass? Golden rod blossomed in patches. She had to admit it was pretty, but still. It looked like a tramp camp. She shuddered. What the hell had she agreed to anyway? There wasn't anything worth two cents in this old place. She probably couldn't even make anything selling the fixtures. Worn wood and dirty glass challenged her sweet memories of golden days. The milk case was so filthy she couldn't see inside. Didn't matter as there were no cartons of fresh juice or chocolate milk waiting to quench a summer thirst.

"The yard isn't as hopeless as it looks. We'll weed whack the weeds down then turn over the soil and plant grass. You'll see, by spring you'll have a beautiful lawn and a place to plant a garden. You can even grow and sell your own herbs."

"What makes you think I'm moving in here and going to run this poor-excuse-for-a-store?"

His eyes widened. "If you're not, then what are you doing here?"

"I'm taking this eyesore off your hands. I'm buying it from you, getting it presentable, and selling it as fast as I can."

She turned to go inside. He grabbed her elbow. "You're not staying?"

"That was never part of the plan. You said fix up the old place and sell it. Not stay here, sink into oblivion, and run a general store."

"I thought you liked it? You did when Gram was running it. You talked about taking it over one day."

"Yeah? See how well that idea panned out?"

"I thought you wanted to escape from your life."

"I did. I do. But not forever. I want to have a life, but I don't want to be Gram."

"Why not? She was a happy woman."

"Not so sure. Her daughter died. Her granddaughter deserted her. She didn't seem so happy."

"She did to me."

"Ah, well. We'll have to agree to disagree. I want more out of life."

"Don't we all? What exactly do you want?" He stood, feet spread apart, arms folded across his chest.

"Good question. I don't know." She faced him. *Not telling him I want a family, kids.* "I'm hoping to find out here."

He snorted. "Why should you?" His face clouded, his brows knitted. "Whatever the hell you want, it sure isn't here, is it?"

She reached out and touched his forearm. "Honestly? I don't know. All I know is I need this quiet time to figure it out."

His expression softened. "Sorry. I don't mean to push you."

"Yes, you do. You always have. Probably the best thing. Though it makes me want to slug you."

He laughed. "Some things never change."

She grinned. "Let's go." She entered the main room and looked around. "Hell, I don't know where to start."

Flint tossed a roll of paper towels at her. "Take these. I'll fill the bucket."

When he returned, he opened a package of sponges and handed one to her.

"First the counter. So we can put stuff there." Cassie dipped her sponge into the warm, soapy water.

"Right." She scrubbed. Before she could blink, the pail was black with dirt. "Can't wash away ten years of dirt with one pail."

Flint started the trek to the sink, reminding her of *The Sorcerer's Apprentice*. Back and forth, fill the pail, get a new sponge, empty the pail, and start all over again. Cassie stripped the grime from the glass cabinet doors. "There. Look! Now you can see inside."

"I remember those shelves were filled with canned goods and boxes of Jell-O pudding mix." Flint stopped to stare.

Cassie opened the cabinet, cleaned off the shelf then ran her hand over it. "Gram tucked away a package of butterscotch pudding mix in the back."

"Yeah?"

Her eyes misted. "And when I'd been good, worked hard, she'd break it out and make it for dinner."

"Butterscotch your favorite?"

"Always."

"Me, too. My mother made it, too."

"She make a big Sunday dinner?"

"Used to. I doubt it, now. My parents live in Arizona. Just the two of them."

"When they still lived here, did you go there every Sunday?"

"Nope. I have a life."

"I heard about your life. You're a professional proposer!"

Anger flashed across Flint's face. Then his dark eyes gleamed. He dipped his sponge in a pail of clean sudsy water and flicked it at her.

"Oh! You dirty rat!" She grabbed a handful of water and threw it at him.

He retaliated, wiping a wet hand down her cheek. Within seconds, it was a water fight. Cassie hid behind the counter, hoarding three saturated sponges. Flint had control of what was left in the pail. Soapy suds clung to his scruffy face. Cassie pointed and laughed.

He put a chair up on the small table in the center of the room. "Watch it. I'm bigger than you are."

"Yeah, but I'm faster."

"Not anymore."

"Yes, I am."

Cassie rifled the sponges at him rapidly, one after another as she broke for the door. The surprise slowed Flint. She dashed outside and ran down the street, toward the lake. Her burnished hair came undone from the clip holding it in place and swung free. She raced toward Cedar Lake, her legs pumping hard as she sucked in fresh, country air.

No longer a skinny eighteen-year-old, Flint flew after her. His motion fluid, he gained ground. She glanced back and shrieked. Sweat plastered her T-shirt to her breasts and her shorts to her butt. Her pleas for mercy didn't stop him. Folks in cars pulled to the side of the road and stared.

"Is she okay?" Cassie heard one woman say.

"Go get her, Flint! You're gaining on her," a man piped up.

And then there it was. The lake. The water so cool, calm, and serene. Heat traveled up until even her ears felt hot. She got to the edge of the lake, sloughed off her sandals, then dove in.

Flint stopped short, shucked his jeans, socks and shoes, and followed her.

WHEN HE SURFACED, HE looked for Cassie. Though her head was visible, she pawed at the water. Wet clothing weighed a swimmer down, even a strong swimmer.

"You okay?" He pulled up alongside her.

"No," she sputtered.

He slid an arm around her middle and hauled her up against his side. "Hang on."

She clung to his shirt. He glided slowly to the ladder. Gripping her upper arm, he eased her closer until she could grasp a rung. Hanging on, she gulped air.

"You all right?"

She gripped his shirt, pulling him up against her, and kissed him. It wasn't a passionate kiss, more like a thank-you. He didn't care. He'd take any kiss he could get. Then she shoved him under water. He popped up, shaking his head, laughing.

"You haven't changed."

"Caught you off guard, didn't I?"

"Everything you do catches me off guard." His gaze connected with hers.

A blush colored her cheeks. "Yeah, well, don't get used to it." She brought her knees to her chest and pushed up on the ladder. In a hop-skip, she stood on the dock, drenched clothes clinging to her body like a second skin. She pulled at the garments, but they snapped right back.

"Thanks for improving the view." Flint stood next to her.

Could he ever get the picture of her almost-naked body, dripping wet, standing in front of him, inviting him to love her, out of his head? Nope. No way. The image was burned into his brain. Slender but inviting was how he'd describe her. His dick was ready, willing, and able to accept an invitation right now.

"You, too," she said, staring first at his chest then at his crotch. His boxers hid nothing.

"Damn!" He picked up his clothes, holding them in front of his groin. "Let's go." He glanced back to make sure she was behind him then headed for the store. Cassie, holding her arm over her chest and her shoes in front of her private parts, followed him.

First one inside, Flint stood behind the counter, ripped off his boxers then jammed his wet legs into his jeans. He struggled to get the garment over his damp hips.

"Not bad. Not bad at all." Cassie leaned over, staring at his butt, and grinned.

Not used to being commando, Flint pushed his dick aside to avoid a horrendous caught-in-the-zipper agony and closed his pants. He peeled his shirt off and spread it over the back of a chair. The heat of her stare drew his attention. He turned to find her face red and her eyes wide.

Trapped, checking him out. He grinned. Every man's dream to be checked out by a chick like Cassandra Wells. He shifted his weight.

"Cold?"

She immediately cast her gaze to her chest.

"No, no. I don't mean that. You're shivering."

"It's cold in here."

"Especially when you're soaking wet. Let's go home, change, get lunch, and then finish up here for today."

She nodded. He snatched his T-shirt off the chair and looked around. "We got about half the first layer of grime off."

"On about half the stuff in here."

"Good start. Let's go." He opened the door for her and followed along. His mother had raised him to be polite—"ladies first" and all. But the bonus was being able to watch Cassie from behind and zero in on her delicious butt, small, tight, and damn cute in those clingy, wet shorts. He savored the moment, almost bumping into her when she reached the truck.

"Sorry." Heat climbed his neck. Did she catch him looking? He opened the door, threw his shirt in the back, and slid behind the wheel. They drove in silence for a while.

"I haven't had a water fight since I left Pine Grove." She combed her fingers through her hair.

"Nothing better on a hot day." He kept his eyes on the road.

She reached over and rested her cold hand on his warm forearm. He glanced over. Her eyes wetted. Turning away from him, she blinked rapidly.

"What's wrong?"

"Nothing. I forgot about the things I liked in Pine Grove." She pushed the heel of her hands against her eyes.

He smiled. "We had fun."

"Fun. Yep. Fun. I haven't had much fun in sixteen years."

"No?" He raised his eyebrows.

"Nope. Just work. Work, work, work. Dancing lessons. Singing lessons. Rehearsals. People breathing down my neck every waking moment."

"Including Basil?"

She laughed. "Oh yeah. He breathed down my neck, too, but for different reasons."

Once again, he saw color in her cheeks. He laughed. Basil was out of the picture now, right? Hey, he shouldn't be getting any ideas. No matter what memories he had of their times together, now Ms. Cassandra Wells was way out of his league. Respect. He needed to respect who she was now and not treat her like the cute teenager who'd made his blood hot.

"People grow up. Life gets in the way."

"Exactly. Life got in the way. My life. And maybe it's time for a change." She sat back, still covering her chest, and gazed out the window.

A pulse in his dick drew his attention. He and it should ignore what she'd said. Change didn't include him. Cassie had to sort her life out and decide what she wanted. And he'd put every cent he had on her not wanting him.

Chapter Seven

Once at Flint's house, Cassie decided to let him take charge in the kitchen. "Since you don't think I know one end of a can opener from the other, you can do lunch." She sniffed.

"Okay, okay. I take it back."

"Too late, mister." She sashayed over to the refrigerator. "I'll do drinks."

"Fine." He jammed a can of tuna in the can opener.

"I love tuna fish sandwiches!"

"Sucking up will get you nowhere," he growled.

Cassie laughed as she filled two glasses from the pitcher of iced tea in the fridge.

They took their lunch to the deck to eat outside amid the warmth of midday. He moved the small table into the shade of a maple tree.

"Why aren't you married?" she blurted out.

His gaze shot up, connecting with hers. Cassie picked up half of her sandwich, wishing she hadn't spoken. Best to keep food in her mouth and shut up before she ruined a good thing.

"Why do you ask?"

Well, you opened the topic, Cassie—no going back now. She swallowed. "Most guys are married by now."

"Not me. Not yet anyway. Only a few false starts. Doesn't mean anything."

What are *false starts?*

"Nothing really. I was engaged a couple of times. No big deal." He picked up a carrot stick. "Weren't you?"

"Me? No. Once, yeah. One time." Yeah, having the tables turned didn't work for her. "So a couple of times, huh?"

"What difference does it make?" Flint took a bite of his sandwich.

"What the hell happened?" She resumed eating.

"Nothing." He waved her off. "Made the wrong choice. Didn't go through with it, so no harm, no foul."

"No harm, no foul? How far did you go?"

"What's it matter?" Picking up his glass of tea, he avoided her stare.

She eyed him. "You didn't go through with it...twice?"

He cleared his throat as he reached for another carrot stick. "Er, three times."

"*Three* times? I thought you were the serial proposer with two, but three? You take it to a new level."

His gaze shot to hers. "Who told you?"

"Marty."

Flint fisted his hand. "I'll kill him."

"Did you go all the way to the altar *three* times?"

"Only once before I changed my mind."

Her mouth fell open. Her brain remained stuck on *three*.

"Okay, okay. I know." He shifted in his seat. "Can we change the subject?"

"No. And the other two times?" She continued her interrogation.

"I came to my senses before wedding plans were made."

"Thank God. Three times? Wow." She shook her head. "Three times. Damn."

"Don't rub it in. I've taken plenty of shit about it already. You don't have to pile on."

"Who were these women?"

"No one you know." He refilled his glass and hers.

"No one from school?"

"Nope. Well, no. Not true. Becky Lawson came to Pine Grove senior year."

"Becky? Becky? Don't remember a Becky." She finished the last bite of half her sandwich.

"You didn't know her. She was a counselor in sleepaway camp every summer."

"Was she hot?"

"They were all hot. Do you think I'd marry anyone who wasn't?" His voice rose.

"Don't get upset. It was only a question. Not an accusation. Besides. You didn't marry them."

"Not because they weren't hot."

"Oh? Then why?"

"When I figure it out, I'll let you know. You're pretty nosy today. Finish up and let's get back to work."

"Sure, sure. I always know when you're hiding something."

"Do you?" He cocked an eyebrow.

"Yeah. I used to. And I always dug it out of you. This won't be any different."

"Things change, Cassie. I'm not the same, naïve, goofy kid. Not putty in your hands or the hands of any woman anymore."

"I see. Three struck out after being engaged."

His face grew stormy. "Shut the fuck up, okay?"

She held up her palms. "Okay. Sorry. No more. Won't mention it again."

He snorted. "As if you could avoid needling me about anything until you get what you want."

"Good memory. I'll lay off. I'm not the same, ball-busting teen I used to be, either."

"Glad to hear it." He popped the last bite in his mouth, grabbed a carrot stick, and stood up.

After they returned to the kitchen, Cassie loaded the plates into the dishwasher, and when she finished, Flint added the glasses. Then he laced his fingers with hers and headed for the door.

Once in the truck, he faced her. "No more questions. Okay?"

"Okay."

He started the car and headed for the store.

When they got inside, Flint poked around in the back. "I found another bucket. Let's divide stuff up. Which do you want, the floor or the milk display case?"

"Floor. I need the exercise."

"Done." He handed her a mop. She filled the bucket and toted it to a corner.

"Music?" Flint set his phone on the counter.

"What do you like?" She shoved the mop into the hot, soapy water.

"Music from your last show." He fiddled around with his cell until she heard her own voice, loud and clear, singing, "Be My Man."

She froze. "How do you know?"

"If you're gonna talk, you're gonna ruin the song."

She waited until it finished then paused it. "How do you know?"

"I went to see it."

"You did?"

"Twice." He left the room. The sound of the water pounding the bottom of the bucket echoed in the empty room.

Emotion gathered in her chest. Turning away from the doorway, she stared at the mop. Flint had been coming to see her on Broadway? Why didn't he come backstage? Why didn't he try to get in touch with her?

A lump as big as a watermelon lodged in her throat. She'd done the show four years ago. Flint had cared so much he had the music?

Did he still care? Did he care enough to walk away from three women because of Cassie? When he returned, softly singing the lyrics to the next song, she faced him.

She wasn't quick enough to wipe a tear away before he spotted it. "What's wrong?"

Words crowded in her throat but couldn't get past the lump. She simply couldn't speak. Blinking away the wetness, she tore her gaze from his and focused on the mop. Bending down, she moved the metal piece around until it wrung excess water from the mop. She straightened and began to wash the floor.

"What?"

All she could do was shake her head.

THE MINUTE HE RETURNED with the bucket and got a glimpse of her face, he knew. He knew she knew. Damn! What an asshole he was. Why did he have to play her music? What did he think, she was an idiot? She couldn't add two and two and come up with four? No one else had. Well, Marty had.

When Flint had driven into the city or taken the bus to see her shows, he'd told everyone he was cultivating printing business in Manhattan. But Marty had known the truth. And Flint had seen every one of her shows and her movies. Sometimes, he'd drive to another town to see her movie over and over.

And the movies made of her musicals. Damn, he knew every word of the soundtrack. In the shower, he'd sing it himself. He loved the music but especially her voice. There was a sweet quality to her soprano. Or was he the only one who heard it? Nah. It was why her shows and movies were so successful. Cassie had a gift, and it reached people all over the world.

He may have blown his cover, but he'd be damned if he'd admit it. Let her guess. He'd never own up to the fact Cassie Wells was responsible for his three broken engagements. He'd rather die than admit it. Every time, he'd yell at himself, call himself names. "Stupid, foolish, idiot, asshole, fucking moron groupie."

It didn't matter how mad he got at himself, his heart had other ideas. He couldn't reason with it, trick it, or strike a bargain. He'd had three pretty, sweet women who were intelligent—except they'd fallen for him—and he'd walked away each time.

Let Cassie guess. He'd stonewall her all the way. She'd never know the truth. He strode over to the counter and switched the music to ragtime jazz by Scott Joplin.

"You used to like this."

"Still do," she choked out, turning away from him.

Like a nimble football player, he'd recovered his own fumble. Cassie danced around with the mop. He enjoyed watching her move. Her graceful moves drew his eye. While his hands may have worked on the case, his gaze followed her around the room.

"I thought you didn't like rehearsals."

"This is a free-form thing. No pressure."

"Okay. Right."

After his mistake with the music, their conversation dried up. They listened to the jazz and worked away, cleaning. Before long, Flint could see progress. They peeled away the grimy surface of the neglected space to reveal some of the charm of days gone by.

"Got any wood polish?" Cassie wrung out her mop and went in the storage room.

"In the truck. Be right back." Flint retrieved a box with other cleaning supplies: glass cleaner, wood polish, and silver polish. Cassie rummaged through it until she found what she wanted.

"Oh yes! Old English! I'm gonna go over these scratches first. Then put on polish." She got down on her hands and knees, lovingly swabbing shallow gouges in the floor as if they were tender cuts and abrasions on a child.

Flint finished up the second case and plucked the bottle of glass cleaner from the box. He shined up the glass until it gleamed.

"That looks amazing," she said, turning her head.

"Thanks. These came pretty clean. Should I turn them on?"

"Why not? We can keep water cold in there."

"Good idea." He bent over and plugged in the machine. The motor jumped to life. Flint smiled. Maybe this old place wasn't a lost cause—yet.

"It works! I can't believe it." She pushed to her feet.

I've got a couple of water bottles in the truck."

They spent the rest of the afternoon washing, polishing, and reminiscing.

"Where's all the cheap candy Gram kept in these things?" Cassie reached in to clean one of the big glass jars.

"We ate it." Flint chuckled.

"That was the best. Tootsie Rolls were my favorite."

"Yeah? Starburst was mine."

"Do you remember the time I put liver in a Tootsie Roll wrapper and gave it to Cabot Tremont?"

"He barfed for a week."

Cassie bent over, making retching noises, imitating the boy. Flint burst out laughing. They worked, talked, and joked until after six. His cell rang. Flint recognized Marty's number.

"Where the hell are you?" his brother demanded.

"We're at the store. What's the problem?" He wiped a wet hand on his jeans.

"Dinner in fifteen. And you'd both better be here."

"Okay. Sorry, Marty."

"Did you hear?"

"Yes. Dinner in fifteen. We lost track of time."

"Spare me what you were doing, okay? Just get your asses back here."

Click.

Cassie and Flint stood at the door and surveyed the shop.

"Looks a helluva lot better than it did." He smiled.

"Yeah, but it still looks tired out."

"Walls need work." Flint shifted his weight.

"Yeah, fresh paint." Cassie bit her lip.

"Wood paneling needs refinishing."

"Floor, too."

"New cash register?" Flint cocked an eyebrow.

"I'm dumping this one from the Dark Ages."

"Come on. We've gotta go."

They piled into the truck and were back at Flint's house in five minutes.

"Oh my God. You two are taking showers before you sit down to eat. Look at you. You look like you fell into a mud puddle."

"We did. Gram's mud puddle." Cassie grinned.

"Go on. I'll keep it warm for a little longer."

Flint sniffed the air. "Greek casserole?"

"Yes. Hurry up!"

Cassie scurried into her bedroom and closed the door. Flint took the stairs two at a time.

ABOUT NINE O'CLOCK, Flint pulled out a glass pitcher from the fridge. "Iced tea?"

"Did you make this?"

"Yep. And with mint from the garden. It's hot in here. Let's go outside."

He poured three glasses and put them on a tray. Cassie held the door open. There were four white wicker rocking chairs on the wraparound front porch, flanked by matching, wicker tables. Cassie plopped down on a chair, resting her bare feet on the porch railing.

Flint sat next to her. The door banged open, slamming into the house, and Marty grabbed the third chair.

"Effing hot in the kitchen."

"I keep telling you to grill outside on hot days."

"Like you tell me to do everything." He glared at Flint.

"Boys, boys. Come on. It's too hot to fight." Cassie sipped the cool drink, savoring the flavor and the memories the taste conjured up. "Damn, did your mother teach you how to make this?"

"Since you're asking, yes. She did." Flint took a swig.

"She made the best mint tea ever."

"She taught me to cook because Flint didn't want to learn," Marty piped up.

"I learned the important stuff. Iced tea, brownies, and a wicked mojito."

Cassie listened to the crickets and gazed at the dazzling array of twinkling stars. The night sky was clear. The bright, round moon dominated the blackness. She swore if she reached out, she could touch it.

Hot days tempered by cool nights reminded her of summers in Pine Grove. The sun would shine until it simply couldn't anymore, burning and blistering everything in its path until the relief of nightfall. Rainy days brought rest, reading, and working in the store.

"I'm gonna do it," she spoke to herself.

"Do what?" Marty asked.

"I'm gonna restore the shop. Bring it back to life."

"Really? It's gonna cost a ton," Marty pointed out.

"So what? I can afford it. A tribute to Gram."

"If you're not gonna run it, why bother?" Flint asked.

"Hmm. No. I can't run it. I'll sell it. If it's fixed up, I shouldn't have any trouble finding a buyer, right?"

"Oh sure. People are lined up around the effing block to own a general store in a small town in the middle of nowhere and work twenty-four seven."

Cassie clicked her tongue. "Flint, always the pessimist."

"And what if you don't sell?"

"You sound like my father." She imitated his deep voice. "And what if you don't get the part?"

"He asked you that?" The question came from Marty.

"Every time. And I always got the part. Well, almost always." She chuckled. "All the important ones."

"So, you'll dig up an alternate plan if you can't find a buyer?" Flint faced her.

"My brother taught me not to worry in advance. He'd tell me there'd be plenty of time to worry about not having a buyer if I don't get one. I don't have to worry ahead of time."

Silence settled on the little group. They rocked and drank, each lost in their own thoughts.

"I know just the guy to do the work." Marty put down his glass.

"Who?" Flint asked.

"Will Lennox, Jess's brother."

"Oh yeah. Right. I hear Nate Travers is working with him. They're good. But don't fool around with Nate, okay?"

"Why?" Cassie raised her eyebrows.

"He's a heartbreaker." Flint's gaze connected with hers.

"Oh, and you're not? Three broken engagements? I guess it takes one to know one."

Marty laughed.

"Fine. You gonna be annoying? Do it yourself. Do it all yourself." Flint pushed to his feet and strode to the door.

Cassie jumped up to block his path. "I'm sorry. I shouldn't have said that."

"No, you shouldn't. You don't know anything about me or my life for the past sixteen years. Stop judging me."

"Okay. You're right. I'm sorry." Her tone softened. She rested her palm on his cheek.

"Forgiven. For now. Don't do it again."

"Who's gonna run our business while you're renovating the store?" Marty cast a suspicious eye on his brother.

"Will and Nate are gonna do the renovation. I'm going to help Cassie supervise."

"Oh, I see. Yeah. Right." Marty shook his head.

"Can't you take over for a few days?"

"Of course. Just be honest. Don't pretend you're going to be at the office when you're not."

"Okay, okay. Don't be a fuckin' pain in the ass."

"I'm not. I'm your partner."

"I can do it. As long as I can reach you by phone in case there's a problem. I can handle it. I deal with producers and directors all the time." Cassie finished her drink.

"He doesn't want you alone with Nate Travers, Mr. Seduction."

"And what's wrong with that?" Flint threw a steely glance at his brother.

"Be honest, Flint. Tell her it's because you want her for yourself. You've been waiting sixteen years to say it. So say it, damn it!" Marty pushed to his feet and stalked across the porch and into the house, slamming the door behind him.

"IT'S NOT TRUE. THINKS he knows everything. He's a pain in the ass." Flint rubbed his forehead, hiding his eyes. How could he face Cassie, now the truth was out? He didn't want her to know. Damn it, he had his pride, didn't he? Back in the day, she read him like a book. He'd never been able to hide anything from her. Would it be true now? No way would he chance it. Her penetrating stare had stripped him bare more times than he cared to recall. He'd expected her to become a prosecuting attorney, not an actress.

As the silence wore on, the air thickened between them. She squirmed in her seat then glanced at her watch.

"I'm going to read for a bit then go to sleep. Big day ahead. Good night, Flint."

He sighed. Thank God she'd given him a way out. "Sure, sure. Good night."

She rose from the chair, grabbed Marty's empty glass and her own, then went inside. He headed for the steps and a walk in the cool night air. His head buzzed, thoughts traveled through at warp speed. No way could he sleep now.

He ambled down the quiet street. Farmhouses trimmed with gingerbread, drab Cape Cods, and mini-Victorians in bright colors trimmed in white resided peacefully, shoulder to shoulder. The McKay dark-blue house with white trim and shutters ruled over a bigger lot with more elbow room. He passed his favorite house—a tall, yellow Victorian with white trim.

When he was a teen, Flint got odd jobs from the couple in that house. Along with his paper route, he earned enough to take girls on dates for a burger or a movie. Independent, even as a lad, Flint loved making his own money. He and Marty had pooled their extra cash and started a baseball card collection together.

Marty! Since when did he get such a big mouth anyway? Flint fisted his hands by his sides. His little brother could think up new ways to tempt Flint into punching him out. If Flint didn't put his foot in it, Marty would do it for him. But this was the worst.

It wasn't like he'd told Marty how he felt about Cassie. His brother was pretty smart, he must have put the pieces together. Hell, Flint didn't figure it out until his last broken engagement. Sure, he'd had feelings for Cassie for years, but she was famous—he didn't have a chance. Why would a lingering crush keep him from getting married to someone else? He needed to stop getting engaged and breaking it off. After wracking his brain for a couple of months, looking for the reason why he kept backing out, he figured the best way to find out was to see a shrink. On the sly, he'd visited a therapist.

The doctor had put his finger on it pretty quick. Flint had never gotten over Cassie.

"You're idealizing Cassie. Expecting other women to make you feel the same way she did. Consider reconnecting. Perhaps spending time with her would convince you she isn't the same person and maybe you can get the closure you need to move on."

Yeah? Easier said than done. How do you approach a successful, famous actress with an idea? "Excuse me, Ms. Wells, would you mind spending a weekend with me so I can find out what a rat you really are and fall out of love with you?" He chuckled at the memory. But the doc had found the cause, even if he didn't have an easy fix.

The silence of the night soothed him. He loved Pine Grove, not only because it was familiar, but because there was a truth here among people making their living from the land or clashing with the elements, fighting to survive, thrive, and find happiness. Pine Grove was a town devoid of pretense, airs, or whatever you want to call it. Damn, the place was real—beauty, warts, and all. And he counted on it, every day of his life.

It didn't take long for Flint to realize walking down the block wouldn't solve his problem, so he returned home to find his brother on the porch. Marty pushed to his feet.

"What the fuck do you want? Haven't you done enough harm?"

Marty gripped Flint's arm. "Look, I'm sorry. Sort of."

"Sort of?" Flint cocked an eyebrow.

"Yeah. I shouldn't have told your secret, but maybe it's good to have it out in the open. Face it and get over it."

"Really? Making Cassie feel like she's responsible for my fucked-up life?"

"Come on, Flint. Don't be a dick. You know what I mean. Now you can talk about it with her. Find out how she feels."

"I know how she feels, Marty. She was engaged to another guy like five minutes ago. Doesn't that pound it into your thick head she's not exactly pining over me?"

"Okay, okay. Maybe. She's free now. And she's here."

"Oh, and you expect the broken-down store and this poor little town will put a spell on her, convincing her to give up her fancy life, put on overalls, and become a hick's wife?"

"When you put it that way, it doesn't sound plausible."

"Ya think?" Flint shook his brother's hand off. "I'm going to bed."

"Truth is better than secrets. Denial never won a woman or brought peace. You never know. Maybe she still has feelings for you?"

"Yeah? And maybe eagles will become vegetarians. Good try. Good night, Marty."

Still steamed, he barely kept from socking his brother. And Marty's stupid rationales. What a fuckin' idiot! How could they possibly be related? Flint slammed into the house and climbed the stairs two at a time.

Chapter Eight

The slamming of the door didn't wake Cassie because she wasn't asleep. Could Marty have been right? Did Flint still care for her, love her? Gooseflesh stole up her arm. Memories of her regret at leaving him and the tiny town she'd come to love flooded back.

She'd begged her mother for one more night before leaving.

"Producers won't wait, Cassie."

"Please, Mom. Just one more night."

"So you can spend it with the farmer?"

"He's not a farmer."

"Might as well be. You're destined for bigger, better things."

"You don't know Flint. He's kind and sweet."

"Yeah, yeah. And I know how hormones rule when you're sixteen. You'll see, in a month you won't even remember his name."

"Don't say that! I'll never forget him. Please, Mom."

"Okay, okay. I'll make something up. On Thursday, at eight a.m., sharp, we head for New York."

"Deal."

"You promise?"

Cassie had swiped her finger across her heart. "Promise."

She couldn't bring herself to tell Flint it was their last night. What if he had pleaded with her to stay, maybe even proposed marriage? What would she have said? How could she explain she'd be going off to do something she'd been trained for since she was a little kid? Would he understand? She'd doubted it. Did she want to leave?

She hadn't been given a choice. And if he'd proposed...she'd shoved the thought out of her mind.

She'd packed a midnight snack, and they had stolen off to find an empty field where they could be alone. In the cool August night, they had made love three times. Lying on a blanket, snuggled against his warm body, she'd listened to him sketch out plans for their future.

"And then, we'll have a baby. Maybe two or three. You're gonna make a great mom."

Her heart had broken at the sincerity in his voice. Up until her mother had received the phone call, a future as a performer had been a pipedream. She'd tossed her lot in with Flint, believed in him. He was real, his plans were real, something she could hold onto. With one phone call, everything had changed, and she didn't have the heart to tell him.

They'd stayed up all night. He returned her to her bed at six. Her mother woke her at seven. They'd packed the car and hit the road. Two days later, Cassie had tried to write him, but the words always came out wrong. She'd cried to her mother.

"You've got a great future. You're a gifted actress, with a voice like an angel. Don't throw it all away, sweetheart. You can be somebody, make a fortune and have a beautiful life. If Flint really loves you like he says he does, he won't stand in your way. He'll applaud you and wish you success."

She'd believed her mother. But her mother had been wrong about one thing. Cassie had never forgotten Flint. He owned a special space in her heart, and she'd wondered about him, from time to time. Where was Flint? Was he married with six kids? She'd assumed he'd found another woman to share his dream. Although it hurt her heart a little, she wished him only happiness.

But now she was reprising an old role. Could Flint still love her? Had he been carrying a torch for her all these years? She stood at a crossroads, not knowing which path to take.

Her mind wandered back to their last night. By then, Flint had become a good lover. She recalled the tenderness of his touch, how he'd excited her quickly and brought her to completion so unselfishly. She remembered the hardness of his body, his pecs and abs, so taut and powerful. She closed her eyes and let her mind recreate the feeling of him inside her. Oh God, her whole body heated, and her hips bucked at the thought.

Throwing the covers off to cool down, she wondered what it would be like to sleep with him again. He looked good, better than he had at eighteen. He'd filled out, his chest was broad and lightly covered with dark hair. His biceps bulged a bit, filling the sleeves of his T-shirt. His dark hair flopped carelessly over his forehead. Damn, he looked good.

Then it hit her. *I guess I never really loved Basil. How could I, if I'm so attracted to Flint? Basil did me a favor. Marriage to him—with or without kids—would have been a disaster.*

Turning her thoughts back to Flint, she figured, by now, he'd probably become a true expert at sex. The idea turned her on. *No way! I'm here to fix up the shop, sell it, and get the hell out of town—back to my life.*

She ground her teeth at the vision of endless rehearsals, people telling her what to do, dieting, weigh-ins, her mother harping, nagging all the time, and no sex. She didn't want the old life anymore, but what life did she want? She had no clue. After all, it was the only life she'd known for years.

She yawned. Her eyelids grew heavy. There'd be plenty of time to figure it out tomorrow. Like Scarlett O'Hara. She'd deal with her life and Flint McKay tomorrow.

THE NEXT MORNING AT eight fifteen, Flint's hard rap on her door woke Cassie. "Rise and shine, princess."

He chuckled at the muffled response. "Time to get up."

The door cracked open. A tousled, sleepy woman wrapped in a blanket looked up at him.

"I called Will Lennox. He's meeting us at the shop at nine. Pancakes are on. Get dressed. We've got work to do."

"Okay," came the mumbled reply then the door shut in his face.

Knowing Cassie slept in the nude made his dick twitch. Damn. She'd been naked on the other side of the blanket. If it had slipped out of her grasp, she'd have displayed everything, in all its sexy, curvy glory to his hungry eyes. The idea had him reeling. He turned on his heel, mentally begged his dick to forget what he saw, and returned to the kitchen.

"She up yet? She coming?"

"Yep."

"First come, first served." Marty shoveled three golden-brown hotcakes on a plate and handed it to his brother.

"Have to hand it to you. No one does these like you."

"Thanks. You called Will?"

"He and Nate are coming at nine thirty."

"I thought you told Cassie nine?"

"I did. This way, she'll move her butt."

"Sneaky. Very sneaky." Marty filled another plate and set it down next to Flint then poured three for himself.

Ten minutes later, Cassie slid into the chair next to Flint. She wore a low-cut T-shirt, showing cleavage, and tight jeans. Flint's gaze swept over her body like a device looking for mines. It lingered on her chest. He recalled how fine her breasts were, well-formed, full, and firm. His fingers tingled slightly at the memory of the smooth skin and the hard nipple. He coughed then cleared his throat, while attempting to drag his eyes from her curves.

"You're not sick, are you?"

He shook his head. Nope, nothing wrong with him tearing her clothes off and making passionate love to her wouldn't cure.

They finished eating and loaded up the truck with more paper towels and soap. Arriving at nine, Cassie lugged supplies in then looked around.

"Where's the contractor?"

"He's not coming till nine thirty."

"You lied to me?"

"Didn't exactly lie. Fudged a little. Didn't know you could dress so fast."

She laughed. "After all the quick changes I've had to do on stage, I'm the fastest dresser you'll ever meet."

The bell on the front door tinkled, and two men walked in. One man, blond and good-looking, spoke first.

"I'm Will Lennox. This is my partner, Nate Travers. You must be Cassandra Wells."

She shook his hand. "Nice to meet you."

Nate's eyes lit up as he moved to shake her hand. He held it too long. Cassie pulled away first. *Stupid asshole. Doesn't know what not to do.* Flint chuckled to himself. Maybe Nate wasn't going to be such a threat after all.

Threat? Hell, Flint didn't have any claim on Cassie. Wasn't even interested in her anymore, was he? Who wanted a famous wife? Eating dinner out interrupted so she could sign autographs? Or having her flitting off to Europe or other sexy places with other men to make a movie? Not him. Hell no. No way. She wasn't the same, sweet, unspoiled child he'd fallen for, was she? He sighed. Perhaps the whole being-in-love thing was over?

"What do you want us to do?" Will asked, pulling out a notebook and pen. Flint hauled four stools out from the office. The three men and Cassie sat at the small soda fountain. Will faced her.

"I think she wants the place restored, right?" Flint glanced at her.

"Back to the way it was."

"So floor refinished, walls painted. What else?"

They went through item by item the changes needed. Will took notes while Nate drooled over Cassie. Flint watched, getting new respect for her and the way she handled Nate. She didn't really flirt, but she didn't get mad, either. She manipulated him with her smile.

If Nate Travers assumed she'd meant something she didn't by her attitude, it was his own fault. He watched the actress weave her invisible web around the young man, who had no idea what was going on.

"This it?" Will put the pen in his breast pocket.

"I think so."

"We'll work up an estimate and email it to you." He rose.

"After we take 15 percent off, as a courtesy," Nate put in.

Will glared at his assistant, who didn't notice. "Come on, lover boy. Let's go." Will stood up and motioned to the door.

"How long will an estimate take?" Cassie followed them out.

"A week?"

"Gives us time to get the place ready," Flint put in.

Cassie nodded. Flint locked the door after Will and Nate left.

"That went well." He leaned against the door.

"Do you really think they'll take 15 percent off?"

"If Nate has any say in it, yeah. You had him eating out of your hand."

"Hmm. Funny. I play a role from one of my movies and guys seem to fall in line, like dogs waiting for a treat."

"You do it well. Haven't used it on me yet, have you?" Flint cocked an eyebrow.

"Don't need to."

He laughed. "Am I easy to maneuver?"

"Reasonable."

"Thanks."

She curtsied.

"If you don't mind, I'm going to swing by the office and see what's going on. I'll be back this afternoon. Okay?"

"Of course. I appreciate the time you've given me. This isn't your headache. It's mine. You've already done way more than your share."

"I'll be back." He closed the door gently behind him.

LOOKING AROUND, SHE sighed and hoisted her butt up on a chair at the counter. Swiveling around, she faced the empty store. Dust particles no longer glistened in the sun. She could breathe just fine. The patina had worn off the wood floor, the old refrigerated case looked tired.

There was a wall of shelves her grandfather had built. She never knew him. He'd passed on before she'd made contact with her birth family. The paint on the shelves had faded. The color scheme for the store had been a bright, cheerful blue and white. Now washed out, the blue had lost its luster, and the white had grayed from dirt and age.

"Blue and white. What do you think, Gram? Maybe, beige and white now? Something more modern?" She smiled. "Beige and black? Beige and black trim?"

That would do it. She put the cast album from her last Broadway musical on her phone so she could sing along as she worked. After filling the bucket with warm, sudsy water, she hit play, grabbed the sponge, and climbed up on the stepladder to reach the top shelves.

Before she was even through the first two songs, the water was black with dirt. Down she went, got new soapy water, and climbed up again. She spent the morning singing, cleaning, and trekking up and down the steps. By noon, the bookcase was clean enough to be primed and painted.

Cassie washed up then headed down the block, looking for a place to grab lunch. She spotted The Cozy Café. After wiping her hands on her jeans, she went in.

"Oh my God, if it isn't Cassie Wells! I'll be darned." Laura Dailey dried her hands on her apron and hugged the girl.

"Good to see you, Mrs. Dailey. Still baking?" The aroma of butter and sugar made her stomach rumble.

"You bet. Call me Laura now. You're older. Hungry? Got a batch of scones fresh from the oven. Sit down, sit down." Laura handed Cassie a menu.

"Starving." Cassie took a seat at a table for two by the window already set up with utensils and water. Sun gleamed off Cedar Lake. An eagle swooped over the water looking for lunch.

"I recommend the roast beef on a croissant. Amy makes the roast beef herself and slices it real thin."

"Can you join me?" She put the green-and-white checked cloth napkin on her lap.

Laura returned to the kitchen for a moment. "Amy gave me the green light. Haven't seen you for many years. But I've been following your career. We're real proud of you." Laura took the other seat.

"Thanks."

"Whatcha doin' next?"

"Fixing up Gram's store." Cassie sipped her water.

"Really? Fixing to run it or sell it?"

"Sell it." Cassie's gaze wandered to the walls. Oil paintings of farm scenes added charm to the café.

Laura nodded. Amy brought their food.

"Those paintings were done by local folks. We've got lots of talent in Pine Grove." Laura beamed with pride.

"Nice." She tucked into her meal. "Mmm. And this is the best roast beef sandwich I've ever eaten."

Amy smiled then dropped the bill on the table. Cassie reached for it, but Laura put her hand over it first.

"My treat."

"No, Laura. Really."

"Don't argue with an old woman. How's the store comin'?"

"I need paint." She checked her phone for the time.

"You gonna paint, yourself?"

Cassie nodded.

"Ever painted before?"

"Nope." Cassie stood up.

"You go on down to Peters' Hardware. They got a new guy. Real good-lookin'. He knows all about paint. His name's Brady Atchison. Tell him I sent you." Laura also rose to her feet.

"Okay. Thanks."

Cassie dropped a ten-dollar bill on the table and hugged Laura. "Great to see you."

"Your grandmother would have been so proud. Keep it up." Laura smiled.

Cassie headed down the street to the hardware store. A bell tinkled when she opened the door. Blue eyes looked up from a ledger on the counter when she walked in.

"Howdy. Can I help you?" A blinding smile from a gorgeous man stopped her.

"I'm looking for Brady Atchison?"

"You found him. What can I do for you?"

Cassie barely ripped her gaze from his wide shoulders and tight T-shirt. Clean-shaven with short blond hair, Brady stepped from behind the counter.

"I need paint." Cassie stumbled over her words.

"What kind of paint?" He moved closer.

"Uh. I don't know."

"Indoor or outdoor?"

"Indoor," she replied.

"Are you painting, or is someone else?"

"I'm painting. I think."

"Ever painted before?"

"No. But how hard can it be?"

He laughed, a deep baritone laugh from his six-foot-two-inch frame. Cassie thought she'd melt.

"Can you show me what I need?"

"Little lady, I can not only show you, but I can tell you how to paint, too."

"Are you an expert?"

"I'm experienced." Brady's gaze swept over her like a warm blanket. "You look familiar."

"We've never met."

"I know you from somewhere."

Cassie turned her brightest smile on him. "Now how about you showing me how to paint?" She stepped closer and looked up into his eyes.

FLINT KNOCKED ON THE door. When he laid eyes on Cassie, his mouth fell open.

"What the hell happened to you?"

"I decided to paint the shelves. Don't they look great?" She brushed back her paint-splattered hair from her forehead.

"You're covered."

"I know. Never done this before. Brady showed me how. I don't think there's a neat way to paint though." She padded across the room in bare feet spotted with beige paint. Hoisting herself into a chair by the fountain, she gazed at her work.

"Brady?"

"Yeah. The cute guy at the hardware store."

Flint cringed. "You didn't fall for his lines, did you?"

"We talked about paint. He gave me a discount 'cause he likes my movies. What do you think?"

Flint let out a breath. He chuckled. "That you match the shelves perfectly. Stand over there. Go ahead. You'll be camouflaged."

Cassie looked down at her jeans and shirt. "Oops."

"Oops is right. I hope you bought water base paint." He took a wet sponge and ran it down her backside. She jumped. "Hey!"

"Testing to see if it'll wash off."

"And?"

"You bought the right stuff."

"I need a shower." She took the sponge from him and wiped her hands.

"And your clothes need to be hosed off."

"What are you doing here?"

"I was going to ask you to dinner, but..."

"It'll probably take me two hours to get cleaned up. Why don't we order pizza?"

"Works for me." Flint pulled out his phone.

"I have some questions, too."

"What do you want?" He held the phone to his ear.

"Meatball, mushrooms, and peppers."

He placed the order, added a six-pack of beer, and put his cell down. "Okay. What do you want to know?"

Cassie hoisted herself onto a tall chair and faced him.

"What happened to Gram's house?"

Flint eased down into the seat next to her. "When she got sick, she had to borrow pretty heavy against it to cover bills. When she passed, the lawyer sold it and paid off the bank. There was only enough left for funeral and burial costs."

Cassie nodded. Her eyes filled with tears. He reached over and squeezed her hand.

"I wanted to come back for the funeral, but I was doing a play in London."

"I know. It didn't matter to Gram. She was already gone."

"I never got to say goodbye." A tear slipped down Cassie's cheek before she brushed it away.

"She knew you were headed for success. She accepted your days here were over."

"Did she?" Cassie's gaze connected with his.

"Of course. She bragged about you all the time."

A conversation he'd had with Cassie's grandmother popped into his mind.

"Don't fret, Flint. Cassie's a big star now. She's got more important things to do than hang around here. She's too big for this little town. She's made something of herself. Pretty darn good, considering her start in life."

"You're proud of her."

"Darn right I am."

"Guess you made the right decision," Flint had remarked.

"About giving her up?" Gram cocked an eyebrow. "I miss her, but I don't regret it. Best decision I ever made. With her mother passed, I couldn't bring her up right. Give her stuff. Her parents have given her the world, developed her natural talents. Do you think she'd be a big star if she lived with me? Hell, no."

"She was damn proud of you."

"Sometimes, I wonder what would have happened if she hadn't given me up for adoption."

"I remember her saying, it was the best decision she'd ever made."

"Really?" Cassie turned hopeful eyes his way.

He covered her hand with his. "She knew she couldn't give you much. She told me so. It must be hard, not having met your biological parents."

She nodded. "At least I know who my mother was. Gram used to talk about her all the time. I felt like I knew her. But she never mentioned my father. Always said she didn't know who it was. But I didn't believe her. Gram could be cagey."

Flint laughed. "Oh, yes she could. When she wanted to know something, she didn't stop until she'd pried it out of you. But return the favor? Never. She didn't gossip. And I bet she knew everybody's secrets."

Cassie laughed. "I bet she did."

A knock at the door interrupted them. Flint paid for the pizza and beer. He set it up on the counter. Cassie pulled paper plates from the bag. They took slices and ate quietly. When he'd finished his first piece, Flint spoke.

"There was one thing."

"What?"

"At the end. She said something I couldn't figure out."

"What?"

"She said. 'Hidden' then 'tell Cassie,' but she never finished the sentence."

"You were with her at the end?"

"Not the very end. But I did visit her in hospice."

Cassie put her head down on her arms and cried. In a muffled voice, she said, "That was so kind of you. So, so, very nice. Special. Thank you."

"I liked her. A lot. She was good to me." Flint moved closer and took Cassie in his arms. She sobbed against his shoulder.

"I wish I could have been here."

"It's not your fault. She understood."

"Maybe."

Cassie pushed out of Flint's embrace. He fished a handkerchief from his back pocket and offered it to her.

She wiped her face. "I'll buy you a new one."

"We'll throw it in the machine."

"Whatever."

They each took another slice.

"This is so good. I never eat pizza."

"Why not?"

"My weight."

"You're too skinny."

"Thanks." She punched him gently in the arm.

"I mean it. Dr. Flint prescribes a piece of pizza every day."

Cassie took a swig of beer. "I don't drink beer, either. Too fattening. This is so good!"

Flint kept his trap shut about her eating and drinking habits and chowed down. When he was almost finished, she piped up.

"Hmm. I wonder what Gram meant when she said 'hidden'?"

"I meant to ask her, but nurses came in and got busy. I had to leave."

"Gram loved old movies. She used to tell me stories about them. Sometimes recite the whole plot."

"The whole plot?" He raised his eyebrows.

"Yeah. And one day she said, 'They always hide things in the same place in the movies.'" Cassie tilted her head. "No. She couldn't mean? Could she?" She pushed to her feet. "Is the same furniture still here?"

"Yes."

"All of it?"

"I think so. Why?"

"Come with me." She crooked her finger at him and headed for the back of the shop. Through the archway were several rooms. One had a door. It was a small space but big enough for a desk, chair, lamp, and file cabinet. Cassie stopped at the desk. Flint lounged against the doorframe.

"Okay. So?"

"She said they always hid stuff in the same place in the movies. They tape the envelope with incriminating evidence to the bottom of a drawer. She said no one ever looked there except the hero." Cassie reached her hand under the center drawer. Her fingers touched something.

"Oh my God. No. No way. No." She shook her head.

"Oh, come on. She couldn't have." Flint moved into the room. He yanked the old drawer out of the desk and turned it upside down, spilling old postage stamps, pennies, nickels, paper clips, and push-pins in assorted colors. A yellowed envelope lay snug against the wood. She ripped it away.

"Cassie Wells," she read the front of the envelope.

"Go ahead. Open it." Flint stood next to her as she ran a finger along the edge then stopped.

Cassie shook her head.

"Why not?"

"I don't know. I think maybe it's something I don't want to know."

"It had better not be another will. Do you want me to open it?"

She nodded.

Flint took it, slipped a finger under the flap, and unsealed it. There was a sheet of paper inside. He took it out, unfolded it, and handed it to her. She sank down on a chair to read. Flint stood behind her, reading over her shoulder.

To Cassie,

I'm sorry to have kept this from you. I should have told you long ago. I hope you'll forgive me. I've always known who your father was. He died before your mother. It was a tractor accident. She said he was fixing to marry her, but then he got killed.

I'm ashamed to say, after he died, I never told his parents. I didn't want them to fight me for custody of you. With DNA testing, they could have proved you belonged to their family as much as mine. I'm sorry

I deprived you of a set of grandparents and maybe cousins, too. I don't know how many are in their family, I knew I had to be the one to raise you. Or at least make sure you got to a fine home.

That I did do. I met with a few families before I picked the Wells for you. And I made a good choice. I looked forward to your visits every summer. So proud of how well you developed, how happy and talented you were. I knew then I had done the right thing.

You probably won't find this until I'm gone. So there's no harm in telling you now who your daddy was. His name was Charlie Briggs. He was only seventeen when the tractor killed him. Your momma confessed to me he was the one. As much as they tried to hide, I'd see them together, so I figured he'd be it. She made me promise not to say anything. But I think you have a right to know.

His parents, Charles, Sr. and Winona Briggs may still live in Pine Grove. Or they may have moved away. I'm sorry I kept this information from you for so long. I was so afraid of losing you.

Do whatever you want with this. I'm so sorry Charlie and your mother never got to know you. They'd be so proud of the beautiful, sweet, talented daughter they made! I know I am.

Please forgive me. If you find them, I hope they welcome you.

Your loving grandmother,

The letter was signed "Gram" in a wobbly hand. Cassie sank down on the floor, staring at the paper.

"Holy shit," Flint muttered.

"Exactly."

Chapter Nine

Time stood still. The air thickened and breathing became an effort. She slumped against the back of the chair, her gaze darting around the room as she tried to accept the information she'd received.

"My father? Seventeen." She stared at the paper, unable to move.

"You okay?" Flint's big hand squeezed her shoulder.

"Charlie Briggs." In her mind, she heard her grandmother's voice reciting the words in the letter. Softly, Cassie repeated every word, struggling to accept it.

"Cassie?"

"Huh?"

"Snap out of it."

She stared at him. Flint wandered over to the front window and stopped.

"There's a Winnie Briggs, works part-time at Java the Hut." He rubbed his stubbly chin.

"Winnie? Like short for Winifred?"

"Or Winona?" Flint faced her.

"Oh my God! She's here. Still here." Cassie covered her mouth with her hand. Tears welled in her eyes.

"But I don't know about a Charles. Let's Google him." Flint slid his cell from his back pocket. He typed and tapped. "There's an obit for a Charles Briggs, Sr."

"Oh no! I missed him?"

"Looks like it. But Winnie. If she's really Winona, is still alive and still here."

"She works at Java?"

Flint nodded.

"What are we waiting for?" Cassie jumped up, stuffed the letter in her pocket, picked up her purse, and headed for the door.

"Don't you think you should clean up a little before going over there?"

"Oh yeah. Right. Let's go home." She pushed so hard the screen door banged against the side of the building.

"Gimme the key." Flint locked the door and they got in his truck.

"Briggs. So my real last name is Briggs."

Flint drove in silence. Cassie sat, trying to process what she'd learned. They arrived at Flint's home in five minutes.

"Wait for me. I'll be fast."

"Yeah, right. Be thorough. You want to make a good impression."

"I'm Cassandra Wells. I always make a good impression."

He chuckled.

True to her word, she was dressed with only an occasional telltale swipe of paint on her leg or neck in fifteen minutes.

"Will you take me there?" She folded a sweatshirt over her arm.

"Wouldn't miss this for the world."

She stared at him. "Why do you say that?"

"Because you are going to make the woman's day."

"You think so?"

"I'd place money on it, and I'm not a betting man." He opened the door of the truck and Cassie scooted inside. Before he put the vehicle in gear, he spoke.

"You've got the letter?"

She patted her purse. "Right here."

"Good."

They drove in silence. He pulled into the parking lot and turned off the ignition. Cassie put her hand on his arm. "Wait."

"What?"

"You're going in with me, aren't you?"

"I said I was."

"Oh yeah. Right."

He shot her a sideways glance. "Nervous?"

"Terrified."

"The woman who's faced millions on stage and screen?"

"Nothing ever meant this much before."

"I get it." He got out of the truck and offered her his hand. Cassie took it and squeezed. "Hey! You're cutting off my circulation."

She let go.

"Let's try this again." He laced his fingers with hers. "There. Okay?"

She nodded.

He opened the door, and Cassie stepped through. The tangy aroma of freshly-brewed coffee greeted her, winding its heavenly scent around her like a soft blanket. There was a counter on one side of the small shop and tables on the other. Two women bustled about, one young and one older.

Cassie stared at the older woman, studying her face and figure. There was nothing familiar about her.

"Hey, Flint. Long time, no see," the woman said. "What can I get you?" She plucked a pen from behind her ear and pulled a pad out of her apron pocket.

"I'll have a medium-sized Java special." He turned to Cassie.

"And you, young lady?" the woman asked, her gaze on the pad as she scribbled.

Cassie continued to stare at the woman. The lady fiddled with her unruly grey hair, pushing it back behind her ears, then straightening her apron. She looked at her hands then her feet. "Something wrong?"

"Uh, well..." Flint shifted his weight.

"Are you ordering something or just staring?" Her voice held an edge it didn't have when she spoke to Flint. "Look, you're wasting my time here. Are you ordering or not?"

"I'm your granddaughter," Cassie blurted out.

The woman narrowed her eyes. "I don't think so. I got two grandchildren. Both boys. What's this about?"

"Winnie, she'll have what I'm having. Okay?" Flint steered Cassie to a table, but she couldn't take her eyes off the woman behind the counter. "Uh, maybe this wasn't a good idea."

"She thinks I'm a whack job, doesn't she?"

"Probably."

"Damn." Cassie plopped down on the chair.

Winnie carried their drinks over. "Here you go."

Cassie grabbed the woman's sleeve. "I am your granddaughter. I have a letter. Are you Charlie Briggs mother?" She looked up into the woman's eyes.

Winnie sucked in air. "Charlie? He's been gone a long time. What do you know about Charlie?"

"He was my father."

Winnie's stare bored into Cassie. "You're a liar. Charlie died at seventeen. Never had no kids. Wasn't married. He was a good boy." She wheeled around on her heels.

"No, wait! Really. Look. It's a letter from my grandmother, Frances Meacham."

"Frances Meacham? She's been gone a long time, too. What do you do? Communicate with the dead?" Winnie's eyes widened.

Flint reached out and took Winnie's hand in both of his. "Maybe you'd better sit down."

"I'll get fired if I do."

"I'll explain." Cassie tried to smile.

"My manager's not going to give a rat's behind you want me to sit. Got it?"

"I'm Cassandra Wells."

"The hell you are!"

"She is. Really. Trust me."

At the commotion, the manager peeked out from a back room, then sidled up to Winnie.

"What's going on here?"

Cassie stood up. "Hi, I'm Cassandra Wells. Nice place you've got here. Great coffee! Can I talk privately with Mrs. Briggs for a moment? Would it be okay if she joined us, just for a few minutes?"

"Damn, you are Cassandra Wells, aren't you? Don't look quite the same without makeup, if you don't mind me saying." The woman rested her hands on her hips.

"Not at all." Cassie called on her acting talents to ignore the woman's rude remark and maintain a pleasant expression.

"No problem, Miss Wells. Sure, Winnie. Take your break now. Okay?" The woman smiled and gestured to the empty table.

"Thank you." Winnie sat quickly, as if she played a game of musical chairs and the music had stopped.

The woman returned to the back of the shop.

Winnie gestured toward the letter. "Let me see."

"First, promise you won't rip it up."

Winnie drew up another chair. "Okay, okay. Give it to me."

Cassie handed over the letter. Winnie licked her lips a couple of times as she read. Cassie's breathing became shallow. She listened to her pulse beat faster and faster. If the woman refused to believe Gram, there was nothing Cassie could do.

A few moments later, Winnie put the paper down. Her eyes filled. "So, you really are Charlie's little girl?"

Cassie nodded, her mouth as dry as cardboard.

Winnie stared at her. "Looks like maybe you got Charlie's blue eyes."

"Can you tell me something about him?"

"Got a picture of him, in my bag in the back. Guess I didn't know my son like I thought I did. Why didn't he tell me?"

Cassie shrugged. "Doesn't matter now."

"Matters to me. So, Frances kept you to herself, huh? Cut me and Charlie Senior out of the picture?"

"I guess."

"Figures. And look at you now. A big movie star?"

"Well..."

"You don't look like it."

Cassie shrugged. "No makeup."

"What do you want from me? You're all grown up. Not like I can take you to the circus or anything. If we even had a circus here. How are your parents? Good to you?"

"Very. I'd like to know more about you. About Charlie, my dad."

"You keep sayin' it, and it sounds so funny."

"I know."

"Guess we got something in common." Winnie checked her watch. "My break's over."

"Will you have dinner with me?" Cassie twisted a tissue in her hand.

"Dinner?"

"Let me take you out. To Homer's, maybe?" The words came out too fast.

Winnie shrugged. "Why not?"

"Tomorrow night?"

"Okay. I get off here at seven thirty. Too late?"

"It's perfect. Can you meet me at Homer's?" She stuffed the tissue in her pocket and smiled.

"Sure."

"By the way, what do you want me to call you?"

"How about Winnie? It's my name."

Cassie's shoulders drooped a little.

"I mean, it's not like I can bounce you on my knee or anything. Ya know? Granddaughter? You're all grown up."

"No one ever outgrows the need for grandparents." Cassie's voice shook a little.

"I guess. See ya at seven thirty." Winnie pushed to her feet and headed back to the counter.

"Please bring a picture of Charlie, my father." Cassie downed her coffee, left a generous tip on the table, and rose to leave.

Flint chugged the rest of his. "Ready?"

She nodded. When they returned to Flint's place, Cassie went up to her room and closed the door. Totally drained, she flopped down on the bed and was asleep instantly.

"DO YOU WANT ME TO COME with you?" Flint asked.

Cassie shook her head. "Nope. I can handle it."

"You're sure?"

"Yeah. But can you pick me up?"

"Of course. Text me when you're ready."

She nodded. One more look in the mirror satisfied her. She'd put on full makeup to convince Winnie she was really Cassandra Wells. She wore a slightly frilly white dress, off the shoulder with a ruffle around the neckline. Three-quarter sleeves, waist pinched in to show off her curves. The skirt fell a bit below the knee.

"You look great. Hot date?" Marty said, banging through the screen door.

"Dinner with my grandmother."

"You having a séance?"

"My other grandmother. It's a long story. Ask Flint. I gotta go."

She climbed into the truck and shut the door. Flint put the vehicle in gear and pulled out of the driveway. Cassie's emotions bounced all over the place. Her nerves worked overtime, sending a trickle of sweat down between her breasts. Optimism fought with pessimism. Would Winnie accept or reject her? Was she playing along to hit Cassie up for money?

After years of being ripped off more than once by a fake friend, Cassie had grown leery of strangers and people professing friendship.

Flint pulled into Homer's parking lot and put the truck in park. "We're here."

"Yep." Placing her hand on the door handle, she hesitated.

Flint leaned over and brushed her lips with his. His gaze connected with hers. "You okay?"

She grabbed his shoulder and pulled his lips to hers again. He increased the pressure and she opened. His heat warmed her. His chest pressed lightly against her breasts. Her nipples hardened. Damn, Flint could still take her from zero to sixty in seconds.

He sat back, staring, his eyes dark with desire. "I could make out with you all night. But you've got someone waiting."

"Right. Right." She took a deep breath and swallowed.

He cupped her cheek. "It's gonna be okay."

"Yeah. You're right. I know it is. Maybe." She pulled the handle back and slid down from the truck.

"Text me and I'll pick you up," he hollered through the open window. She nodded and opened the door to the restaurant.

Winnie Briggs sat at a table for four by the window, nursing a beer. Creases on her forehead deepened. Cassie guessed she must be at least seventy. She walked over and pulled out a chair. As the legs scraped against the floor, Winnie looked up.

"Hi. You're here."

"Didn't you think I'd come?" Cassie sat down.

"I've been thinkin'. Sure took you a long time to hunt me up."

"I didn't know about you until I read the letter.

Do you have any pictures of Charlie, my father?" Cassie hesitated. Her nerves kicked up. She picked up the napkin and wiped her upper lip.

"I do. So hard to imagine you being Charlie's girl. Charlie and that little slut. I told him to stay away from her. But he didn't listen. Obviously." Winnie chuckled, tossing a sly glance at Cassie.

"That little slut was my mother. And she died, too."

"Don't mean no offense. I remember reading about it in the paper. After Charlie's accident."

"She loved your son. That's why she chose to have me instead of getting an abortion. Gram said my mom confessed her plans to elope with Charlie."

"Really? Damn. You're full of surprises." She shifted in her seat.

"Maybe because you hated my mom."

Winnie's eyes filled. "I didn't hate her. But Charlie was so young. With his whole life ahead of him. Too young to settle down with one girl." She sighed. "I wanted so much for him. See the world. Find his place before he married and had a family."

Cassie put her hand on Winnie's forearm and gave a gentle squeeze.

Winnie covered it with her own and smiled. "Too late for regrets. He did what he did. You're here now. Time to get on with things."

"Look. If I'm an inconvenience, I can go away. I mean, it's not like we've known each other for years. I have parents and had a wonderful grandmother. I don't want to interfere in your life. Maybe it's best if I go." Cassie pushed the chair back. But Winnie's hand on hers stopped her.

"Don't go. Don't mind me. I brought pictures. Let me tell you about Charlie. Your dad. He was a wonderful person."

While Winnie rifled through her enormous handbag, Cassie studied her face. The skin drooped. Lines at the corners of her mouth matched those on her forehead. Poorly dressed in a faded T-shirt and a skirt appearing to be homemade, Winnie looked worn-out.

She jabbered on about Charlie's achievements in sports and his huge circle of friends as she fished out snapshot after snapshot. Her face lit up. Cassie figured he was her pride and joy. What a horrible blow to lose him so early in life! Tears stung at the backs of Cassie's eyes. What if Charlie had lived? Would he have wanted her? Would he have stepped up and been her father? Would she have grown up in Winnie's house?

"What'll it be?" Homer stood at their table, pen and pad in hand.

Winnie glanced up. "Cheeseburger with fries and another beer, Homer."

"Same for me." Cassie gave the man a winning smile. "And bring me the check."

Winnie eyed her then lifted her gaze to the restaurant owner. "Well, hell. Then I'll have a piece of Laura Dailey's cheesecake, too."

Cassie laughed. Homer took the order and left. Winnie rocked her chair forward.

"Come here. Closer. Let's start at the beginning. Charlie was the best-looking baby in the hospital."

Cassie's chair touched Winnie's. The older woman gave a running commentary on each photo. Winnie's eyes sparkled, an energy emanated from her.

As she bragged shamelessly, Cassie smiled and leaned back in her chair. Warmth and love washed over her, as if her father had been there. She felt his presence through his adoring mother. Was this what it was like to have a child? If she became a mother, would she love her child so deeply? Her stomach clenched.

BY EIGHT O'CLOCK, THE two women had eaten Homer's last two pieces of cheesecake. Winnie licked her lips. "Laura Dailey knows how to bake."

"Best cheesecake ever."

"And you've probably eaten cheesecake all over the world, haven't you?"

Cassie sensed heat in her cheeks. "I've been a few places. But haven't had cheesecake anywhere but here."

"Why the hell not?"

"Have to stay slim. Can't gain weight."

"You stay in this town, you'll gain weight. We got the best food." Winnie sat back, resting her hands on her sizeable belly.

Homer dropped the check in front of Cassie, who scooped it up, flipped a credit card from her purse, and handed it to him.

"Great meal," she told him, then turned toward her grandmother. "Thank you for coming. And for telling me so much about my dad."

Winnie leaned forward. "Would you like to keep a picture?"

Cassie clasped her hands together. "Can I?"

Winnie scooped a fistful from her worn bag and set them on the table. "Which one?"

Cassie leafed through the small pile and stopped at the one of Charlie smiling, wearing his football jersey. "This one. Is it okay?"

"Sure. I have plenty. He would've liked you. Always had a soft spot for pretty women. Your mom coulda stopped traffic. Didn't think she'd stay with Charlie. A woman who looked like her would have men chasing her wherever she went."

"Sounds like Dad was a guy she'd never leave."

"We'll never know, will we?"

A pang of sadness pierced Cassie's heart. She'd never much missed her biological parents because her adoptive ones were so present and caring. For a moment, the loss squeezed her heart. Emptiness filled her.

"Thanks, again, for dinner." Winnie pushed to her feet.

"Can we stay in touch?"

"Sure. I live here. I've got two daughters. They both have kids. I don't know as they'd have time to meet a new niece or anything. But you and I can talk. Come by The Hut anytime."

"Thanks. I will. I understand. Maybe this is something you'd like to keep between us."

"Maybe. Let me think about it."

"Of course." Cassie's eyes wetted for a moment then she averted her gaze and plucked her phone from her purse.

"You texting Flint? No need. I'll run you over to his house. You shackin' up with him?"

"He's an old friend."

Winnie laughed. "Yeah. You could do a lot worse. He's no Academy Award winning actor or director or anything. But he works hard. Got a good business. Keeps his nose clean and is nice to folks. You could do a lot worse." She shrugged. "Just sayin'."

Cassie couldn't help but grin. Typical grandmother—trying to fix her up with someone she was already half in love with anyway.

"And he's a volunteer fireman, too. Saved a lot of folks."

"Really?" She grinned. "I'm not surprised."

"Yep. You can count on Flint." Winnie preceded Cassie out of the restaurant.

She got in Winnie's ten-year-old Toyota and gave her Flint's address. When they pulled up in front of the house, Winnie turned off the ignition.

She sighed then faced Cassie. "I hope you're not disappointed."

"Disappointed?"

"Yeah. Meeting me. I mean, I'm not a fancy person."

"No, I'm not disappointed at all. Thank you for sharing so much about my dad. I feel so close to him now. I know it's been a shock, me popping up out of nowhere. I'm grateful you've given me this time."

"Would you like to come to Sunday dinner at my house? If they're not doin' anything, I could invite Charlie's sibs."

"That would be wonderful. But if they can't come, I understand." Cassie swallowed. In her heart, she didn't but wouldn't admit it. Maybe Winnie had changed her mind about her new granddaughter?

"Let me check with everyone first."

The women exchanged cell numbers, hugged, and Cassie got out of the car. She stood at the front door, waving until Winnie was out of sight.

"I guess dinner was a success," came a deep voice behind her.

Cassie jumped. "Flint McKay! How dare you sneak up on me?"

He shrugged. "I just opened the door."

"I didn't hear you. Yes, we had a good time. Look. She gave me a picture of my dad."

She offered him the photo.

"Good-lookin' guy."

"Thanks. He played football for the high school."

Flint returned the picture. "Come inside, it's gettin' cold. Fall's coming early this year."

"Fall? Like in changing leaves? Oh heavens!" Cassie clasped her hands together in front of her chest.

"You haven't seen the leaves change?"

"I lived in Southern California. No leaves changing there. I never stayed here long enough."

"You'll love it."

"I can't wait." She folded her arms across her chest. Flint snuggled her into his shoulder as they walked inside.

"See? I told you it's cool."

As long as she could share body heat with him, she didn't care how cold it got.

Chapter Ten

"I'LL MAKE A FIRE." Flint headed to the living room.

"I'll get a sweater." Cassie's footsteps sounded in the hall.

"So, when are you going to return to the office, full-time?"

Flint glanced over his shoulder to spy his brother lounging against the archway connecting the living and dining rooms.

"What do you mean? I came in yesterday."

"Yeah. For an hour or two."

"It was more than that." Flint placed three logs on the grate.

"No, it wasn't. You're preoccupied with Cassie."

"So? I can still do my job."

"Bullshit."

"Come on, Marty. Gimme a break." Flint rolled up some newspaper and lit it. Then he thrust it up the chimney to create a draft.

"Look, if you've got something going with her, it's okay. But it's hard to believe she's going to dump a big career to stay in Pine Grove and bake cookies."

"Who said anything about baking cookies? Bet she doesn't even know how."

"You know what I mean." Marty plopped down on the sofa.

Flint shoved the flaming newspaper under the logs and closed the screen. He straightened.

"Come on, Marty. I'm not leaving town. I'm not giving up the business."

"Then what *are* you doing?"

Flint shook his head. "No clue."

Before Marty could respond, the town fire alarm siren sounded.

"It's my day. Gotta go." Flint grabbed a jacket and his keys. "Please explain to Cassie."

"Okay."

In a flash, he was out the door and climbing behind the wheel of his truck. He sped to the firehouse. Three other men were there, donning their protective pants and jackets. Two more men arrived after Flint. He changed and took his place on the fire engine.

The vehicle roared out of the garage and headed for a farmhouse three miles away. When they arrived, smoke billowed out from the kitchen window. Flint and his buddies entered the house. Two men headed for the kitchen while Flint and a co-worker checked the other rooms, looking for people and pets. The men contained the fire, then put it out. After two hours on the scene, they returned to the firehouse, and Flint headed home.

Cassie sat reading by the fire. "Marty has gone to bed."

Flint glanced at his smoke-stained face in the hall mirror. "I'll grab a shower and join you."

He hustled up the stairs to the bathroom. Flint ran the water, waiting for it to get hot. He stripped off his clothes and stuffed them in a plastic bag. Keeping them separate meant not getting smoke smell in Marty's underwear. Flint chuckled to himself. Marty could be such an old biddy about shit like that.

He stepped under the shower. The minute the warm water hit his body, he remembered Cassie sat downstairs. Dressed in a T-shirt nightgown and flimsy robe, she'd wrapped a blanket his mother had crocheted around her legs.

The gown didn't hide the fact she didn't have a bra on. Flint picked up on those things. Slender as a blade of grass, her breasts still bounced when she walked. He loved to watch them and fantasize.

Thoughts like these in the shower woke his dick up. Blood pumped to the neglected member. No, no, not now. He wanted to get downstairs, sip tea, and maybe make a play for Cassie. He'd held himself in check long enough. Too many days with her teasing him in her bikini, or Cassie covered only in a towel, smacking into him in the hall. He'd barely been able to contain his lust. Now it was time. With Marty safely out of the way and the fire casting an inviting glow, he'd make his move.

As much as he refused to admit it to Marty, Flint had always known he still loved Cassie. He'd been the proudest guy in Pine Grove when she'd hit the big screen and started winning awards and acclaim. He'd never admit to anyone it was Cassie, or his love for her, that had busted up his previous trips to the altar.

He washed quickly, tried to calm his dick, and grabbed a towel. The woman of his dreams was downstairs, waiting for him—whether she knew it or not—and he'd better get going.

RESTLESS, CASSIE PUT down her book, took a sip of tea, and stared into the fire. Watching the yellow, orange, and red flames lick the logs put her in a sort of trance. The day had been exhausting and exhilarating. New energy burned inside her.

Her mind roamed to the image of Flint in the shower. She sighed. And he was doing it without her. She'd been waiting for him to make a pass. She'd been surprised and disappointed when he didn't. She figured, after all these years, his passion had fizzled, sliding into friendship.

Sure, he wasn't Basil. What he lacked in fame she'd put money on him making up in the bedroom. Basil had been more in love with himself than her. But Flint? If she remembered correctly, there was nothing selfish about the man. After all these years, she figured he'd have chalked up a truckload of practice.

She got goose bumps wishing for long nights making love, cuddling, and snuggling. Basil had been affectionate and met her basic needs. Now her bed was cold and empty. Imagine, a famous, beautiful movie star pining away alone in bed?

At the sound of a heavy footstep, she looked up. The man she wanted descended the stairs, slowly, wearing a terry robe and rubbing his head with a hand towel. Was he naked underneath? Probably. Heat flowed to the juncture of her thighs. What could be more romantic than making love by the fire? She swallowed as she watched his easy, loose-jointed gait.

"Brandy?" he asked.

"Definitely."

He stopped at a sideboard doubling as a bar and retrieved two small snifters. As he approached her, towel slung around his neck, wet hair tousled, holding a brandy in each hand, Cassie shivered. Now, if only he'd drop the robe.

"Here. This should warm you up."

You should warm me up! "Thanks." She took the glass, keeping eye contact.

"What? Am I showing? Is my head on backwards?" He raised his eyebrows.

Heat filled her face. She lowered her gaze to the glass and brought it to her mouth. Flint sat on the rug next to her chair.

"Good." She licked her lips.

"Dad always bought the good stuff."

She noticed him rearrange his robe, covering his privates. He *was* naked underneath. The heat in her body doubled. She leaned over and ran a finger through his hair.

"There's nothing sexier than a man straight from the shower."

"Really?" His brown eyes darkened as they made contact with her blues.

"Really."

He straightened to kiss her. Cassie bent down to reach him. He cupped his fingers around the back of her neck, holding her still while his lips, warm and inviting, coaxed hers open. Inhibitions melted under Flint's heat. She relaxed and leaned into him. She slid her hands under his robe and behind his neck. He tilted his head.

"Why don't you come down here? It's warmer."

"I'll bet it is."

He laughed. "I dare you to find out just how hot."

"A dare? I never turn down a dare." She eased down next to him. Opening his robe, she slid her hands up his chest. When she made contact with his pecs, a muffled sound came from his throat. Cassie inched closer.

"I want you," he whispered. He ran his lips along the side of her jaw.

"Feeling's mutual." She sucked in air, her eyes wide.

"Really?"

"You're repeating yourself."

He chuckled. "Beautiful." He rubbed several strands of her hair between his fingers. "Come here." He rose to his knees and tucked her beneath him. The fireplace couldn't compete with the heat generated between Flint and Cassie. She raised one knee, her foot coming to rest against his thigh.

"I'm here. What are you gonna do about it?"

A sexy chuckle emanated from deep in his chest. "You'll find out."

Flint laced the fingers of both his hands with hers and raised them above her head. Propping himself up, he lowered his head until their mouths met. Cassie arched into him, her breasts pushing into his chest. She raised her hips slightly until she could feel his erection. The hardness ignited her fire. Flames of desire could only be extinguished by Flint taking her, hard and fast. She groaned.

He released her hands and bent his head to her neck. His hands ripped her robe open.

"Take it off."

"The nightgown?"

"And anything else you're wearing."

"That's all."

He grinned, shooting a salacious look her way. "Good."

After she sat up, Cassie pushed the robe off her shoulders. She yanked the hem of the short gown up over her rump and then over her head.

Flint sat back on his heels, watching. "Beautiful."

Suddenly shy, she covered herself with her hands.

"Don't. You're spoiling the view." He eased her hands away, dropping them at her sides. "I could look at you all day, every day."

"And you're dressed? Come on, mister. Sauce for the goose."

Flint shed his robe and heaved it on a chair.

"You've filled out a little since high school." She checked out his form with hot eyes.

"Working out'll do it."

"Nice," she said, inching closer, resting her palm on his chest.

"Yours are as great as I remember."

"You remember?" Damn, did he have an image of her naked fixed in his brain?

"I've never forgotten for one moment. The time we spent together..."

"You mean the time we spent having sex."

"That, too. I remember everything."

"Everything?" She cocked an eyebrow.

With a hand on her knee, he opened her legs and settled between. "Everything. Want me to show you?"

"I thought you'd never ask."

He shook his head. "Still a smart-ass."

"Always."

He leaned down to kiss her. She flung her arms around his neck and pulled her breasts to his pecs then she raised one leg and hooked it around his waist.

"Are you protected?" he whispered, panting.

"Yeah. Pill."

"Great!"

He slid his hand down her thigh, resting his thumb on her slit. Holy Hell! But he didn't stop there. He glided it down her wetness and inside. Her hips bucked. She cursed and shut her eyes. Need spiraled up inside.

Leaning back on his haunches, Flint gripped her waist lightly. He brushed her lips with his, then kissed down her neck, and kept going. When he reached her breasts, he stopped to pay homage. He kissed each one, sucking briefly on one nipple, then the other.

"These are amazing," he muttered then continued kissing down her body.

When he reached her mound, he looked up. His eyes made contact with hers. She ran her fingers through his short hair. He grinned then returned to his task. When his tongue made contact with her flesh. She moaned, her breathing ragged.

"Oh my God." The words blended together in a guttural sound emanating from deep in her throat.

He didn't stop. Flattening his tongue against her, then moving it in circular motions ratcheted her heat to unbearable.

"If you don't stop, I'm gonna come."

"Do it."

"I want you. Inside. Before I..." She could barely speak. He pushed up, hooked her legs over his shoulders.

"You're mine." He directed his dick to her entrance and plunged in.

"Oh, hot damn!" Tension coiled in her belly.

"You okay?"

"Amazing." She blinked, swallowed, and stared. Her insides burned then his hips started slowly pulling out then thrusting back in.

"More." She gripped his shoulders, pressing her fingertips into his flesh.

"Hey, watch it."

"Sorry. Faster. Harder."

He shifted his weight and sped up. Within seconds, the orgasm building, growing, burst forth. She squeezed her eyes tight while electricity shot through her body. Flutters sent wave after wave of pleasure through her all the way to her fingertips.

"Holy shit." His deep voice brought her back to Earth. She watched him squeeze his eyes shut.

When Flint bent his head, sweat dripped from his forehead to hers. He groaned then closed his fingers over her arms. Silence, except for the sounds of shallow breathing.

Cassie lay flat, her head resting on the rug.

"Hey. You. Amazing woman. Still the biggest turn-on in the world."

She bent her head forward and smiled at his flushed face.

"You've learned a few things."

"Ya think?" Hissing softly, Flint pulled out of her. "You're with me tonight."

"In your bed?" Her eyebrows rose.

"Tonight and every night. Get your stuff from the guest room."

"Aye, aye, Captain."

He grinned a lopsided grin reminding her of him at seventeen. "Any objections?"

"None."

Within five minutes, she'd joined him upstairs. Flint had washed up. His hair was combed, his face dry and rosy, and his teeth freshly brushed. Even the sweat on his brow was gone. He stood, feet apart, wearing only boxers as he greeted her with a kiss. Her heart flipped. She could barely tear her gaze from his chest. Muscled with a light covering of dark hair, it invited her touch. She couldn't resist as she sidled up closer. Her palms flattened against his pecs.

"Do you like this?"

"Are you kidding? Always." Covering her little hand with his, he sandwiched it against his body. His skin warmed her.

He closed his fingers around her breast. "I don't need an engraved invitation."

His touch sent a shiver down her spine. With Flint, she wasn't *Cassandra Wells, movie star.* She was simply his Cassie, best buds and lovers from way back. Flint snaked his arm around her middle.

"It's late. Time for bed." He took her hand.

Cassie slid in first, Flint followed, then pulled up the covers. When he eased onto the pillows, she snuggled up to him. He opened his arms, and she rested her head on his shoulder. He folded her closer.

"Nice," he muttered.

"Does this mean we're living together?"

"What?"

"Does it?" she pressed.

"Well, not if you don't want it to."

"I mean, technically, we *are* living together."

"Technically, yeah."

"And now we're sharing a bed."

"Yeah."

"So, I guess it does."

"But you're not staying, are you?" He rolled up on his side and faced her.

"You mean forever?" She pushed up on her elbow.

"Yes. Well, maybe," he backpedaled.

Heat stole into her face. Had she thought about staying there forever? Of course. But she'd never tell him. Besides, she hadn't made up her mind.

"Forever is a long time," she stalled.

"Of course. It is. Yep." He looked away.

Cassie took his chin and turned it to face her. "Are you saying you want me to stay forever?"

Silence greeted her. He lifted his gaze to meet hers. It was a warm, questioning, probing look, but he said nothing.

She grew impatient. "Well?"

"Let's figure this out tomorrow."

"That's not much of an answer."

"Okay, then." He sat up straight. "Are you saying you're ready to commit to staying here forever?"

Typical of Flint to bounce the ball back into her court. She gazed down at her hands. "I don't know. You haven't asked me to. So how can I have an answer?"

"And if I had? Would you say *yes*?"

She brought her gaze up to face his. "You're right. Let's talk about this tomorrow." She reached over and clicked off the bedside lamp. Lying flat and staring at the ceiling, she tried to sort out her thoughts. Was she ready to give up the career she'd worked so hard for? Or was this simply a vacation? A respite from the pressure, the publicity, the lack of privacy—temporary or permanent? She needed this. But was it forever? Damned if she knew.

Flint eased back down and pushed up on his side. He slipped his hand under her gown. Smoothing his hands over the planes of her body, he skimmed his palms down over her soft skin.

"Sleepy, darlin'?" His voice lazy, provocative, low, and sexy.

"Not particularly." She faced him.

"How about..." She put her fingers over his lips then replaced them with hers. As if someone had sounded the starter bell, Flint woke up. He slid his arm around her and pulled her back toward him until they were glued together. Cassie raised her leg and hitched it on his hip. He moved his hand down to her rump.

"Damn. This is the cutest thing." He squeezed, wrapping his fingers around her cheek before sliding them down and in to caress her sex.

Cassie jumped.

"Problem?"

"Just startled."

He chuckled. "Prepare yourself."

She wound her free arm around his chest and raised her chin. Flint lowered his mouth to hers. Need grew in her until she could barely contain it. His dick hardened against her leg as he probed her with his fingers.

"Take me. Damn it. Do it," she whispered into his mouth.

And he did what she asked.

Chapter Eleven

He awoke at three and headed for the kitchen. Standing at the window in his boxers, he toyed with a glass of water. It wasn't thirst waking him up. It was his brain.

What the fuck was he doing—asking her to stay? *She's Cassandra fucking Wells, and I'm...nobody.* And forever? He shook his head slowly. What a fool he was. As soon as he said it, she balked. She had a career, a big-ass career, and who was he? A printer and part-time fireman.

Right. Stay here with him forever. What a joke. And he was the jester, the clown who'd said it. She'd picked right up on it, and, like a wild horse, shied away from the idea instantly.

A nobody like Flint McKay wasn't going to throw a harness on Cassandra Wells. No, sirree. She needed to run free, to take any fantastic thing offered. What did he have to offer? Life in exciting Pine Grove, a general store, and maybe a couple of kids. Oh, and his undying love forever. But it didn't stack up to a starring role on Broadway or in a movie, did it? Not by a long shot.

Oh yeah. The store. They needed to complete the sale before she continued with the renovation. She'd offered him twice what he paid for it, but he couldn't make a profit on her. If she paid what he did, he'd be square.

He wondered who'd buy it when it was all fixed up? Sure be worth a whole lot more than he paid for it. Smart move on her part. Another way she outclassed him. He could have renovated it and resold it, but he didn't think of it, did he?

To be totally fair, he wanted to return it to her as is, rather than fix it up in a way she might not like. He couldn't return it to her for the price he paid if he renovated it. There was being nice to save the old place from demolition, and there was taking a big financial hit for a rich woman. He was kind, but he wasn't stupid.

He took a slug of water and strolled over to the other window. The word "forever" came to mind again. He wanted forever, and he wanted it with Cassie Wells. And he'd show up on time for the wedding, ready to rock and roll.

He chuckled to himself. It would never happen, but who would it hurt if he fantasized about it—for a while? After all, she was in his house, in his bed. He sighed. A vision of Cassie in an apron, waiting for him at the front door, flitted across his mind's eye. He laughed. She'd never be the little lady in the kitchen and a siren in his bed. She'd be fun, unpredictable, smart, funny, and sexy. What else could he possibly want?

He finished the water and trotted back to the kitchen. After rinsing out the glass, he returned to the bedroom. Stifling a yawn, he hesitated, watching Cassie sleep. Relaxed in slumber she resembled the sweet teenager he'd fallen for. Gone were any elements of glamour. Her natural beauty shone through. Her blonde hair spread out across the pillow, her lashes resting against her cheek caught his eye.

Although she carried herself with confidence, once asleep she resumed her inner child, vulnerable, soft, and gentle. He knew she'd hardened up—had to if she wanted to be successful in such a competitive world. But now, it had melted away. This was the girl he'd loved all these years.

He wanted to touch her but didn't want to wake her. She changed position, uttering a small moan. Flint slid between the sheets. As if on instinct, she knew he was there, she inched closer, touching him. He rolled on his side and slung an arm over her middle. A small sigh fluttered from her throat. No matter how long he'd live this dream, he'd relish every second.

Closing his eyes, he took a breath. The warm, slightly sweet scent of Cassie drifted to his nose. Inhaling deeply, he smiled, kissed her hair oh-so gently so as not to wake her, and closed his eyes.

CASSIE SHOOK OFF HER habit of sleeping late, formed by late-night Broadway performances. The sun peeped in, and she greeted it with a grin. Jumping out of bed, she padded to the door and grabbed Flint's terry robe. Wrapping it around her, she tightened the sash and headed for the bathroom.

One peek in the mirror and she was surprised to see a glow of happiness on her otherwise sleep-deprived face. Maybe her skin tone needed work, but her eyes sparkled like never before. Was it due to Flint McKay or simply great sex? Maybe both. Or great sex with Flint McKay.

She giggled at her image in the mirror. After washing up, she headed downstairs. It was six, a bit early for her lover, but perfect for Cassie. She put up a pot of coffee, turned on the radio, and did bending and stretching exercises to music.

Although she had decisions to make about her future, no sense letting her fine-tuned body go to pot. Keeping up on her exercises and watching her diet had become second nature, and she didn't intend to let it fade away.

Taking a break, she filled a mug with the hot brew and doctored it to the way she liked it. She skipped up the stairs, careful not to spill. Standing in the doorway, she watched Flint sleep. Damn, he looked so cute—all warm, cuddly, and vulnerable. A devilish idea landed in her brain. It was time to get up. She put her mug down on the dresser and fished her phone out of the pocket of the robe.

Fiddling with Pandora, she finally located a march by John Philip Souza. She blasted the music and pranced around the room. As the first cymbal crashed, Flint bolted upright and out of bed.

"What the fuck?" he hollered.

"Time to get up, sleepyhead. The day's a-wastin.'" Cassie grinned.

"Why you little devil." Flint was after her in a nanosecond. Cassie ran, squealing, around the bed with Flint in hot pursuit. She jumped on the mattress, but halfway across, he landed a flying tackle. She fell, giggling, into the softness of the pillow top. His weight pushed her down. He laced his fingers with hers and stretched her arms above her head.

"What the hell? It's six thirty. Girl, what are you doing?"

"Early riser."

"That makes one of us. Geez. I need my beauty sleep."

"Time's a-wastin', Flint."

"Oh yeah?" He trapped her legs between his. A spark of mischief lit up his eyes as he lowered his mouth to hers. Releasing her hands, he balanced himself above her. Cassie eased her arms around his neck and parted her lips. His tongue entered.

Arching against him, desire rose in her loins.

"Well, well, well. Isn't this cozy?" A deep voice interrupted the lovers.

"What?" Flint yanked his mouth from hers and pushed up.

Marty stood in his boxers, arms folded across his chest. "Aren't you two just too cute. Have you looked at the clock? What the hell?"

Flint rolled off Cassie, who fussed with the robe, covering herself again.

"What are you doing here? And what business is it of yours what time we get up?"

"I don't give a rat's ass, Flint. But when you're laughing and screaming and making the floor shake... There are other people in this house."

"People? Do you have a girl in there?"

"I do not."

"So roll over and go back to sleep."

Cassie pushed to her feet. "I'm sorry, Marty. You're right. We shouldn't be so noisy. I wanted to get Flint up to do some exercise."

"He was, weren't you, my brother?"

Cassie laughed as Flint's face reddened. "Shut up, Marty," he muttered.

"Why don't you go back to bed, Marty? We're up now, right?" She glanced at Flint who gave a slight nod. "We'll go make breakfast and be quiet as mice. Come on."

"I'm up. Are you going to exercise?" Marty faced her.

"Sure. Do you want to join me?"

"Yeah. Let big brother make breakfast."

"Sounds like a plan. Okay, Flint?"

He ground out words she couldn't understand and slipped on a T-shirt.

"Okay, then. To the living room. I've got just the right music here." She fiddled with her phone as she followed Marty down the stairs.

"I need my own place," Flint mumbled, shaking his head and heading for the kitchen. "I really need my own place."

BY EIGHT, FLINT AND Cassie left Marty singing in the shower as they pulled out of the driveway, heading for the store. They took several trips hauling supplies inside before they'd emptied the vehicle.

"Will called yesterday. They finished spackling the walls. They're ready to paint. But I told them I want to do it."

"More painting?"

"I liked it. It was fun. So I'm gonna paint the walls, too."

"Paint the walls. Okay."

"They picked up the paint for me."

Flint shook his head. "People do things for you, don't they?"

"I'm paying them."

"True."

"So today we paint."

"We?"

"You said you'd help."

"True. I did. Okay."

"By the way, I never paid you. How much do you want for the place?"

"Only what I paid."

"And it was?"

"Thirty-five thousand."

Cassie made a noise with her tongue. "Unbelievable the place went so cheap."

"I was lucky."

She rummaged through her purse and plucked out a checkbook.

"Wait, wait. We need papers. Title. Deed. And stuff."

"Can't I just write you a check?"

"You can, but we need a contract and shit to make this legal."

"Who do we call? What do we do?"

"I'll call Grey Andrews. He's the town supervisor. He'll set it up."

While Flint was on the phone, Cassie looked around. They needed to paint the walls quickly so the contractors could refinish the floor. She wandered around the place, imagining new shelves, a couple of light fixtures, and what she'd need to display goods. Display goods? What the hell did she know about running a store? Nothing. Maybe she could sell it to someone, once it was fixed up. Maybe even make a little profit? Or at least recoup what she put in anyway.

The outside of the sorry shop had peeling white paint. The shutters were faded. She made a face then crossed the street and took a long look at the building. Color schemes flashed through her mind. While she hadn't lived in a house in years, flitting from city to city for a play or movie shoot, she'd liked the colors of the houses in New England. Narrowing her eyes, she chose a deep, barn red with white trim and black shutters.

They'd need professionals to paint the outside. No way would she be risking her career by getting up on a ladder to scrape down these walls. Her career? Hmm. Her mind left the store and zeroed in on acting. Her mother had texted her about a hundred times about new offers. Especially the offer to take her Broadway role to the screen.

She'd loved the play and had hoped to be offered the screen role, too. Would she leave Pine Grove to go back to the grueling life of a movie shoot? She chewed her lip. Although she'd thought she'd made up her mind, the movie role was choice—could she pass it up? And for what? Flint didn't want to have forever with her. Last night, he'd hemmed and hawed, giving her a "maybe," then avoided a direct answer. She couldn't count on him, could she? What would it be like to move here on her own? She'd always been with her mother, father, or brother. The thought of being alone sent a shiver up her spine.

"All right." Flint interrupted her thoughts. "Grey's gonna set everything up. End of the week, we'll meet with him and Drew Armstrong, best attorney in town. Then dinner out to celebrate. Okay?"

"Sounds good. I was thinking about what color to paint the store."

"I thought we already were painting the store."

"The outside. The outside is pathetic. I can never sell the place looking like this."

"Oh, so you've decided to sell it?"

"Can't run it myself."

"Why not?"

"I'm an actress. I don't know anything about running a store."

Flint nodded. She stared at him, but he didn't meet her gaze. There was something going on, but she wasn't sure what.

"So, you're definitely leaving, then?"

"I didn't say that."

"Selling the store?"

"I don't know what I'm doing, Flint. Okay?"

He raised his palms. "Hey, don't get mad at me. I'm not making you sell the place. I'm not making you leave."

"And you're not making me stay, either. Let's go." She strode into the building, toed off her shoes, and picked up a roller. "You edge, I'll roll."

"Aye, aye, Captain." Flint saluted, put his shoes behind the counter, and picked up a paintbrush.

"If you mean to be funny, you're not."

"Then I'll just do as I'm told and shut up." His expression grew stormy.

She rested a hand on her hip. "You know, if you're gonna be annoying, why don't you go to your office today instead? Huh?"

"Good idea. I just might."

"Well, go ahead. I can paint this place without you."

"You can do everything without me, if you want." He threw down the brush.

"And I can live at the hotel, too."

"Go ahead. Pay a fortune. Give up free room. Seems pretty stupid to me."

"Oh, so now I'm stupid?" She crossed her arms over her chest.

"If the shoe fits, darlin'."

"Don't call me *darlin'*."

"Fine. But you didn't mind me calling you that last night." He pushed by her.

"Yeah? Well. Last night? Well, yeah. Last night." Before she could get her words to come out right, he was halfway to the truck. She followed him outside. "Go on!"

"You started it."

"And I suppose you're finishing it?"

"Yep." He yanked open the door and got in. After slamming it, he gunned the motor, and roared away from the curb.

"Speeding! They got laws here, Flint!" she hollered after him. But he drove away without looking back.

Cassie sank down on the curb, her face in her hands. What had she done? She'd picked a fight with him for nothing. Or had he picked a fight with her? Now she had to move out of his bed and into the hotel. Didn't she say she would? Damn. It was the last thing she wanted.

If he wanted her to stay, why didn't he ask her to? If she did, would he propose? Did she want to marry him? Not if he'd run off in a huff whenever they argued. Did she even know Flint anymore? Would marrying him simply be running away from a life too stressful? Would it simply be a snap-decision solution that would turn into disaster? Maybe marriage should be put on the shelf for now.

Her cell rang. She looked at the screen. Her mother. Shit, exactly what she didn't need.

ANGER BURNED IN FLINT'S chest. What a self-righteous little spoiled brat! Who did Cassie think she was? Her successful career didn't make her better than anyone. Not better than him anyway.

Bossing him around? Telling him what to do? He shook his head. Nope, no, no way would he be her cabana boy. He'd painted rooms in his folks' house. He knew exactly what to do. What did she know? Nothing. She'd never painted shit.

Attitude, she still has the same attitude she had when she was sixteen. Sassy little Cassandra Wells knew everything. Or she'd strutted around like she did. He pulled into the parking lot of the old Victorian house where he had office space.

An image of Cassie at sixteen in the backseat of his car flitted through his brain. He laughed. Yeah, she'd pretended to know all about sex, too. How to do it. He'd laughed at her, making her mad. She'd fastened her bra and stormed out of the car. Fortunately, he'd caught up with her in time. Walking barefoot down a dark street at one in the morning wasn't safe.

He'd cajoled her into the car. Yes, he'd apologized. He shook his head at the memory. She'd been crying. He'd wiped away her tears, found the perfect parking spot, and made love to her.

His anger faded, leaving yearning. God, he couldn't get enough of her then. The feel of her soft, tender skin against his had spiked fire in his loins. And damn, the girl could kiss. He licked his lower lip. She hadn't lost it. Trudging up the steps, he regretted leaving. Last night had been like a dream. He'd relived it several times before they locked horns.

Now, she was pissed and would probably move to the Inn. She could afford anything. His hot temper had taken away her reason to stay with him. Anger at himself roiled around in his gut. He opened the office door so hard it banged against the wall. Marty appeared in the arch separating their offices.

"What the hell?" Marty's hands set on his hips.

"What?"

"What's wrong with you?"

"I've been stupid."

"Should I alert the media? Oh, wait. You being stupid isn't news."

"Lay off." Flint slapped his jacket on a hook by the door and strode to his desk. He dumped his butt in his chair then turned on his computer. "What's going on?"

"If you'd spend a day or two here, you'd know."

"I'm asking, Marty!" Flint's voice rose to the rafters.

Marty ambled over to the coffeemaker and poured himself a new cup. "I've been researching the market."

Flint raised his eyebrows. "And?"

"There's a ton of business in New York City."

"What does it do for us?"

"We can undercut the printers there and pick up enough work to keep us going for years."

"And you know this, how?"

"As I said, if you were listening. I've been doing research. Calling city printers and getting quotes. Jesus, they are ripping the shit off people."

"Oh?" Flint focused on his brother.

"Yeah. The quotes I'm getting, we could do the job for half and still make a profit."

"But delivery?"

"That's the problem. One of us would have to drive the job into town, or we'd have to hire a driver. I think outside shipping might be too expensive."

"Hmm. Okay. But for a smaller job, we could ship, right?"

"Right. UPS would work."

"And how do you propose to pick up this business?"

"Advertise."

"That's expensive."

"Advertise on Craig's List. At least start there. If we can pick up business, it'll be worth it to spend some money on advertising."

"Okay. Go for it." Flint pushed to his feet and ambled over to the coffeemaker.

Marty rested a hip on his brother's desk. "I'm not going ahead with anything until I know where you stand."

"What do you mean? I'm here, aren't I?"

"I don't know. Are you? Or is your head still at the store with Cassie?"

"I admit I've been spending some time helping her out, but it's over." Flint took a swig of his beverage.

Marty stood up. "What do you mean, it's over? Did you break up with her?"

"There's nothing to break up. Cassie's renovating the store and selling it. Then she's leaving. End of story. She can handle the renovation and the sale. She doesn't need me."

Marty's eyebrows rose. "Leaving?"

"Yeah. Like, goodbye forever."

Did she say that? Had they talked about forever, or did he imagine it?

"What the fuck did you do?"

Flint faced his brother. "Huh?"

"Everything was going so good with her. What did you do?"

"Way to be supportive, asshole. I didn't do anything."

Marty shook his head. "I don't believe it."

"I didn't, damn it!" Flint slammed his mug on the desk, spilling the liquid. "Shit!"

Marty grabbed a roll of paper towels and tossed it to his brother. "You must have said something."

"Okay, well. Maybe. She said something about forever, and I...? Well, I said maybe."

"And?" Marty prodded.

"And she said, 'Are you asking me to stay forever?' and I kinda didn't answer. Then she said forever is a long time. Which kinda means 'no', right?"

"She doesn't want to stay?"

"We talked around it. Never got a straight answer. She put it off. So if she's not staying, that means she's leaving, right? Going back to being Cassandra Wells? If she is, the sooner, the better."

"You can't mean it."

"I can and do. I'm over her. It's time I get on with my life."

"I don't believe it. You were so close. Really." Marty shook his head. "I'm sorry, Flint. I thought you two were made for each other."

"Yeah, well, Cassie's made for stardom, and I'm made for Pine Grove. Where's the mail?"

Marty handed a stack of envelopes to his brother and returned to his desk. Flint pretended to focus on the letters in his hand. Under Marty's stare, blood rushed to Flint's head.

He'd lied to Marty, first time in a long time. No way was he over Cassie. But he wanted to be, oh hell yes, he wanted to be. Because then the pain in his chest would stop and he could think about something besides her luscious body and throaty laugh.

"Flint?"

He looked up. "You can lie to yourself all you want to. But you're not fooling me. You'll never be over Cassie Wells. So why don't you stop trying and make a play for her. A serious play."

"Like what?"

Marty lowered his gaze to his computer. "Proposing marriage might be a good place to start."

"HI, MOM. WHAT'S UP?"

"Hi, Darling. Have you had time to think over what we discussed? I have several tempting offers here."

"Back-to-back movies?"

"Yeah, well, maybe. But you don't have to do all of them."

"Only three of the four?"

"You read my mind."

"I'm not ready to do that. I may never be ready." Cassie sighed.

"Aren't you coming back?"

"I don't know. Not yet anyway. I'm fixing up the store."

"But you're going to sell it, right?"

"Probably."

"Probably? You haven't busted your butt for all these years to become some insipid country shopkeeper!"

"Now, Mom. Calm down."

"I mean. It's not only your life being taken over, it's mine, too. And your father's, and your brother's."

"Stop! All of you have profited very well from my career. So don't make out like you've sacrificed your entire life for me."

"Well, I have."

"No. You haven't. Look, I gotta go. The paint is drying, and I have walls to do."

"But, Cassie—"

"Stop bugging me, Mom. I don't miss the rehearsals, the classes, busting my ass, and being tired all the time. I like it here. So leave me alone, okay? I'll tell you when I'm ready to come back."

"It had better be soon!"

The line went dead. Her mother had hung up on her.

Cassie sucked air through her teeth. She hated when her mother did that. She put her phone down and hugged her knees. Stay in Pine Grove and do nothing? Or go back to making movies, doing plays, and grinding herself into the ground?

Her family had high expectations, ones she found impossible to live up to. Her eyes filled. Flint had walked out on her, her mother was pissed, and Cassie had nowhere to go, no friendly shoulder to cry on. She put her head down on her arms and cried.

"Hey, there. Cassie? What's wrong?"

She looked up into the sympathetic blue eyes of Winnie Briggs. Blinking sent the tears cascading down Cassie's cheeks. Struggling for words, she gulped air.

Winnie got down on the curb next to her and took Cassie into her arms. "There, there. Come on, honey. Whatever it is, it can't be so bad."

Warmth from the friendly embrace triggered emotion in the young actress. Unable to hold back, she sobbed. Winnie shoved a tissue in her hand.

"Come on. I'll buy you a cup of coffee." The women stood. Winnie slung her arm around Cassie's shoulders and guided her to a car. When they got to Java the Hut, the women got out. "My shift doesn't start for twenty minutes. Wanna tell me what's going on?"

The women sat in a corner booth. Cassie took two shuddering breaths then her words poured out in a jumbled mess.

"I want to stay, but Flint doesn't want me here. My mother wants me to come home and do three movies. But I don't want to. Flint wants me to run the store, but I don't want to. Everybody's telling me what to do. I don't know what I want to do." Tears started anew.

Winnie signaled to the waitress. "Connie, can we have two coffees, please?"

"Sure thing." The waitress looked askance at the sobbing girl sitting across from her friend.

"Don't mind her. She's having a little meltdown."

The women sat quietly. Cassie twisted up two paper napkins, crumbling them on the table. The beverages arrived. Winnie took a long look at Cassie.

"I see your dilemma. Are you sure Flint doesn't want you to stay?"

"He got mad when I said I didn't want to run the store. He called me stupid, too."

"He's the stupid one." She patted her arm. "But I saw the way he looked at you. The man's got it bad."

"Then why doesn't he say something? Do something?"

"Like what?"

"Propose? Well, maybe at least ask me to stay?"

"Would you say yes?"

"I don't know." Cassie stared at her mug.

"Don't wish for something unless you really want it."

"I don't know what I'm doing. I got into a fight with Flint and threatened to go to the hotel. So now I have to. But I liked staying with him."

"He has his faults, but he's a good man."

"I know. I know." Cassie put her hands over her face.

"What were you doing in the old store?"

"Painting. Renovating."

"Why don't I run you over there. After my shift, I'll pick you up and take you to the hotel, if you still want to stay there. Okay?"

Cassie nodded, and on the ride to the store, she stared out the window. "Thank you, Winnie."

"You're welcome. I hope you patch it up with Flint. If it's what you want."

"I do. I think it's the only thing I know I want."

"Good place to start." She patted Cassie's hand then put the car in park. "There you go, missy. I'll check on you at five, when I get off."

"Thank you so much." Cassie hugged her grandmother.

"You're welcome."

Chapter Twelve

F lint steered his truck toward the store. A few hours of paper-work and time to think had cooled his head. Apologizing didn't come natural to Flint. Being the oldest, he'd always been the one to give the orders and make sure others obeyed.

But Cassie was a different animal. His grandfather would have called her *headstrong*. Cassie had a mind of her own, something Flint never thought he'd like in a woman. He admired Cassie for her opinions and the will to get what she wanted out of life. There was something downright sexy about a woman who wasn't leaning all over him, wishy-washy, waiting for him to jump-start her life.

He needed to treat her nice and find a way to undo the harm he'd done. *Good luck with that*, he told himself. He parked then approached the door slowly, searching his brain for the right words. He knocked.

"Come in."

Cassie turned. She had paint smeared across her cheek and in her hair and a roller in her hand. When he spied her feet covered in paint, he figured she'd stepped in the roller pan. He chuckled, recalling he'd done it once or twice himself.

"What are you laughing at?" Her frown, so mock serious compared to her hair dotted with splatter from cream-colored paint.

"Nothing. Nothing."

"So I got a little paint on me. Got the floor covered. It's not a problem. You want something?" She put the roller down and rested her hands on her hips, leaving more paint on her clothing.

She looked so cute, like a little kid who got into a can of paint and had a field day. He wanted to hug her and kiss her, but her stormy expression didn't invite familiarity. Besides, he didn't want to become the same color as the walls.

"How you doin'?" He thought he'd start gentle.

"Fine. Got the back room painted. Blue. Only one more wall here to do."

He eyed the wet walls. "You're doing a good job."

She gave a half smile but lowered her hands and relaxed her stance. He took a deep breath.

"As I said before. You want something?" Her tone softened.

"Wanted to give you a ride home is all. I mean, if you're ready to leave."

"I've got a ride, thank you. So you can toddle on home." She made a gesture.

"A ride? With who?"

"And this concerns you how?" She turned her back to him and ran her roller through the paint.

"Come on, Cassie. Stop playing games. Not everyone who offers you a ride is safe."

She whirled around to face him. "I'm not twelve. I can take care of myself."

"Well, shoot me for trying to do the right thing here." Anger flamed in his chest. "Who you ridin' with?"

"My grandmother."

"Gram? She's gone."

"No. Winnie. My *other* grandmother." Her haughty expression made him want to grab her and spank her.

"Well, pardon me. Guess she's safe enough. So, you don't need me."

For a moment, she chewed her lip. "Not for a ride, I don't. Winnie's coming around five thirty. She's going to take me to the Inn."

Didn't that seal the deal? She'd gone through with the idiotic plan to move out of his house and into the Inn. Anger turned to hurt. "Really? You going to throw away your money on a room? It isn't cheap."

"I'm not poor. I can afford it."

He glanced around at the work they'd done on the store. "It's going to take a couple of weeks for this place to be ready."

"So?" She rested her hand on her hip and shot him a defiant glare.

"You're still mad?"

She didn't answer.

"Oh, baby. Look. I'm sorry I fought with you this morning. Can't we bury the hatchet? Can't we forget it?"

"Forget you don't want me forever?"

"I never said that."

"You calling me a liar?"

Frustration bubbled up inside him. "No. I'm not. I'm saying we weren't communicating very well this morning. Come on. Come back to the house with me. Let's patch things up."

"What'll I tell Winnie?"

"She'll understand."

"She sure will. I got off early. Go with Flint. I got grocery shopping to do anyway."

They turned to see Winnie in the doorway.

"Better for you to ride with him." She waved as she turned toward the road.

"Okay. Thanks, Winnie," Cassie called after the woman.

Flint silently thanked her. "You coming with me, then?"

"If you can wait till I get cleaned up." She washed out the roller and the pan then set them outside to dry.

"No problem." Flint wandered into the office. "Place looks real good. You're doing a fine job."

"Thanks." She went into the bathroom and shut the door.

He heard the strains of a favorite Christmas song. Cassie had a beautiful voice. When she came out, her face scrubbed clean, her multicolored hair pulled up into a ponytail, she appeared as young and fresh as a teenager. His heart lurched. Could she be even more beautiful without a lick of makeup?

"Ready." She put her painting clothes across a chair then met his gaze with wary eyes.

"Good. Taking anything with you?"

"Nope. I'm coming back tomorrow."

"Okay." He nodded and held the door for her.

The ride home was quiet. Once inside the house, Flint took her elbow. "Can I talk to you?"

She followed him into the den. He shut the door. "Sit."

She followed his instructions. Flint took the seat next to her and cleared his throat.

"Look. No reason for you to go to the Inn. Please stay here. If you don't want to bunk in with me, you can return to the guest room. But I really want you to stay."

"Even if I don't sleep with you?"

"Honestly? Of course I want you to sleep with me. But if you don't want to, I accept that. I still want you here."

CASSIE SUCKED ON HER lower lip for a moment. The last thing she wanted was to move out. With all her traveling, she'd rarely been alone. Someone from her family always went along. The Inn, as beautiful as it was, would be cold and lonely.

"Okay. I'll stay."

He grabbed her and hugged her tight. Her eyes drifted shut. His masculine scent mixed with a faint remnant of aftershave and a little sweat met her nose. That's him. That's Flint. And she loved the way he smelled. He pushed away, still holding her upper arms. His gaze sought hers.

"With me? Or in the guest room?"

Part of her wanted to torture him by selecting the guest room. Hell, truth was she wanted him as much as he wanted her.

"With you."

His grin widened and his second hug morphed into bone-crusher status.

"Sorry, sorry." He stepped back.

Marty burst through the doorway. "Nice, nice. But what's for dinner?"

"Dinner?" Cassie and Flint looked at each other.

"Right here," Marty said, pointing to the refrigerator. "Flint is supposed to be cooking tonight."

Watching Flint's confusion, Cassie hid a smile behind her hand.

"Screw it. Cassie's decided to stay. Let's go to Homer's and celebrate."

Marty grinned and shook his head. "Always a way out. Okay, but you're paying."

"Yep. I am."

A text from her mother grabbed Cassie's attention.

Mom: *When are you coming home?*

She paused for a moment before replying.

Cassie: *No clue, Mom. Relax. Things are good.*

"Let's take my car." Marty rattled his keys.

"Then I can drink." Flint patted his brother on the shoulder then held the door for the others.

"Cassie rides shotgun."

Grumbling, Flint got in the back.

As the car pulled out of the driveway, Cassie looked out the window. Leaves were changing colors. She noticed the difference from day to day.

"I've never seen the leaves change."

"Really?" Marty took a quick glance at her then focused on the road.

"Grew up in Southern California. Never stayed here long enough to see fall. It's beautiful."

He pulled into Homer's lot and parked. At the door, Flint requested a table near a window.

Homer swung by with a small pad and pen.

"Since Flint's paying, may I recommend the filet mignon?" Marty suggested.

"Go ahead. Then it's hot dogs and beans all next week," Flint piped up.

"Will you two give it a rest? Geez. I'll have a glass of Cabernet Sauvignon."

"I'll have whatever you have on tap. My brother'll have water." Flint grinned.

"Stuff it, Flint. I'll have a Coke, Homer."

"Coming right up. Specials today are lasagna, stuffed shrimp, and pumpkin pie."

They placed their orders. Snarky shots zoomed between the brothers. Cassie grinned. Anyone who didn't know them would think they hated each other. She knew better. There was something comforting about their banter, their easy friendship.

She realized Marty cared deeply for his brother and cast a jaundiced eye on Cassie. She noticed him staring at her from time to time, almost as if he wanted to ask her something but never did. Marty had something on his mind about her, and it bothered her. Afraid to ask him, scared it might be angry or hostile, she let it lie.

The longer she stayed, the more uneasy she became around Marty. Why couldn't he come out and ask her? Did he think she'd stomp on his brother's heart? Maybe he didn't know her very well. Or didn't know that Flint had a problem with commitment. Well, after three broken engagements, what else could it be?

Chapter Thirteen

After dinner, Marty dropped them home then went out with friends. Dancing up the walk, singing the song from her show, lightness filled Cassie. She continued to move as Flint jammed the key in the lock.

"How about a glass of wine?" He turned on the lights in the living room and kitchen.

"Sure." She plopped down on the sofa.

Flint pulled out a bottle from the liquor cabinet, yanked out the cork and poured two glasses. Then he joined her on the couch.

"I didn't know you drink wine." She took a sip.

"Sometimes. I drink lots of stuff." Flint built a fire.

They drank in silence for a bit.

"Do you want kids?" She blurted out the question then covered her mouth.

"Where'd that come from?"

"Well, do you?"

"Of course."

"How many?"

"Two would be good. Maybe one to start?"

"Yeah. Okay. Two."

"Or three, if the two are great. Do you want kids?"

"I do."

"How can you do that and be Cassandra Wells?"

"I like being plain old Cassie Wells."

"Do you? Could you ever live in a place like Pine Grove?"

She nodded. "I love it here. The leaves change."

"Every October. Like clockwork."

They finished their wine. He glanced at his watch.

"Bed?" He cocked an eyebrow and glanced at her.

"Thought you'd never ask."

"Come." He swept her into his arms, scooped her up, and carried her to bed. Giggling, Cassie kissed his cheek and fastened her arms around his shoulders. His strength awed her. Feeling his arms beneath her knees and shoulders started her motor.

Flint eased her down on his bed. "Do you need help?" He reached for the button on her blouse.

"I can manage, but if you tackle the bottom buttons and I do the top, I'll be undressed in half the time."

"Sounds like a plan." He knelt on the bed. As soon as the blouse was open, he peeled it off.

Flint undressed her with glee, kissing every inch of skin. When he discarded his T-shirt, pants, and boxers, she flattened her palms on his chest. The feel of his muscles moving beneath her hands flipped her switch. The more she touched him the higher the flames grew.

He paid attention to her breasts, kissing them, then closing his lips over her nipples. With each tug, her desire increased, the tension inside her coiled tighter.

"Flint," she panted. "Enough. Do it. Do it. Take me. Do it!"

He flipped down on his back, closing his hands over her hips. "Come here, baby." He picked her up and settled her over him. She parted her legs and he eased her down, grabbing his dick to guide it into her.

"Ride 'em, cowboy!" she howled as he lowered her, filling her completely. "Damn!"

He hissed as her tight wetness gripped him. She closed her fingers over his shoulders and bounced her butt up and down on him.

"I'm going to ride you hard." Each time she rose up, she contracted her muscles to squeeze him.

He groaned, closing his eyes. Cassie heated to almost unbearable. Finally, she leaned her forearms on his chest, pushed up on her knees, and bobbed her butt up and down on him rapidly, increasing the speed as her body hit the breaking point.

As the orgasm took over, she pushed down against him, arching her back, her breasts standing proudly before him. Her eyes drifted shut as a moan escaped her throat. As pleasure zoomed through her veins to every part of her body, she slowly opened her eyes.

Flint stared at her with hot eyes. She started up again, but he took control this time, moving her up and down to his rhythm. His lips captured one nipple as his hand slid up her side. He grabbed her breast, cupping it. Then it hit him. He roared once and held her down on his dick.

Sweat broke out on his forehead and pecs. Cassie danced her fingers through his chest hair. He eased his hands up to her head, bringing it toward him. He planted a sweet, gentle kiss on her lips and muttered, "I love you."

As if someone had dumped a bucket of ice water on their heads, Flint and Cassie's eyes opened wide. She jumped slightly.

"I, I, I..." he stuttered.

"I know. I love you, too."

Silence. He slid his palms slowly down her chest, stopping to give a gentle squeeze to each breast. "You're beautiful."

She leaned down, pressing her mouth to his, holding him tightly between her thighs. He caressed her back as she probed with her tongue. Needing air, she popped up, with a quick gasp. Staring at him, she smiled. "I feel great."

"Me, too."

She dismounted slowly. He trotted off to the bathroom. When he returned, it was her turn.

"I've turned on the electric mattress pad."

"With the heat we created, do you think we'll need it?"

He chuckled. "It gets pretty cold here at night."

She relished cuddling up to him. His body was like her own personal electric blanket. Cassie got into bed and pulled up the covers. The room had cooled. She shivered then inched nearer where he could sling an arm over her. She snuggled into him and he switched off the light.

"Cassie, I..."

"It's okay. Me, too."

"Goodnight."

"Goodnight, Flint."

Not thinking about forever, Cassie let the warmth of Flint and the mattress pad sink into her bones. She'd think about the challenges she faced tomorrow and enjoy the here and now.

THE NEXT MORNING, FLINT dropped Cassie at the store then went to his office. He opened his computer and grabbed a stack of bills. Paperwork was his least favorite part of the job. After ten minutes, he pushed to his feet and turned to Marty.

"Do we have a job running downstairs?"

"Every day for the next two weeks."

Flint gave his brother a thumb's up. He descended the steep steps to the basement and flicked on the light. His ears picked up the low hum of printers in action. They had invested in quality, high-speed printers, for both black-and-white and color jobs.

Flint maintained the machinery and supplies, while Marty set up the jobs. The printers were spitting out color flyers for a store in Oak Bend. Three more jobs waited in the wings, ready to go. He checked the counter—five thousand more to print. It would be done in two hours.

While his body was in the office, his heart stayed in the store with Cassie. While Marty visited a new client, Flint needed to set up the next few jobs. One for a thousand color brochures. And six smaller jobs for 500 sets of instructions. When the printers ran, money came in.

Still, he wanted to pick up a roller and paint alongside Cassie. Last night he'd confessed he loved her. She'd said it back, but did she mean it? And what did it matter? She'd be leaving as soon as the place was sold. Words of wisdom he imagined his mother would say came to him. *"Enjoy the good times while they're here."*

He'd try, though it wouldn't be easy to roadblock thoughts about the future. Cassie flitted from movie to movie from stage to stage, as the offers came in. Could anyone in show business plan their future? Probably not. Flint planned.

He'd started saving in high school. Although he didn't know what he wanted to do, he knew doing anything, like having his own business, would take money. He'd been working, planning, and saving for years. And now he had a successful business, a home, a good life. All except for one thing. Love. He didn't have a woman to call his own.

Flint checked the paper trays and refilled the ones that were low. He checked the setup for the next job, making sure he had all the materials he needed, then he tramped upstairs. Before he made it to his desk, Marty cornered him.

"What's going on with you and Cassie? You said she was moving to the hotel. Now she's back in your room?"

"Yeah. So?"

"So?"

"She's staying with me." He raised his chin a touch and rested his hands on his hips.

"You two could be a little quieter, you know. Keeping me awake."

Flint grinned. "Jealous?"

"Just looking for a good night's sleep."

"Sure, sure. Find the right woman. Better than a sleeping pill." He elbowed him. "Move. I've got bills to pay."

Marty dropped another small stack of envelopes on his brother's desk. "Here."

Flint made a face then perused the mail. "Hey, some of these are checks."

"Thank God. I'll deposit them today."

He handed his brother the ones with checks and opened the checkbook. Flint hated paying bills, but it had to be done. His mind kept drifting back to Cassie, sleeping peacefully beside him. Her skin, her hair mussed from sleep, her drowsy eyes looking lazy and lustful at the same time. Had there ever been a more seductive woman? Not in his lifetime.

A KNOCK ON THE DOOR interrupted Cassie cleaning her brushes.

"Hi." Will Lennox stood outside the screen, holding a carpenter's box.

"Will. Hi. Come in."

"You said you'd be ready for me today."

"Yes, well, we've fallen a little behind."

"Let me take some measurements, then. When do you think I can get in?"

"I'm going to finish the walls today."

"Okay. A day to dry and then I'll come in and do the floor."

"Perfect."

After Will finished and put his measuring tape away, Cassie's stomach rumbled. She checked her watch. One o'clock. Her cell rang.

"Have you eaten yet?" It was Flint.

"I was about to go out."

"Let me buy you lunch at The Cozy Café."

"Best offer I've had all day."

"I'll pick you up."

At the honk from Flint's truck, Cassie waved. He drove on less-traveled streets, homes to large farms. Cassie took in the brilliant reds, golds, and oranges of the changing leaves.

"It looks like a movie set."

"I took the scenic route. Look at 'em now. One good windy, rainy day and all the leaves will be on the ground."

"Really?"

"Yeah. It takes its own sweet time getting to this point, and then wham! All the branches are bare. Fall is over in a heartbeat and winter's here."

The Cozy was busy. Flint parked on the street. Cassie hugged herself against the chilly air.

"Don't they know about autumn here?"

"What do you mean?"

"Isn't this winter weather?"

Flint chuckled. "Not up here. It's fall weather."

"How cold does it get in winter?"

"Colder. A lot colder. Trust me. It must be forty degrees today."

"To a Southern California girl, that's cold."

"Come on. Coffee'll warm you up." He held the door open.

The charming café stood on the edge of the water. There was a deck attached, jutting out into Cedar Lake. Tables were set up there.

"Are people still sitting outside?" She glanced out the French doors.

"Yep. We're pretty hearty."

She nodded.

"I've got a table with a view opening up," said Laura Dailey, menus in hand.

A couple pushed past Cassie and Flint, heading to the door. Laura cleared the table.

"Two coffees, Laura." Flint studied the menu. "What's your soup today?"

"Amy made a lovely chicken corn chowder. We have fresh ham salad today, too. Whatcha havin'?"

"Soup sounds good. I'll have a cup and the ham salad on rye?" Cassie handed the menu back.

"Soup for me, too. A bowl. And the roast beef hero."

"Got it. Thanks."

Laura scurried into the back, only to reappear seconds later carrying a pot of hot coffee. She filled their mugs then left.

Cassie added milk and sugar. Wrapping her cold fingers around the warm mug, she took a sip. She looked around the room, her gaze stopping at a bulletin board. One flyer had a big headline, "Square Dance."

"A square dance? Really?" She chuckled.

"Oh yeah. Forgot about that. It's a fundraiser. We charge ten bucks and have a raffle. Money goes to pay for our holiday shit."

"Shit?"

"Sorry. I mean the Thanksgiving dinner."

"Do you go to the town dinner or have your own?"

"I go there and help serve."

"Nice."

"It's not the same, having it at home, since my parents moved to Florida."

"You don't get together with friends?"

"Nah. They all have family. Marty and I work at the firehouse dinner. We've got a lot to be thankful for."

Cassie nodded. She had a lot to be thankful for, too, didn't she?

"Will you even be here for Thanksgiving?" He cocked an eyebrow.

She shrugged. Thanksgiving hadn't been on her radar since she was a kid. Every year, she'd have a performance to do, or rehearsal or it would be a travel day. If she was free, she and her parents would go to a restaurant.

"Thanksgiving doesn't mean much to me."

He stared hard at her. "That's too bad. If you're still here, come to the firehouse with me."

"Okay. What about the square dance? Are you going?"

"Wouldn't miss it. Will you go, too?"

"Me? Square dancing?" Cassie burst into laughter.

Their soup arrived. She picked up the spoon.

"Never been to one?"

She shook her head and tasted the soup. "Wow. This is great."

"Laura and Amy are the best cooks in the county."

They ate in silence.

"Come on. Come with me."

"Where?"

"The square dance. It's this Saturday. You'll still be here, right?"

"Right."

"You're coming. Remember it's a fund-raiser."

"I'll bring money."

"I didn't mean that." He waved her off. "I meant it's a community thing. For the good of the town."

"Okay, okay. I'll go. Geez." She rolled her eyes. "Can't a girl eat her soup?"

He squeezed her hand and smiled. Then he raised his eyebrows. "Thanksgiving?"

"We'll see about that."

He took a bite of his sandwich, chewed, swallowed. "I heard Will was over at your place."

"Is nothing private in this town?"

"Any reason Will being at your place should be private? Was Nate with him?" His expression clouded.

"Of course not. Will's doing the floors."

"Yeah. That's what I thought."

They finished eating. Flint paid the check. "Where to?"

"I'm done painting. Back to your place?"

"Sure thing."

He parked in the driveway.

"I'm going to take a walk then read before I start dinner." Cassie got out and leaned against the car. "I think it's my night."

"Marty'll be happy about that." Flint turned the truck on and rested his arm on the open window.

Cassie squeezed his forearm briefly before he drove away. She sighed and entered the house. Although she'd enjoyed her time in Pine Grove, whatever would she do if she lived here full-time? She pulled one of Flint's jackets from a hook, grabbed her camera, then went outside.

She ambled through the backyard to the woods. The riot of color stole her breath. She snapped photo after photo of trees, leaves, farmhouses, and the occasional Victorian she passed. She sure didn't have this in Southern California.

"I'M GOIN' HOME." FLINT closed his briefcase and headed for the door.

"Who's on for dinner?" Marty faced his brother.

"Cassie."

"Oh. Text me if I need to bring home a pizza."

Flint laughed. "You have no faith."

"I'm a realist. Meatball or pepperoni?" Marty smiled.

Flint chuckled and closed the door. Cassie was no cook. She swore she could burn water. He'd left a few beginner cookbooks on the counter, hoping she got the hint. He pulled into the driveway and parked. The front door wasn't locked, so he walked right in. Damn! Something smelled real good. He peeked into the living room.

Sound asleep, Cassie was curled up on the sofa, an open book lay on the floor by her hand. She'd wrapped a blanket around her and tucked it under her feet. She looked so innocent and pure. He chuckled.

There was nothing innocent and pure about this girl. Not that he minded. She'd been around the world more than once, could converse in several languages, sing like a songbird, swear like a sailor, and dance like a ballerina.

He tiptoed into the kitchen. Smart girl, she'd filled the Crockpot and it took care of the rest. He lifted the cover and spied chicken, veggies, and some kind of sauce. Perfect. He'd whip up some rice and *voila*—dinner.

He pulled a bottle of beer out of the fridge. Stealing into the living room, he toed off his shoes, eased his butt into a wing chair, and rested his feet on a small stool. Damn, he could get used to this.

No way! She was leaving. She'd said so. He'd never have this, and the sooner he realized it, the better. But, damn, he wanted it, wanted it bad. When he finished his beer, he got up and made a fire in the fireplace.

The clinking of the screen disturbed Cassie. She shifted position, moaned once, sighed, and continued sleeping. The crackling of the fire inspired him. He moved to the sofa to get a better view of the flame—or that's what he told himself—and snuggled up to her as best he could. She stretched then rested her head in his lap and continued to snooze. He fell asleep, wrapped in dreams of domestic bliss, taking pleasure from an ordinary, peaceful, passion-filled life.

At the slamming of the front door, Flint jumped.

"Something smells good!"

Rubbing his eyes, he focused on his brother. "Do you have to come in here like a fuckin' Mack truck?"

Cassie stretched and opened her eyes.

"Sleeping? It's dinnertime. Wake up, Sleeping Beauty." Marty laughed.

"I oughta slug you."

"We had to get up sometime." Cassie fell back against the cushions.

Marty set the table. Flint made rice, and the trio sat down to eat.

"Are you going to the square dance, Marty?" Cassie asked.

"I don't know."

Flint looked up. "Why not?"

"Isabelle might be there."

Cassie looked up. "Who's Isabelle?"

"His old girlfriend. She dumped him."

"She didn't dump me."

"She gave you the ring back."

"Yeah, well..."

"She's an idiot, Marty. I've told you a thousand times. She was lucky to get a guy like you to look at her twice."

Marty gave a brief smile then lowered his gaze to his plate.

Cassie patted Marty's hand. "I have to agree with Flint."

"Anyway. I'm not up for running into her."

"Are you sure she's going to be there?" Flint asked.

"Hank is going to be calling, isn't he? They're together now. Or so I've heard."

"Well, fuck her. Go anyway. You might meet someone else." Flint took a forkful of food.

"Who? Who is there in this hick town of 10 people, eh? There's no one, Flint. No one. You know that."

"Flint ran out on three women, so there must be someone here for you."

Marty burst into laughter. "I can always count on you, Flint. Whatever I've screwed up, you've already screwed up worse."

Flint's eyes crinkled. "Someone's gotta set the standard for bad around here."

"And it's always you."

The brothers laughed.

"Beer?" Marty asked.

"Why not? I'm not driving."

Cassie watched with big eyes as the men ragged on each other. When the meal was finished, they cleaned up, still trash-talking and laughing. For a moment, she envied their easy camaraderie. She and her brother, Brian, were formal with each other. Brian kept his private life to himself. She sighed. It must be nice to be regular people. She picked up her book and padded upstairs.

Chapter Fourteen

Flint opened the double door to the Pine Grove High School gym. He, Cassie, and Marty stepped inside. They stopped at the table to buy tickets. She spied a donation jar, reached into her wallet, and dropped sixty dollars in.

"Thank you! The money is for the free Thanksgiving dinner at the firehouse." An older woman sitting at the table smiled up at Cassie.

The reflection from the colored lights strung around the cavernous room bounced off the shiny gymnasium floor. A voice came over the loudspeaker.

"Allemande left with your left hand, into a grand right and left." The caller at the mike spoke loud and clear. In the center of the room, men in jeans and T-shirts swung women in brightly colored dresses. Their full skirts billowed out as they twirled and danced.

Laughter punctuated the caller's commands as people went left instead of right or to their corner instead of partner.

"Three tickets, Agnes." Flint reached into his back pocket.

"You buyin' for me, Brother?"

"Yep."

The trio entered the room. Country music on the fiddle got Cassie's toe tapping.

"Check out the baked goods table." Marty motioned to the others. They wandered over. The long table covered in a white cloth, sported dozens of cupcakes, frosted in chocolate, pink, or white icing. Four cakes commanded attention. There was a chocolate, a red

173

velvet, an angel food, and the one that caught Cassie's, eye—a six-layer white coconut cake.

"Wow! Look." She pointed to the coconut.

"Laura Dailey's pride and joy." Marty smiled.

The tired voice of a woman sitting behind the table grabbed their attention.

"Cake is three bucks a slice. Cupcakes, two bucks each. Brownies are a dollar."

"One of each."

The woman's eyes widened. "Really?"

"Just kidding. A cupcake and a slice of the chocolate cake," Flint said.

"A slice of coconut cake for me." Cassie said.

"Two brownies."

"Marty always has to be different." Flint chuckled while he unwrapped his cupcake.

"You two bicker like an old married couple." Cassie picked up a plastic fork.

The trio stood to the side and watched the dancing. The lively music had Cassie's hips moving to the beat while she relished the moist confection.

When they finished, the woman behind the table handed out wipes. "Here you go."

"Let's see what you got, McKay." Cassie took Flint's hand and headed for the dance floor.

Marty hugged a wall. Cassie kept an eye on him. She overheard the woman at the refreshment table.

"Laura Dailey's niece is over there with her two kids. Why don't you ask her to dance?"

"I don't know her."

"I'll introduce you."

"I don't think so."

Cassie took a spot across from the cake table to watch Marty. A pretty redhead sashayed up to him.

"Who's that?" Cassie whispered to Flint.

"Who?"

"The redhead?"

"Isabelle Townsend. Marty's ex."

"She doesn't look very ex right now."

The music started up, keeping Cassie from overhearing their conversation. She saw the woman lean over and whisper in Marty's ear. He shook his head then made a beeline for the dance floor. He approached a pretty blonde with two kids in tow. She thought she heard him introduce himself and ask the woman to dance.

Cassie raised her gaze to the redhead. She crossed her arms over her chest and shot daggers at the blonde. Cassie poked Flint in the ribs and pointed to her.

"Aren't you supposed to be bowing to your corner?"

"What?"

Flint laughed. "You gotta listen to the calls and pay attention, sweetheart."

"Okay, okay." Determined to worm the whole story out of Marty later, she got into the spirit and joined in the lively dancing. Cassie wasn't used to being out of her element on the dance floor, but she picked up on the commands quickly.

"Not bad for a novice."

"Not bad. I'm doing better than you."

Flint laughed as he joined arms and swung her around. Cassie closed her fingers around his forearm. Every time they touched her body temperature rose. When he put his hands on her waist for one move, her nipples tightened. Her man, in his plaid flannel shirt and jeans, stole her breath.

Being among strangers made her nervous. It calmed her to have him there. Basil had provided some comfort when they spent nights in strange hotels. But he'd take off whenever he had an interview or photo op and never worried about her.

Not Flint. He checked up on her. Made sure she didn't take a ride from a dangerous person, or the contractor was on the up-and-up. At first his attitude rankled her. Before long, she realized it wasn't that he didn't think her capable of taking care of herself, but rather, as he put it, he "didn't trust the world" when it came to Cassie.

The dancing got her blood pumping. The more she moved, the more turned on she got. Yes, she wanted Flint, but she'd have to wait. Tapping her foot, she asked him, "Is this the last one?"

"Yeah. Too bad."

She shot him a flirtatious look.

"Or not. Whatever." He gave her a questioning glance.

Cassie sidled up to him, slipping under his arm and snaking her arms around his middle. She squeezed. "When can we leave?"

He raised his eyebrows. "In a hurry?"

"Maybe." She peered at him from under her black lashes.

Cassie couldn't wait to get outside. The early November night was cold, but it felt good. Marty joined them. Flint kept singing "Buffalo Gal" as he danced his way to the truck.

"Who were you dancing with?" Cassie directed her question to Marty.

"I shoulda known you'd be poking your nose into his business. Can't even wait until we get home, can you?" Flint stared at her.

"No biggie. Her name's Jenny something. She's Laura Dailey's niece. Here for the weekend."

"Pretty."

Marty nodded.

"Who's the redhead, and what did she want?"

"That's Isabelle. We dated for a while. Then she got engaged to somebody else."

"She's married?" Cassie's eyebrows shot up.

"Not anymore. She dumped him and got a good settlement."

"Oh, a gold digger." Cassie nodded.

"Marty dodged a bullet."

"Didn't feel like it at the time." Marty shuffled along, sliding into the backseat.

"Did she break your heart?" Cassie turned to face him. Flint put the truck in gear.

"What do you think?"

"I think the McKay men manage to find women, get engaged, even multiple times, yet never close the deal. Why aren't you guys married?"

"If I was, you wouldn't be here," Flint spoke up.

"Unless you were married to her." It was Marty from the backseat.

Laughter cut the tension. Cassie stopped probing and faced forward. These two men were a mystery. Was Flint waiting for her all these years? Impossible, right?

She leaned over and whispered in his ear. "I gotta get you home."

"Girl, I'm doing the speed limit."

"Hey, you two. You're not alone here. Save it for the bedroom."

Cassie sensed heat in her face. She edged over to hug the door until they pulled into the driveway.

AT ODDS FOR A WEEK while the contractors worked on the store, Cassie took up cooking. She watched cooking shows on daytime TV and bought cookbooks at the local bookstore. Every night, the McKay men came home to a new hot meal. Some days the meal was a success, others, they ended up going out for pizza.

Flint admired her determination, but he knew gourmet chefs were not born in a week. He played along, pleasantly surprised by her tasty concoctions. He and Marty took turns cleaning up. Both men were relieved not to have to wrack their brains for dinner ideas at the end of the day.

Best of all was having her in his bed every night. Although she'd always been a willing partner, her sexual appetite almost matched his. Sometimes she'd be up late, trying out a new recipe, not coming up to bed until the middle of the night. Then he'd feel cold hands on his butt or slithering up his back. He'd roll over, and she'd be ready to rock and roll. Sure he'd wake up exhausted in the morning but with a smile on his face.

Thanksgiving was only a few days away. He had to get in gear for the big dinner at the firehouse. There was shopping and planning to do.

Lying in bed after making love, Flint broached the subject.

"How would you like to help with Thanksgiving dinner at the firehouse?" He didn't expect her to agree.

"Sure. Do you want me to cook? Find a cool recipe and make something?"

"Uh, no. We need shopping and hauling, and setup, and clean up. Dish washing. The women who did the cooking last year are doing it again this year."

"Oh. Okay." Her smile drooped.

"You'll be working with me. Okay?"

"Sure. Why not? It's not like I've got something else to do."

"What do you usually do on Thanksgiving?" He put up a fresh pot of coffee.

"Grab a burger. Eat in my dressing room. Sometimes we had turkey sandwiches. When I was on Broadway, we always had a show on Thanksgiving Day. Doing a movie? I'd sometimes be on location in a foreign country. Thanksgiving isn't celebrated everywhere."

"Really? That's terrible."

"You don't miss what you've never had."

"Haven't you ever wanted to have a normal Thanksgiving?" He took their mugs from the table.

"Sure. I used to. When I was little, we'd get together with aunts, uncles, cousins, and a huge turkey. The whole thing. But not since I was sixteen. It's only one day. I got over it."

"And now?"

She shrugged. "I don't know. I suppose it's nice. Might as well be doing something useful, like helping out at the firehouse. I don't have anywhere else to go anyway."

"What about your parents? Your brother?"

"My parents are in Paris and Brian's going to be with his wife's family."

Sadness crept into his heart. He cupped her head and pulled her into a hug. Thinking back on all the warm, wonderful Thanksgivings he'd had with his brother and his parents. And cousins, aunts, uncles, too. There'd be too much food, and football games, jigsaw puzzles, and tossing a ball outside if there wasn't snow. Wonderful memories flitted through his brain. Cassie had none. An ache passed through his chest.

"People think movie stars have it so great." He shook his head.

He filled their cups, added milk and sugar to hers, and handed it over. As nonchalant as she tried to sound, she couldn't hide a hint of moisture in her eyes. Suddenly, he wanted to have the biggest, loudest Thanksgiving in the world in his house, just for her.

The meal at the firehouse was about other people and plain hard work. He always collapsed with a beer and a football game when he got home.

"What time is the event?"

"We have it early. One o'clock. Then everyone who works can get home for some family time. Or a Thanksgiving of their own."

"Sounds good. I'm down for it."

"When do we have to get started?"

"Tomorrow morning."

"What time?"

"Seven?"

"Better get to sleep then." She scooted down, pulling up the covers. Flint spooned her and the couple fell asleep.

THE ALARM WOKE THEM at seven. They dressed and headed for the kitchen. Cassie made coffee and cracked a couple of eggs in the frying pan.

"Let's get started on the shopping list." Flint grabbed a pad and a pen from a drawer and sat at the table.

"Let's see, twenty turkeys." He wrote it down.

"Twenty?" Cassie filled two mugs.

"We're expecting a hundred people."

"That many can't afford Thanksgiving?" She added milk and sugar to hers.

He nodded.

"That's terrible."

"Jonas Barley's giving us 12, and Amos Winfield is donating eight. We pick those up early Thanksgiving morning."

"How early?"

"Hmm. About five or six."

"What's next?" She brought the beverages to the table, grabbed the pen and took over the paper. "Watch the eggs."

Flint pushed to his feet. "This is the stuff we have to buy. Yams. Regular potatoes. Onions. Canned green beans. Cranberries. Cream of mushroom soup." As he talked, she wrote. "Oh, and paper plates and plastic knives and forks. Somewhere I've got the exact amounts from the recipes from last year. The same ladies make the same stuff every year." He flipped the eggs over and pulled plates down from the cabinet.

"Okay. Where do we go for all this?"

"Samson's, it's a big box store."

When they finished the list, breakfast was ready.

"Nearest one is about an hour away. Maybe a little longer."

"We'll let's go, then." Cassie took the last bite of egg and drained her mug.

A sleepy Marty scratching his chest joined them.

"We're going to Samson's." Flint put the plates in the dishwasher.

"Okay."

"Here's breakfast. Coffee's still hot." Cassie grabbed her coat and tossed one to Flint.

They climbed into the truck and headed for the highway. Cassie fiddled with the radio. The soundtrack for one of her movies came on. She sang along. They arrived at the store by nine, but long lines had already formed. Time slipped away.

The truck pulled into the driveway at Flint and Marty's house at six o'clock. It was pitch black, and Cassie was bone weary. She dragged herself to the front door. Oh, yes, something smelled good.

"Where have you two been? Dinner's ready." Marty stood in the archway to the kitchen.

"Took us the whole damn day to buy everything and haul it to the firehouse." Flint sank down on a chair at the kitchen table.

"Beer, anyone?" Marty stood at the open fridge.

Cassie smiled. "Hell, yes."

Marty deposited a beer in her hand and one in Flint's before he brought a chicken and rice casserole to the table. While they ate and drank, Flint and Cassie recounted their day. Finding the food at the huge store had taken forever.

"Why don't they just have one effing Thanksgiving aisle? With all our stuff in it?" Cassie grumbled.

"That's not the way it works."

"I got that. But why not?" She took a forkful of food.

"Cassie was great. Once she stopped bitching, we got it done."

"Bitching? The guy wouldn't get his lazy butt out of our way."

Flint laughed.

"So, what's next?" she asked.

"Picking up the turkeys tomorrow morning."

"Ugh. At five."

"Laura said by six. It would give them enough time to get 'em cooked by one."

"Early to bed, you guys. And no fooling around." Marty hid a grin.

"Fooling around? I'll be lucky if I can crawl upstairs and fall into bed." Cassie groaned.

When they finished dinner, Marty offered to clean up.

"Are you coming tomorrow?" Cassie asked him, before heading upstairs.

"Yep. But I get there later. I'm in charge of the setup."

"Oh. Good. Night."

"Good night, Cassie."

She peeled off her clothes and fell into bed. Flint spooned her, and she was asleep before he could kiss her good night.

THE ALARM WENT OFF at five. Cassie rolled over to face the window. It was pitch black outside and chilly inside. Flint's warm hands rubbed gently up and down her torso.

"You starting something?" Her voice was raspy.

"Nope. Wish we could. My way of saying good morning."

"Ugh. It's dark outside. Cold in here and we have to get up."

"Yeah. But you'll see. It'll be a fun day."

"Fun?"

"Trust me."

She made a clucking sound and pushed the covers down. "I get the bathroom first."

"Be my guest."

"Oh, hell, I really am your guest, aren't I?" She stopped.

"Oh, God, no. No bad puns. Not at this hour. Please." He groaned, pulling the covers over his head.

Cassie chuckled as she scampered across the cold wood floor. After a quick shower, she dressed in jeans, a sweatshirt, and heavy socks. She padded down to the kitchen and got coffee started.

"I'll make eggs," came from the husky voice of her lover.

They ate and drank in silence. Cassie peeked at the window. "Sun's coming up."

"Grab your jacket. Let's go. We don't want to keep those turkeys waiting."

He shot her a grin and held the door open. Cassie was too sleepy for music, so they rode in silence. At each farm, they were invited in for coffee.

"No time. Thanks anyway, Martha."

"Are you really Cassandra Wells? You don't look like her."

"That's what they tell me. Thanks for the turkey."

By seven, they had unloaded the birds, one at each house. The "ladies who cook" as Flint called them, had already preheated their stoves. Most of the food was farmed out to be cooked in various homes in town. Laura Dailey took over baking the pies. As they drove to each farm, one by one they spied lights coming on in house after house.

The ladies had to get these dishes out of the way so they could cook for their families. At eight they had a break and returned home.

Holding a cup of coffee, Marty greeted them. "You're done, Brother?"

"Yep."

"We don't have to do anything?" Cassie asked.

"Not until eleven thirty."

"I'm going back to sleep. Please set the alarm." Cassie yawned.

"I'm right behind you." Flint followed her up the stairs.

Cassie shed her clothes and crawled into bed. The sheets were cold, but then Flint joined her. He was a regular heat machine. They snuggled together.

As soon as she heard Flint's soft snore, her eyes opened. Her body needed relaxation, but her mind wasn't tired. Lying on her side, she stared out the window. The sky was gray with a few darker clouds moving in. Now and then a stray snowflake flitted by the window. She shivered, pulling the covers tighter around her.

What was it like to have a real, American Thanksgiving? She tried to remember back when she was a young teen. Of course, she'd been bogged down with acting classes, dance classes, and singing lessons for forever. But before she actually started performing, they'd had Thanksgiving, hadn't they?

Shutting her eyes, she dialed back her memories. Yes, in the old house. The small one they owned before her parents hit it big as agents and she got her first big role. It was a cute house, three bedrooms, one bathroom. The backyard was the best part. There was a swing on a huge tree limb. Her father grew tomatoes and cucumbers in a small garden.

Ah, yes, the aroma of the turkey roasting in the oven—could she remember it? No, but she recalled how hungry she got, smelling all those good things coming from the kitchen. Her mother still cooked in those days. And her father was home by six fifteen every night.

Brian played baseball, and they watched family shows on television after dinner. Her grandparents, her adoptive ones, would join them for the holiday. She remembered her father struggling to put the wooden leaves in the table to make it big enough. Her mother went to her special drawer for the white Irish linen tablecloth and the good silver.

When they hit it big, the first thing her parents did was dump their quaint little house for a much grander one—a modern home with plenty of glass and three bathrooms. Cassie sighed. She never liked their new house much. But the first one—she never forgot.

She had tucked away the dream of an old-fashioned Thanksgiving with the one of a simpler life and a family of her own. Some day she would have one, with turkey, stuffing, and cranberries. Longing filled her heart and tears clouded her eyes. She had much to be grateful for, yet there seemed to be so many people who had so much more. She dozed.

The alarm went off. Flint's hand on her shoulder roused her.

"It's showtime." He stirred behind her.

"Oh God. Don't say that to me."

They got dressed, made the bed, and shrugged on heavy coats. From the house to the truck, a bitter wind nipped their faces. Flint blasted the heat as he drove to the firehouse. There were already four cars in the lot. He parked as close to the door as he could. Cassie ran inside.

"This California girl is not used to this weather. Damn, it's cold!"

"Welcome to Pine Grove," said Ivy, one of the ladies sharpening a carving set.

Tables had been draped with white cloths. Marty was setting plastic utensils, paper plates, and napkins out. Huge aluminum-foil pans, loaded with side dishes from Brussels sprouts to salad, took their places one after the other on the long tables. A handful of the women who cooked stayed to serve.

"If we move the sprouts next to the Caesar salad, and then the carrots, one person can handle those three dishes." Cassie nodded as Flint rearranged food and set up the serving order. "This is how it works. You come in, pick a place to sit, grab your plate, and get in line."

She nodded. "That works."

He turned to call across the room to his brother. "Marty! Can you handle the to-go orders?"

Marty nodded.

"To go?"

"Some people have family at home who can't get here. So they pick up dinner to go. We don't have a lot of those. But there are always a few."

Cassie glanced around the room, watching people pulling all the parts of the event together. "This is amazing."

"Keeps me busy."

Flint headed for the door to help a woman struggling with a giant pot of soup. Dish after dish arrived until there was no room left on the long tables. She inspected the mouthwatering, homemade food, including cranberry sauce, creamed onions, creamed spinach, Brussels sprouts, green bean casserole, grilled carrots, candied carrots, mashed potatoes, sweet potatoes, candied yam medallions, stuffing, eight pies, and ten platters piled high with sliced turkey. All the aromas of the delectable food made her stomach rumble.

"Marty, we're gonna need another table." Flint gave the order. Cassie set it up.

And then the parade of hungry people began. It started as a trickle. A couple of people right at the stroke of one. But the small stream became a flood when the clock struck the half hour. The line grew and grew, snaking around the side wall, threatening to burst out the door into the frigid air.

Cassie mimicked Flint. She took over three pans, doling out portions of side dishes to hungry country folk. She and Flint moved quickly, smiling, asking people what they wanted. A couple of the older men flirted with Cassie, embarrassing her.

One old geezer had no shame. "I'll take turkey with a side helping of you, missy."

Flint jumped in. "Sorry. She's already spoken for."

"Do you know how lucky you are, Flint McKay?" The old man turned a cold eye on Flint, then turned a warm one on Cassie.

"I sure do. Brussel sprouts?"

One or two of the women refused to believe she was the famous actress.

"You're not Cassandra Wells. She's a lot prettier than you," an older woman said.

"Some nerve. Pretending to be a famous actress," another mumbled loud enough for Cassie to hear.

Cassie shrugged. Maybe that was an improvement over being beset by fans looking for autographs?

Three of the older ladies made comments to Flint about her, asking him was he fixing to marry this one, and would he actually show up this time?

"Well, Flint, is she number four?"

"How about it? Gonna marry this one, too?" The women chuckled.

The poor man turned all kinds of colors but kept dishing out food.

By three o'clock, the place had emptied out. A few townsfolk stayed to help clean up. Most scurried home to their families and their own Thanksgiving celebrations. Cassie washed serving dishes, serving spoons, carving sets, water pitchers, iced tea pitchers, coffee mugs, and anything else that came her way.

Flint and Marty collapsed the tables and put them away. They left the tablecloths in a heap for Martha to launder over the weekend. By four, everyone was gone except Flint, Marty, and Cassie. They doled out the last of the coffee and plunked down on folding chairs.

"Wow!" Cassie blew out a breath.

"We did it." Flint grinned and turned to her. "Did you eat?"

She shook her head. "No time."

"Marty?"

"Nope. I forgot."

"Me, too. The turkeys are gone."

"I think we've got leftovers at home," Marty said.

Suddenly, her eyes filled. She'd been so busy making sure everyone else's Thanksgiving was good, she'd forgotten about her own. Sure, it was important, taking care of others, still a wave of loneliness swept over her as she sat in the chilly cavernous fire department garage.

Chapter Fifteen

"Well, well, well. Look at the three of you. Have I ever seen a sadder crew?"

They looked up. Winnie stood in the doorway, hands on hips.

"I'm sorry, Winnie. The dinner is over."

"Oh, hush up, Flint McKay. I'm not here to mooch a free meal. I'm here to invite my"—Winnie cleared her throat—"my granddaughter and her buddies to my house for a right proper Thanksgiving dinner."

"What?" Cassie couldn't believe her ears.

"That's right. Get your coats. We've squeezed three more places at the table. Family's waitin' and they're hungry, so let's go."

"But what about your children and their children?" Cassie pushed to her feet. "Do they even know about me? I thought you'd decided not to tell them."

"Damn it all to hell. I couldn't keep it a secret. Soon as they found out about you, well, they've been buggin' me. They want to meet you. Not often you get a new family member. Specially one that's famous, and all. So get your butts going. Flint? You know my house?"

"I think so."

"It's the one with green shutters on Vale Street."

"I know Vale," Marty piped up.

"Good. Let's go."

Two tears ran down Cassie's cheeks. She hugged Winnie. "Thank you," she whispered. "I can't wait to meet them."

"Don't go getting all emotional. You might feel different after you get to know 'em."

"They're my blood."

"Got that right. Come on, now, or I'll catch hell for dilly-dallying." Winne stepped back and motioned toward the door.

Cassie grabbed her coat and yanked it on. Questions filled her head.

"Can I ride with Winnie?"

"Sure." Flint gave her a kiss then climbed in the truck. Cassie called to Winnie, who stopped short.

"Wait for me!"

"Climb in, honey."

Winnie's car was warmer than the truck. As Cassie thawed out, she peppered her grandmother with questions.

"How many kids did you have?"

"Five, including Charlie."

"So I have four aunts or uncles?"

"Three aunts. One uncle."

"Will they all be there?"

"Yep. And my two grandsons, too."

Questions poured out like popcorn in a popper. Winnie chuckled but answered each one.

She pulled up in front of a modest white house. "The kids have parked up the driveway and garage."

A wave of fear and shyness engulfed Cassie. "What if they don't like me?"

Winnie snorted. "Are you kiddin'? They'll love you. And if they don't, too damn bad. You're my kin now. So they can lump it."

Winnie exited the car first. Cassie followed slowly. The wind bit through her jacket and stung her face. Why did people live in a climate like this? Winnie opened the door. Cassie heard the buzz of voices halt. There was a hush as she approached. Gingerly, she stepped into the foyer.

Winnie took her elbow and tugged her inside. "You're letting the heat out."

"Sorry," Cassie mumbled, her eyes wide as they flitted over a sea of faces. Tall, short, brown-haired, blonde, dark eyes, light eyes—seemed there was everything in her family. She shrank back flattening herself against the door. No audience in the world could ever be as intimidating as this one. The door opened to let in Flint and Marty. They moved around behind Winnie.

"Don't get shy now." Winnie put her arm around the girl.

"Welcome, Cassie!" someone from the back called out. Others followed. Before long she could barely hear herself think as the cheer from her relatives escalated. Then silence. And they applauded. Cassie covered her face with her hands and sobbed.

Winnie hugged her. "It's okay, sweetheart. It's gonna be okay. You're one of us. Come on in, boys." Winnie motioned to the McKay brothers. "This is Flint McKay and his brother, Marty. Cassie's friends. Where's the turkey?"

"Coming, Mama."

The women brought out dish after dish of delectable food. Winnie's oldest, Jake, carved the bird at the sideboard.

"If only my husband could be here to see this." Winnie shook her head as a tear escaped down her cheek.

"Daddy? What about Charlie?" a woman to her right spoke up. "Hi, I'm Annaleese."

As the dishes were passed, one by one, the people at the table introduced themselves. Spouses indicated who was their significant other. Sitting on Cassie's left, because Winnie was on her right, Flint squeezed her hand.

"You have to try my cranberry relish," said a woman, dishing out a spoonful. Winnie and her brood heaped food on Cassie's plate. She couldn't keep up with the steady flow of this one's homemade rolls or the other one's special carrot casserole.

Cassie ate and ate, not worried for a second about her weight. The food was so delicious, she simply could not stop.

"She's got Charlie's eyes," the oldest male said.

"And his chin, too," piped up a woman across the table.

There were fourteen people jammed together at Winnie's dining room table. Food was passed then placed on the sideboard because there simply wasn't room. Flint and Marty tucked into their food. The conversational ball was carried by Winnie and the other women at the table. Sons-in-law and Jake shoveled in turkey, stuffing, and everything else. They watched the ladies but kept their forks moving.

Cassie had never seen such a family before. There were the occasional disagreements, but no one got nasty. Jake teased his sisters, and the grandkids finished fast and asked to be excused to play video games.

No food had ever tasted as good. This kind of down-home cooking had never been served in Cassie's house when she was growing up.

"Charlie would have been so proud of you," Winnie said, in a low voice. Her eyes filled.

Cassie's brows rose. "You think?"

"I know."

When the family had finished every morsel, two women got up and cleared. Cassie made a move. Winnie placed a hand on her arm.

"Don't you dare. You and the boys here have done enough for one day, working at the firehouse. I bet there wasn't one quiet moment."

Cassie nodded.

"You take it easy. It's time for pie!"

The women brought out three pies. Cassie identified pumpkin, lemon meringue, and apple. She licked her lips. Was it possible she still had room for dessert?

"My favorite part of the meal," one dark-haired woman said. "Winnie's apple pie."

After pie, coffee, and tea were handed out, the questions began.

"What made you look for us?" Jake asked.

"That's a funny story." Cassie's gaze connected with his.

"You're not gonna believe this one." Winnie shook her head.

"Try me. I'm game for anything. Knowing Charlie, Miss Cassandra Wells doesn't surprise me one bit." He grinned.

Cassie looked at Flint. He shrugged. "Okay. Here goes. When I was sixteen, I spent my summers here, working for Gram. My other grandmother..."

By eight o'clock, the crowd thinned out. Cassie hugged Winnie. "Thank you so much. This has been the best Thanksgiving ever."

"For me, too. Except I sure miss Charlie."

"Wish I'd known him."

"Boy, he'd be so proud of you. I am. We all are."

"I love your family, Winnie."

"Your family, too."

Cassie nodded. "I guess they are. They're great. And boy, can they cook!"

Winnie laughed. "You should see our summer barbecues! Will you be here in the summer? How long are you stayin'?"

Flint's stare heated her back. "I don't know. I haven't decided yet."

"Well, I hope you make this your permanent home. We have so much to catch up on."

Cassie's heart swelled. Was it ever too late to find out you belonged someplace?

"Me, too." Flint took her arm.

"Wait! Wait." It was Annaleese. Cassie stopped for one more hug. Joy filled her heart.

Flint helped her into the truck. Marty jumped in the back. They rode slowly home. Once inside, Flint built a fire. The trio, bloated bellies and drooping eyelids, fell fast asleep in the living room. Cassie and Flint snuggled together, and Marty stretched out on the other end of the sectional.

For a moment, she thought she might be in a Hallmark movie instead of her life. Then exhaustion took over.

AT THREE O'CLOCK IN the morning, the emergency siren woke Flint. He yawned and untangled himself as gently as he could. Cassie opened her eyes.

"Emergency," he whispered, grabbing his shoes. He stuffed his feet in his boots and shoved his arms in his coat and was out the door in five minutes. Yawning as he drove, he rubbed his eyes. At least no one was on the road.

"Don't bother changing. It's one sick guy. I called the other guys and told them not to come." Dave, the fire chief, slipped on his coat.

"But not me?"

"Hell no. You got off last time."

"It's Richard, Mindy's cousin," Dave said.

"Is he at Mindy's?"

Dave nodded.

"What's wrong?"

"I don't know. Pain. Mindy thinks it might be appendicitis. Let's go."

Dave got behind the wheel of the ambulance; Flint jumped in the passenger seat. When they arrived, Mindy yanked open the door.

"Hurry. He's in a lot of pain." She fixed her robe and retied the sash.

Wearing a T-shirt and boxers, Richard paced, hunched over, grabbing his gut, moaning. Flint approached him.

"Can you straighten up, please?" When he did, Flint poked him in the area of the appendix and nodded.

"Looks like Mindy might be right. Get a coat. We'll take you to the hospital in Oak Bend."

Mindy helped Richard then opened the door. He climbed in the ambulance and lay down on the stretcher while the other two got up front. Dave hit the siren then stepped on the gas.

They made it to the hospital in record time. After Flint jumped out. Dave put the vehicle in park. The two men opened the door and slid out the stretcher. They wheeled Richard inside.

After checking with the hospital staff, the two men got back in the ambulance. Flint called Mindy.

"Richard's in emergency at Oak Bend General. Looks like appendicitis. They're prepping for surgery. You can probably still call him for about fifteen minutes."

"Thanks, guys."

"You're welcome."

Dave took his time driving to the firehouse. It was almost seven when Flint saw the sun tiptoe over the horizon. He parked the truck and entered the house as silently as he could. When he opened the door, the tantalizing smell of bacon met his nose.

"What?" He looked around.

Cassie padded out of the kitchen, barefoot, wearing one of his T-shirts and leggings.

"You're up? Why?"

"In spite of that enormous meal yesterday, I figured you'd be hungry when you got home."

"Hungry?" His stomach rumbled. "After yesterday, I thought I'd never be hungry again."

Marty joined them, offering a full mug to Flint.

"Oh, coffee! Yes! Oh, yes, yes, yes."

"You went out without coffee?"

"No time."

"Food will be ready in about ten minutes. What was the emergency?"

Flint eased into a chair and, between sips of the hot brew, related the event. While Cassie watched the eggs on the stove, Marty, who'd been tending bacon in the oven, piped up.

"Oh, shit. That's Richard Winslow?"

"Yeah. So?"

"He's starring in Mindy's holiday show."

"Really?"

"She's putting on *A Christmas Carol, the Musical* at the Pine Grove Playhouse. It's set to open Sunday night."

"No way he's going to be performing anything by then."

"What a mess! She'll have to refund everyone's money."

Flint turned to Cassie. "Mindy owns the Playhouse. She directs and produces one holiday show every year. It starts the weekend after Thanksgiving and runs until Christmas."

"Doesn't she have an understudy?" Cassie asked, adding milk to her refill.

"Oh yeah. Gil something. I think he got the flu. That's what I heard at The Cozy." Marty parceled out bacon to three plates.

"There's where you get all your news? Your gossip? The Cozy Café?" Cassie made eye contact with Marty.

"There or Homer's."

She added eggs and passed out the dishes.

"I imagine there's a giant panic attack going on at the Armstrong house right now." Flint picked up a piece of bacon.

"Armstrong? Like the guy who's going to do the sale of the store from you to me?"

"Yeah. Him. Mindy's his wife."

Cassie nodded. Flint's cell rang.

"It's for you." He handed the phone to Cassie.

"No one would call me on your phone. Who is it?"

Flint shrugged but pulled his gaze away from hers. Cassie stared at him as she cradled the phone. "Hello?"

"How would you like to get legal work for free?" said a female voice.

"WHO'S THIS?"

"My name is Mindy Winslow. You don't know me, but your boyfriend rescued my cousin this morning."

"Oh, I heard about that."

"Miss Wells, I'm in a terrible position. I have sold-out performances in my theatre for *A Christmas Carol, the Musical* and I have no Scrooge. I'm asking. No, I'm begging you. Would you please step in and be our Scrooge?"

"What? Is this a joke?"

Flint cringed and tiptoed toward the door until Cassie put a deathlike grip on his arm. He yelped but stepped back in the kitchen.

"Did Flint tell you to call me?"

"Uh, well. To be totally honest..."

"That's what I thought. And he asked you not to tell me, right?"

"You know him well."

"Damn right I do. I couldn't possibly..."

"Yes, oh yes, you could. We'd all help you. I could be over there in five minutes with the script. Our piano player said he'd meet us at the theatre in an hour. Oh, please, Ms. Wells. Please. I'm begging you. It's not only for me, and it's not about money. But the people of Pine Grove look forward to this all year. And the kids. We've got more than two hundred kids coming in the next three weeks. It's only for three weeks."

Silence.

"Can you hold for a minute?" Cassie glared at Flint. He shrugged. She put her hand over the phone and turned on him. "This was your idea!"

Again, he gave her a lame grin and looked away.

"And if I don't do it, I'm the bad guy. The show won't go on because of me. Because you opened your big mouth. Without even asking me."

"Would you have said yes?"

"No."

"There you go. See?"

"You're infuriating, frustrating. You've set me up."

"I'll work with you." He closed his fingers over her arm.

She shrugged it off. "Damn right you'll work with me. You'll be my slave! You'll do everything I say. And you can kiss your office goodbye. Because I'll need you at every rehearsal. And to run lines."

His face reddened. "But I have a business…"

"Not for the next three weeks you don't." She put the phone back to her ear. "You made a good case, Mindy. Okay. I'll give it a try. But I don't guarantee a good performance. And I may have to go on stage holding the script. But Flint has volunteered to spend every waking minute working with me over the next three weeks to make sure I give the best performance possible."

"Oh my God!! Thank you so much. You have no idea. You've saved the theatre and the entire holiday for all of Pine Grove. Thank Flint for me, too. I'm coming right over with the script."

"Good. The sooner I start learning the lines, the better."

"Oh, by the way. Drew said he'd handle the sale of your store, do all the legal work, free of charge. We are so grateful."

"Thank him for me, Mindy. I look forward to working with you." Cassie hung up the phone and shoved it in Flint's belly. He tried to smile, but she glared at him anyway.

"What did you do, Brother?" Marty loaded the dishes in the dishwasher.

"Put my foot in it, I guess."

"But lovely Cassie will make sure we have a holiday performance to remember," Marty said.

"Yeah. Mr. Scrooge has just become Miss Scrooge." Her brow knitted.

Marty laughed. "Good for you, Cassie. You're brave."

"Brave? Or stupid? Take your pick."

"Maybe *you'd* better move into the guest room, Flint," Marty said.

She stalked out of the room and ran up the stairs, slamming the door. In five minutes, it opened. Flint's clothes flew down the stairs, piece by piece, landing in a heap on the floor. Cassie followed. She kicked open the door to the guest room, entered, threw everything on the bed, and stormed out.

"There's no maybe about it." She returned upstairs, again slamming the door.

The house grew quiet.

In Flint's room, Cassie flounced down on the bed and stared out the window. How the hell could she pull this off? A live show requires months and months of rehearsal. She had two days. *Two days!* She groaned and fell back on the bed.

No time to lick her wounds. The script would be there any minute, and she'd better be ready. She hit the shower, hoping to scrub her insecurities away. Working with a small-town director, probably amateur musicians, how could she succeed? And if she didn't? Everyone would say she was too stuck-up to give the show her all.

Hah! Cassie gave every show her all. She shook her head as warm water poured down. She didn't know how to perform any other way. That was the reason she was such a rag when her show closed. Was she fully recovered yet? She wasn't ready to go back to Hollywood, to professional performing yet.

She turned off the shower and stepped into a fluffy towel. Clearing off the fog on the mirror with her fist, she stared at her bare face. She'd been hoping to stay through Christmas. She hadn't told Flint the store was finished. He hadn't asked and she didn't volunteer.

If she'd told him, then she'd have to have the sale and return to California. Wouldn't she? She'd have no reason to stay. And it's not like he'd made any commitment. Besides, how much can you believe a guy who left three women at the altar anyway?

She dried off and slipped on leggings and a sweater. As she toweled her hair, the doorbell sounded. She took a deep breath and let it out. Staring into the mirror, she muttered, "Showtime!" Then ran down the stairs.

When Flint opened the door, Cassie jumped down the last two steps. A young woman with dark hair blew in with a chilly wind.

"Hi, I'm Cassie." She extended her hand.

"I'm Mindy. Nice to meet you."

The woman had an envelope tucked under her arm.

"Coffee? Hot chocolate? Tea?"

"Cyanide?" Mindy countered.

Chapter Sixteen

"It's not so bad." Cassie took Mindy's coat.

"You say that now. But when you're going over lines and cursing a blue streak, then tell me a cyanide cocktail won't appeal."

"Kitchen? Living room?" Flint pointed.

"Oh, scripts are best opened on the kitchen table. And coffee sounds great." Mindy smiled.

Flint prepared beverages then took a seat. Cassie shot him a look.

"What? It's not okay for me to be here?"

Mindy sent a questioning glance to Cassie. "Okay, okay. I guess it is. It's your house."

Flint smiled.

"Me, too?" Marty put in.

Cassie raised her hand. "Wait a minute. This isn't a performance. It's a working meeting."

When she saw the sad look on Marty's face, she relented. "Okay, okay. All McKay boys are permitted to listen in. And I said 'listen.' No talking. No adding your two cents. This is a meeting between two professionals."

The men nodded.

Cassie glared at Flint. "And you're in charge of refreshments."

"Got it."

Mindy took the script out of the envelope. "First thing we're doing is changing the advertising. I need a good photo of you, as well as a headshot for the program. It's too late to change it for tomorrow night, but we'll have the new one ready on Monday." Mindy turned to Flint. "If you guys will print for us on Sunday?"

"Absolutely." Marty nodded.

"We have decided to call you Miss Scrooge, as introducing a husband, even a dead one, at this point would change everyone's lines. With the help of some interns, Drew is going over the script to see how much else has to be changed."

"Are you going to age me?"

"Yes. Do you have a problem?"

Cassie shook her head. "Never done it before. But it's fine."

"Good. We have some makeup students who've volunteered." Mindy thumbed through to the first scene. "Turn to page five."

Mindy read all the parts. After a few pages, she turned the part of Scrooge over to Cassie. Embarrassed in front of Flint and Marty, she spoke up.

"I'm not used to having an audience when I don't know what I'm doing. Could you guys either move your chairs behind me, so I don't remember you're there, or leave the room?"

Mindy stood up. "Why don't we take this to the theatre. It's not as warm and cozy as this kitchen, but it's private."

"I'll leave, I'll leave." Flint put his hands up. "You don't have to."

"Mindy's idea is good. And we can block it out as we go along. Let's go." Cassie headed for the coat closet.

"Good luck, babe," Flint said, attempting to kiss her. She sidestepped out of his reach.

Cassie climbed into the passenger side of Mindy's SUV.

"You have no idea how grateful I am you've agreed to do this."

"I have no idea how I'll learn it all by day after tomorrow."

"Don't worry. I'll be in the wings and coach you any time you need it. Maybe we can have a prop with your lines on it? We'll figure something out."

Cassie took a big breath. "Flint'll run lines with me."

"Doesn't he have to work?"

"I told him he'd be staying home, working with me until I had it down. He agreed."

"Thank God. Having a coach helps."

"Coach? He's already bossy enough."

Mindy laughed and shook her head. "Men."

Could she do this without her mother's help? Caroline Wells had been her daughter's support since day one. She'd been to every set, every theatre, gone on every location with her daughter. Cassie had counted on her mother to make things comfortable and be her cheerleader. This time she'd be on her own.

No way would Caroline fly out to hold Cassie's hand. And when she heard what her daughter was doing, she'd probably have a stroke. Appear in makeup making her old and ugly? Caroline would never approve. Cassie had no intention of telling her mother. The number of texts had dropped to four a day now. Caroline had accepted her daughter taking a break, and Cassie wouldn't upset things with the truth.

The theatre was chilly. Cassie kept her coat on as she strolled down the aisle. Of course, the stage was considerably smaller than Broadway. She mentally kicked herself for not expecting that. The show would have a cozier feel—perfect for Scrooge's story.

The heavy, dark-red curtains didn't add warmth to the room. "It's freezing in here," Cassie said.

"Can't afford to heat the place without people in it. Drew says it's a waste of money, and he's right."

"No problem. Let's get started." She buttoned her coat.

Cassie hopped up the four steps to stage right while Mindy took the stairs on stage left. Page by page, Cassie read Scrooge's dialogue and Mindy recited the rest.

"What about songs?" Cassie bit her lip. It had been quite a while since her last voice lesson or even musical rehearsal.

"The pianist is coming this afternoon. I have the songs in a separate book. It's on the piano."

"Okay. Let's leave it till then."

Mindy shot a thumbs-up.

"Delivery!" a deep, masculine voice rang out.

The women turned to see Flint walking up the aisle, carrying two bags.

"Laura and Amy at The Cozy Café donated lunch. They're so grateful to you, Cassie, for doing this. It looks pretty spectacular. Brisket sandwiches, potato salad, coleslaw, Laura's famous scones for break time. Oh, I almost forgot. Two pieces of the coconut cake you like so much."

"Wow." Her mouth watered.

"And this has two thermoses of hot chocolate. Figured too much coffee and you'd be too wired to remember anything."

The women joined Flint in the orchestra pit. He put the bags on the piano. Cassie hugged her man. "You're awesome. Thank you. And please thank Laura and Amy for us."

"Everyone is behind you. They're grateful you took this on."

"I hope I don't let people down."

Mindy unwrapped a sandwich. "The whole cast is coming tomorrow for a run-through with Cassie."

"How's she doing?" Flint asked, unpacking the beverages.

"Great. She gets it. A real pro." Mindy took a bite of her sandwich.

Hunger gripped Cassie's belly and she tucked into her food.

"Thanks for bringing this. You don't have to hang around."

"Trying to get rid of me, huh?"

She nodded as she chewed.

"I can take a hint." He grinned and turned toward the door.

"Flint is a good guy." Mindy pulled up two chairs.

"I know. He's a little commitment shy."

"Three failed attempts speak for themselves." Mindy opened her container of potato salad.

"We're not long term anyway."

"No?" Mindy shot her a quizzical look.

"I'm heading back home after Christmas Carol closes."

Mindy's eyebrows rose. "That's too bad. I'd love to have a leading lady of your caliber living in town."

"There's no way I can stay indefinitely with Flint." Cassie took a bite of her tasty sandwich.

Mindy nodded. "I get it."

He's never asked me to stay. Just commented on my leaving, like he was sad or something. Cassie sighed. Best to plan to move on.

AFTER EATING, CASSIE and Mindy rehearsed. Despite the chill in the theatre, Cassie sweated.

"I don't know, Mindy. This seems kind of ridiculous. I'll never memorize all this."

"You can take the script onstage with you, if you need to. We'll disguise it as a book. Say, Ebenezer's book of accounts or something. You're doing great."

"Great? I'm drowning."

Mindy grabbed Cassie by the shoulders. "Don't give up. It's much too soon. Let's keep going. We can break at five. Go home, have dinner."

"I can run lines with Flint after dinner."

"Great. Then back here tomorrow at nine? Too early?"

"Hell no."

"I'll have the rest of the cast here. I think we're going to switch Nancy and Don. Don was going to play you as a young man. Nancy can play you as a young woman and Don can be your beau. Let's take a break. I need to call them."

"That won't affect me, will it?"

"No. You'll be watching."

"Good. I can be looking over my lines."

"If I can take you offstage then, I will."

Cassie put her hand on Mindy's arm. "No, that's okay. Leave me onstage. I'll have Scrooge's book. I can look through and prep myself for the upcoming scenes."

"Ebenezer. Shit! We need a new name for you!"

"Go call Nancy and Don. I'll think of something."

Mindy left the stage. Cassie picked up her phone. "Mom will know." She dialed her mother.

"Cassie! Darling! I've been hoping you'd call. Are you booked on a flight home?"

"Not yet. A little glitch."

"Glitch?"

"Yes, and I need your help on something."

Cassie related the story to her mother. "So I need a female name for Ebenezer."

"I can't believe you signed on to do this."

"Mom. It's already too late."

"But, Cassie. You're giving away..."

"I'm doing it, Mom. Now help me find an appropriate name."

"You get paid millions to do live theatre."

"Mom!"

"Okay, okay. Hmm. Let's see. Eleanor."

"Perfect! Thanks, Mom."

"You're coming home for Christmas, aren't you?"

Cassie hesitated. She'd made no plans to fly home. "Well. This goes right through to Christmas morning."

"Cassie!"

"I gotta go." She ended the conversation. Guilt washed through her. Not be with her parents on Christmas? Brian would probably fly out. They wouldn't miss her, would they? But she couldn't shake the feeling she was deserting them. Damn it! Why did life have to be so complicated?

"Okay. Nancy and Don are coming over tonight at eight. I think it will be an easy switch. Let's continue."

Cassie picked up her script and climbed the stairs to the stage. "Where were we?"

"Coming up with a name for Ebenezer."

"Oh yes. I called my mom and she suggested Eleanor."

"Perfect!"

The rehearsal continued. Cassie forced her mother out of her thoughts and concentrated on the play. In an hour, the pianist showed up. They practiced the songs for the rest of the afternoon. At five, Mindy drove Cassie home.

When she opened the door, the smell of something good greeted her. After the huge meal at noon, how could she be hungry again? But she was. Ravenous.

Marty spoke, "Give me your coat. I've got a cup of herbal tea ready for you. Dinner will be on the table in ten minutes. How did it go?"

She staggered into the kitchen.

Flint held a cup and saucer in his hand. "Here. Mindy told me you'd be singing all afternoon. She suggested you might need this."

Cassie took the cup and sank down on a chair.

"So, how'd it go?" Flint leaned against the archway.

"Oh God. I don't know shit. It's going to take me forever. Can you run lines with me tonight?"

"Of course."

"I'm here, too. I can do anything you need." Marty pulled a casserole dish from the oven.

"That smells great. I'm so hungry."

"After what you ate at noon?"

"I know. Right? I thought I'd never be hungry again."

As Marty spooned out servings of the hot dish, he offered his news. "Everything has been changed on the posters and the programs. I'm taking it to press tomorrow."

"You'd better talk to Mindy. She switched Nancy and Don's roles."

"Thanks for the heads-up. I'll call her tomorrow morning. She should see the final version before we print anyway."

Cassie wolfed down her food. Tension coiled in her shoulders and neck. Could she do this? Dinner was over in record time.

"Come on, Flint. We have work to do." She pushed to her feet and headed for the living room. Pushing aside the couch and coffee table, she created an open space.

"Here. You play all the parts. And I'm going to try to remember my lines. Prompt me when I forget, okay?"

"Got it. Can I sit down?"

"No! Stand up." Her voice rose.

"All right. All right. Don't get excited. It's my first time doing this."

"MIDNIGHT. TIME TO PACK it in," Flint said, shutting off the living room light.

Cassie trudged up the stairs, mumbling, her head swimming with dialogue and stage directions. A persistent throb at the base of her skull transmitted pain throughout her body. Speaking in a scratchy voice, she directed weary eyes to him.

"I'll be lucky if I don't have laryngitis by tomorrow."

"You'll be fine. Come on. I'll give you a back massage."

Flint turned on the electric mattress pad to preheat the bed. They undressed in silence. Cassie slipped a little negligee on. The tiny spaghetti straps barely kept the garment covering her breasts. She didn't care. All she wanted was to lie down.

He ripped down the covers and she crawled in. Stretched out on her belly, her face turned toward him, she moaned.

"It's gonna be all right," he said, stripping down to his boxers. He climbed in beside her and pulled up the covers. Scooting closer, he rubbed his hands together before touching her. She lay flat, head on her pillow, arms at her sides.

"I can't do this. Why did I say I would?"

"Yes, you can. And you will. You'll see. I can't believe this is the worst emergency performance you've ever done. Can you move a little closer?"

"No. I can't. I can't move. Aren't you supposed to be sleeping in the guest room?"

"Okay, okay. I'll slide over. If you want the massage, you have to let me in my own bed." He eased the sheet and quilt down to the middle of her back then slid the straps down. Flint placed his palms on her shoulder blades and moved them down, adding pressure.

"Oh God." Cassie closed her eyes. "That feels so good." His warm hands on her skin soothed her muscles. She relaxed. A sense of relief crept over her. He massaged along her spine then up around her neck and shoulders then down to her waist then up again.

Slowly his touch calmed her enough to slip into sleep. Her eyes drifted shut and she lost consciousness. About three thirty, a bad dream woke Cassie. Sweat coated her forehead. When she sat up, Flint stirred. A deep, sleepy voice broke the silence.

"What's the matter? You okay?"

"Bad dream." She lay down, but tension tightened inside her.

"Can't sleep?" he muttered.

"I'm scared."

"What?" Flint's eyes opened wider.

"I'm scared," she whispered.

"Of what?"

"The show."

"Really? You'll be great."

"What if I'm not? Everyone's expecting me to be great. But I don't have enough time to learn the part."

"What I saw looked damn good."

"Will you hold me, please?" Her voice shrank down to almost nothing.

"Sure, honey," he said, his voice gentle. He folded her in his arms and held her against his chest. She slung one leg over his hip and flattened her palm on his pecs. Cassie eased her head next to his neck. The warmth of his body surrounded her. Tension drained from her as she listened to the steady beat of his heart. Its rhythm put her to sleep.

The next thing she knew, Flint whispered.

"Cassie. Baby. Time to get up."

She cracked her eyes open. The clock read seven.

"Do I have to? Can't you tell everyone I died?" She pulled the covers over her head.

Flint peeled the quilt down.

"Come on, baby. There's nothing to be afraid of. Let's run your lines."

"All right. All right. I'm coming."

"We can start now, while you're getting dressed." Flint gave her the first cue.

Cassie responded. Back and forth they went. Then she launched into a short monologue. Flint corrected her. She slipped on her leggings as she recited. He responded. She rummaged through his closet until she found a turquoise plaid flannel shirt. She pulled it off the hanger, all the time speaking her lines. She yanked a T-shirt over her head.

"Line!" She slipped the warm, soft shirt over her shoulders.

"No bra?" He stared at her breasts.

"Don't look. No time for sex. Line!"

They continued, on and on, stopping to refresh Cassie's memory from time to time. They broke to head downstairs to breakfast.

Marty was in the kitchen at the stove. "Bacon and cheddar omelets. You need a good breakfast. It's almost opening night."

Cassie wrapped her arms around her middle. "Don't say that."

"You still have time."

Flint shot a dirty look at his brother.

When the food was ready, they ate in silence, except for Cassie. She kept reciting lines between bites of food. At eight o'clock, there was a honk outside. Marty peered out the window. "Mindy's here."

"I'm off." Cassie shoved an English muffin in her mouth and grabbed her coat.

"Good luck." Flint kissed her cheek.

Cassie threw herself in his arms. "You're the best," she whispered then disappeared out the door.

Chapter Seventeen

F lint watched Mindy's car take Cassie away.

"She's scared shitless."

"No one will know." Marty put the frying pan in the sink.

"I know she can do this. But she has to know it."

"She's a professional. I'm sure they're all scared before a performance." Marty turned on the water.

"Yeah, but no one goes on with so little rehearsal time. She's right—everyone's gonna expect her to be perfect. And great."

Marty nodded. Flint stared at the sky and put his mug down.

"It's not fair."

"Life isn't fair," Marty replied.

"Don't get philosophical with me." Flint put his mug in the dishwasher.

"Look." Marty turned off the water. "This is making the best of a bad situation. I think everyone knows Richard's in the hospital and Gil's got the flu. No one expects her to be perfect. She's not a miracle worker."

"That's not true. She's Cassandra Wells, star of stage and screen. And everyone is going to assume she learned her lines by osmosis in five fucking minutes. There will be expectations." Flint frowned.

"Maybe. Maybe you're right. She'll rise to the occasion." Marty resumed washing a pan.

"I hope you're right. Last night—"

Marty held up his hand. "Stop right there."

"I'm not going to talk about sex. Besides, we didn't have sex last night. You should have seen her. She curled up next to me like a wounded animal."

"She's not used to failure or even a second-rate performance."

"Oh, I know she won't fail. But can she live up to such high expectations?" Tension coiled in Flint's shoulders. "It's a big thing. Big challenge."

"You worried about her?" Marty cocked an eyebrow as he faced Flint.

"A little. Maybe."

"Are you coming into the office today?"

Flint shook his head. "Besides, it's Saturday. I'm going to the theatre. Cassie needs all the support she can get."

"Okay."

"Get those programs ready on time, okay?"

"Got it covered."

Flint patted his brother on the back. "Thanks."

Marty grinned.

Flint stripped down and stepped under a hot shower. The heat and pounding of the water felt good. Why did he care about how Cassie did? She'd be selling the store and leaving soon anyway. He soaped up his hair then rinsed. Of course he cared. She'd been so vulnerable with him last night, it touched his heart.

Flint had never seen her so open. The girl with the snappy comebacks, the independent spirit had crumbled like a piece of burnt toast. And what did he do? He comforted her, loving every minute of it. This was his chance, his first opportunity to be supportive.

But so what? She'd hit the road and expect him to follow? No way would he be Mr. Cassandra Wells. Once again, the tug-of-war in his heart—fall for Cassie Wells and get his guts stomped on or pretend not to care and let her go? Hell, pretending hadn't fooled anyone in the past, had it? So maybe he'd make a play for her, offer her a commitment and see if she'd stay.

She'd said she was ready to settle down. She's complained about the traveling, the exhaustion, the "you're only as good as your last performance" bullshit. According to Cassie, she was ready for another life. Flint pressed his lips together. Time to put up or shut up—make her an offer, call her bluff, whatever way he wanted to put it.

He took a deep breath and turned off the water. Slapping on shave cream, he decided on a totally smooth face. He hummed one of the songs from the play as he shaved. Cassandra Wells might be facing her toughest challenge, but so was he—Flint McKay— facing his, making her his own, for life.

He dressed and drove to The Playhouse. When he opened the door, Mindy called for a break. Cassie didn't stop. She kept speaking.

"Costume check!" a woman in the wings called.

"Come on, Cassie." Mindy shepherded her to the woman holding a big dress.

When Mindy returned to the stage, Flint approached.

"Hi, Flint. What's up?"

"I'm here to help. Anything you need done. Errands run? Something fixed? Anything?"

Mindy smiled at him. "That's great. I'm sure we'll need something. Have a seat. But please, don't interrupt."

Flint shot a thumbs-up. "Hey, is this the dress rehearsal?"

"That's about to start now."

The man at the piano did an exercise. The string trio tuned up, and Flint took a front-row seat.

IN THE DRESSING ROOM, Cassie stripped down for the wardrobe lady. The dress went over her head and was fastened in back.

"Hmm. A little big."

"A little?" Cassie laughed.

She stood still while the woman made a tuck here and a fold there. Mindy entered.

"Marty did this for me yesterday. It's a book. See? It's marked accounts."

"Yeah. Great. So?" Cassie ran her hand over the new book made to look antique.

"Open it."

When she did, she found the script inside.

"See. You can use this as a prop. Hold it the whole time. And refer to any pages where you need help with the lines."

"This is fantastic."

"No one but you, me, and Marty will know what's really in this book."

Cassie hugged Mindy. "This is fantastic."

"You're doing great."

"I've got the songs mostly memorized. I need to practice."

"Right after rehearsal. But I don't want to strain your voice."

"Slept well. I'm feeling okay."

"Sleeping with Flint? I'll bet." Mindy shot a sly smile at her leading lady.

"No, no. Not that." Blood rushed to her face. "He gave me a great back massage. It did the trick."

"I'll bet."

Cassie punched Mindy in the arm, gently, and they laughed.

"Would you mind holding still so I can get this fitted? I don't have much time to make alterations."

"Oh sorry."

"I won't interrupt."

Cassie patted the book. "Thank you so much for this. I'm feeling better already."

"Good. You're gonna be great. I can feel it."

"Thank you so much, Mindy."

"No. Thank you!" The women hugged briefly while the wardrobe woman frowned.

Cassie dug into the script, singing and repeating her lines over and over as the wardrobe lady took in the dress.

"Only this dress and a nightgown. Let's get this off and see if the gown needs fixing."

Cassie put the book down and held her arms over her head. While the fussing continued, she never stopped working on her lines.

When she returned to the stage, the full cast had assembled. As the rehearsal got underway, Cassie lost herself in the character. Straightening up, she projected a haughty, proud, stingy, older woman with a superior attitude. She strode across the stage, cringed at the ghosts of Christmas, and hit all her marks.

"Makeup's coming at six. They'll need to take some time with you."

Peeking into the audience from time to time, she noticed Flint hung on every word Cassie uttered. At the break, Mindy sent him to pick up the programs.

Cassie marveled at her ability to go through this horrendous situation without her mother holding her hand. Flint had stepped in as her support, and it worked. He'd been amazing, more than she'd ever imagined.

Basil hadn't been a man who readily accepted the backseat. Nope. He'd needed to be the star twenty-four seven. But not Flint. He blended into the background, only stepping out when he was needed. Her heart swelled.

Maybe it was why she didn't miss Basil the way she'd expected. Flint seemed to breeze in and simply take his place in her life. He hadn't made a big fuss, or put her down, or told her what to do—not in an obnoxious way. He'd encouraged her. Gratitude filled her heart. But was she simply grateful to a friend or in love with the man? She gave her head a quick shake. There was no time to think about love now.

"Okay, everybody. Break's over. Places, please. Don, I think we left off with you."

Cassie focused on the play. She didn't notice Flint coming or going, but a thermos of chamomile tea with her name on it appeared on the apron of the stage. A box of programs showed up in the wings. Small touches drew her eye but not her mind as she barreled through the play, totally focused and getting better with each act.

At the end, Mindy addressed the cast.

"Sit everybody. Sit." The people sat where they stood. "It's four. Go home. Have dinner and rest. Be back here tomorrow no later than one for a final run-through. Come in costume! We don't have enough dressing room space for everyone. Cassie comes first. Curtain goes up tomorrow at eight sharp! Great job, everyone. Great job."

People gathered their costumes and other belongings and stopped to wish Cassie good luck on their way out. A few asked for autographs.

"Are you okay?" Mindy rubbed Cassie's arm. "Want to go home?"

"Yeah. I think so."

"Fine. Get some rest. You're gonna be great. Don't worry."

Cassie gave a wan smile as a deep voice spoke.

"Ready?" It was Flint.

She nodded. He offered his hand to help her down the stairs then tucked it through his arm.

"I'm not going to talk until I get back to the theatre tomorrow. Want to save my voice. Okay?"

"You know what you need to do."

"Thanks."

He opened the truck door and helped her in. Cassie sat back. Make-or-break time was almost there. She sighed, watching the cold wintery scenery pass by.

"Marty made comfort food. Pot roast and mashed potatoes. Those good?"

She nodded. "No dairy."

"Got it. Tea?"

She nodded again. He took one hand off the steering wheel to squeeze hers. She shot him a shy smile.

One more rehearsal. Showtime was around the corner. A sense of relief washed over her as the tension drained. This was it. Either she had it or she didn't. The crib sheets in the book comforted her. If she floundered, there would be the book and a prompter backstage.

Somewhere from deep inside, she knew she was as ready as she could be. A grin stretched her lips. She'd never done such a serious show or performed as an old woman. This would be a new feather in her cap, if it wasn't a total failure. And she did it without Caroline. Confidence washed through her.

When they got home, Marty carved the pot roast. She ate the biggest meal ever then lay down for a rest. Like a big, warm teddy bear, Flint joined her. Wrapped in his arms, she slept peacefully.

OPENING NIGHT

In the dressing room at the theatre, Cassie yanked off her sweats. The costume lady helped her into the old nightgown first then the elaborate dress over that. It would make costume changes quicker and easier. Then the makeup people took over. As she sat still while they worked on her, she recited her lines. Her fingers clutched the book as if it was her life's blood. Maybe, in theatre-speak, it was. She repeated the soliloquys, mumbling so as not to interfere with the elaborate makeup the art students were applying.

One by one, cast members stopped by to wish her good luck.

"Break a leg."

"Go for it."

"Without you, there'd be no show."

The last one was Mindy. "Good news?"

"There's a tornado heading our way and we all have to seek shelter?" Cassie turned hopeful eyes to her director.

Mindy brushed her arm and made a face. "Gil, the understudy, is getting better. In two weeks, he might be able to come back to the show."

"Switch Scrooges in mid-run?"

"Don't you want to leave early? Then you can have Christmas off."

"By then, I'll have this down pat. I'd planned to stay until closing night."

"Well now, if you don't want to, you don't have to."

"Okay. Thanks. I think."

"When word about Richard and Gil got out, I had a flood of calls of people cancelling their tickets."

"Oh damn. Really?" At the idea of a half-empty theatre, Cassie groaned.

Mindy put her hand on Cassie's shoulder. "That is, until I told them you were taking over. In fact, the theatre is sold out. And I'm sure that's due to you. Thank you." Mindy gave her a hug. "Good luck tonight. I know you'll be great."

When they finished, Cassie went to the wings and peeked out at the crowd. She hid well so no one could see her and only pulled the side of the curtain back an inch or two. The auditorium had filled.

Wait! A man came down to the first row. Cassie couldn't be sure. She squinted. Yes, it was Flint. He motioned and five, no seven, no ten people in the first row got up. They marched back three rows. New people filed in and filled those seats. Cassie shrugged. Pretty strange. But she had bigger things on her mind.

At eight sharp, Mindy stepped out in front of the stage. Everyone took their places. Except Cassie, who was poised in the wings to make her entrance. Mindy announced the program change then ran off stage left. The stage crew turned on the spotlights and raised the curtain.

Bob Cratchit was sitting at his desk. There were some lines from the supporting cast then Cassie's cue. Wearing very high heels to make her appear more imposing than her usual five foot four inches, she strode onto the stage. The minute she appeared the spectators broke into applause.

Cassie glanced at the audience for only a moment, but she noticed the seats in the front row were filled with Winnie and her family. Emotion gathered in Cassie's chest. With a toss of her head, she shook it off and delivered her harsh lines with a stern coldness worthy of any Scrooge.

As the play progressed, she grew stronger, more confident. After sneaking peeks at the book four times in the first act, she didn't need it but once in the second. With guidance from the conductor of the small orchestra, her voice rang out, clear and true.

The lyrics flowed through her seamlessly, like she'd been doing the show for months. Of course, she made mental notes of her weaknesses, vowing to fix them in time for the next performance.

Gazing out at her new family, clapping the loudest, warmed her heart. From time to time, when she made an extra effort to have her words reach the back of the theatre, she looked out and spied Flint, standing there, at the door. He made a thumbs-up sign. How could she go wrong with all this support? It lifted her higher and higher.

When the curtain came down, the applause was thunderous. She got five curtain calls, with a standing ovation at the end—and a bouquet of roses. Her eyes filled as she bowed and then stepped back to acknowledge the supporting cast, the conductor, the orchestra, and the director.

When the curtain stayed down, Mindy rushed up to hug her. Other cast members threw in their congratulations. In her dressing room, she plopped down in a chair while the makeup interns carefully removed their work. There was a knock on the door.

"Come in."

"You were amazing. Awesome! I've never seen such a great performance. You were better than you were on Broadway!" It was Flint. The kids moved away, and he scooped her up in his arms, kissing her soundly. "I'm so proud!" His eyes shone with respect and excitement. "Get this stuff off your face. It's time to celebrate."

Within minutes, she was Cassie in sweats again. He bundled her into the truck and drove to Homers. When he opened the door, the place was packed! People stood and applauded. Winnie rushed up.

"You were great!"

"Thank you. I saw you and the rest of the family in the first row. Thank you so much for coming. It meant so much to me to look out and see your smiling faces."

"We wouldn't miss it for anything. You're a star, honey. And we're all so proud of you."

There was a huge banner above the bar: *Congratulations, Cassie.*

Flint led her to a table where a plate piled high with a huge burger, fries, coleslaw, and a giant Coke awaited. She grabbed the drink and polished off half in about three seconds. Then she looked around.

Flint slid into the seat next to her and put his arm around her.

"I don't know what to say." Her gaze met his head-on. "Thank you. You're wonderful."

"I love you, honey. There's nothing I wouldn't do for you," he replied.

Two tears spilled over onto her cheeks. Seemed like she'd been waiting all her life to hear those words.

Chapter Eighteen

Typical of all her stage performances, Cassie didn't wind down until about two o'clock. They closed Homers then dashed to the truck with a winterish wind nipping at their heels. As they drove through the empty streets of Pine Grove, guided by moonlight and headlights, she sighed. She couldn't stop smiling.

"How do you feel?" Flint glanced over at her for a second.

"Happy. Tired."

He smiled.

She faced him. "It's amazing what you did."

"Me? I didn't do a thing."

"You sat Winnie and her brood in the front row."

"So?"

"And you organized the celebration at Homer's. And I bet you paid for it, too. I'd like to pay you back."

"Forget it. You've already done that. Paid the whole town back."

"Thank you. It was wonderful. I didn't expect it."

He grinned. "Yeah. You were so surprised."

She chuckled. "I was."

"I was impressed with how hard you worked."

"People think acting is simple, easy stuff. They don't know the hours and hours that go into a performance."

"You're a pro."

"I should be after sixteen years, don't you think?"

He parked, and they entered the house quietly.

"Marty is probably sleeping," Flint said, turning the key in the lock gently.

She nodded. They hung up their coats and tiptoed up the steps. All Cassie wanted was to get naked with Flint. They undressed in silence. He doused the light and they eased into bed. Damn! The sheets were freezing. Cassie shivered and grabbed him. Pressing herself to him, desire sparked. She'd thought exhaustion would have wiped out any ideas about lovemaking, but she'd been wrong. She reached down to touch his dick. Obviously, he wasn't tired, either.

"You're kidding." His voice vibrated against her.

"I never kid about sex."

He kissed her, gently at first, nibbling on her lower lip, then more passionately. Cassie twined her arms around his neck. He nudged her legs apart and settled between them. She raised her knees up, sliding her feet along the sheet.

Flint's hands wandered over her torso, follow by his mouth. She closed her knees on him, holding him fast.

"Trapped!" She giggled.

"And loving it," he replied. He flattened himself, grabbing her thighs. He buried his face in her mound.

Cassie arched a bit, groaning. "Yes!"

He busied himself licking her until she began to squirm. "Do it, do it!"

He laughed and sat up.

"No, wait!" She crawled over to him, took his dick in her hand then into her mouth. When she heard him hiss, she almost grinned. Sliding her mouth up and down on him, she added a little extra suction.

"Holy hell!"

She continued quickly. When his hand came to rest on her head, she sped up.

"Enough. Enough. Stop. Please!" He begged her. She sat up and wiped her mouth with the back of her hand.

"Ready?"

"Yes."

Then he was on her, lifting her legs up to her chest, he plunged in, filling her. She shut her eyes and moaned. "Damn. That's good."

"Oh, baby, baby," he moaned into her neck, pulling out and thrusting in again and again. He started off slowly, raising her heat. But as desire spiraled higher and higher, she begged for more.

"Faster. Harder."

Once she gave him the green light, Flint let loose. He upped the pace and the force.

"Oh God," she muttered as need grew. The heat became unbearable right before she slipped over the edge. Every muscle in her body contracted then released, pouring pure pleasure through her. "Shit," she groaned, sweat breaking out on her forehead.

He chuckled and slowed down but only for a moment.

"Oh, Jesus, Christ." His hips hit a steady rhythm for a few seconds then stopped. Flint bowed his head, burying his face in her neck and groaned. She gripped his sides. Sweat gathered between their chests as he reached his climax.

His hot breath fanned over her. He raised his head and kissed her forehead.

"That was fantastic."

"The perfect ending to a perfect day." He sat back and brushed her hair off her forehead.

"I love you," she said.

Silence filled the room.

"Don't say it if you don't mean it." He rested on his haunches.

"I do. I do mean it. You said it. Do you mean it?"

"I think I've always loved you. Since I was eighteen, I've been too stupid to realize it."

"Really?"

He nodded. "But you haven't always felt the same."

"I don't know. Every time I thought about you, I got a warm feeling. I always knew, in the back of my mind, you were a safe place for me. If I was in trouble, I could show up at your door and you'd take me in."

"Your test of love?"

"Sometimes."

"Have you been in trouble?"

She shook her head. "But you never know. Living such a public life, one little slip can land you in big trouble."

"That's a lot of pressure."

Her eyes filled. "Uh, yeah." Emotion choked her.

"Hey, hey. Don't cry. You're not in trouble. I'm here."

He headed for the bathroom. When he returned, he climbed in next to her and took her in his arms. "Come here, baby. You have nothing to be afraid of."

She cuddled into his warmth, resting her hand on his chest. His presence soothed her.

"Tomorrow's gonna be a long day."

"We need sleep," he said.

Flint pulled the covers over them and tucked her head under his chin. Twined together, the lovers fell into a deep sleep.

CASSIE AWOKE ON HER own at eight. She yawned and stretched before turning to gaze at Flint. Last night they had exchanged "I love you's" a second time. What did it mean? Where was their relationship going? Although Cassie had fallen in love with the small town, last night's performance only underscored the fact her heart lay in the theatre, too.

She hunkered down under the quilt and pushed up against Flint to ward off the chill in the air.

"Don't you guys ever turn on the heat in this place?"

"It's on. Takes a while to get up to the second floor."

"Bullshit. I'm gonna catch pneumonia." Cassie jumped out of bed, grabbed a robe, and disappeared into the bathroom.

When she came out, robe fastened securely, towel in a turban, she sashayed back into the bedroom. Flint had made the bed and donned sweats.

"Jesus, woman. You've been in there forever."

"It's hard to wash off my lover," she said, casting flirty eyes his way.

"Don't get me started. My turn for the bathroom."

"I have to go over some lines anyway. Hmm. Do I smell bacon?" She slipped on an emerald-green running suit and socks then danced downstairs. Marty stood in the kitchen over the stove.

"Bacon?" She took a seat.

"And French toast."

"Oh my God. I love French toast! You're a doll." She kissed his cheek as she breezed past to get coffee. "Refill, Marty?"

"Thanks."

The brew warmed her insides. Happiness flowed in Cassie's veins. She retrieved her script from the front hall table and opened it on the kitchen table.

"Going over lines?"

"Yeah. There were a few places where I messed up."

"I didn't catch anything."

"A couple of times I was able to fix it."

"I thought you were fantastic."

"Thanks."

Marty put the bacon on a paper towel to drain then flipped the French toast. The creaking of the old stairs and the sound of a heavy footfall drew Cassie's attention. Flint filled the doorway. She sighed, staring at him so sexy in a tight blue sweater and jeans. Remembering their steamy night together, she grinned. Nothing like a great night of love to make for a happy morning after.

"Breakfast smells great." Flint filled his mug. "More?" Holding the coffeepot, he stopped next to Cassie. She nodded.

While they ate, he ran lines with her. Marty listened. At nine, Flint drove Cassie to the theatre.

"I've got some stuff to do. I'll be back later."

Cassie lingered in the truck. She faced him, took his head in her hands, and kissed him long and hard.

"What was that for?" He raised his eyebrows.

"Because I love you."

His smiled warmed her. "I love you, too, honey. Have a good rehearsal. I'll be back."

She skedaddled into the theatre to get out of the frosty air.

"Mindy! Crank up the heat! I swear I can see my breath."

Mindy appeared from the wings. "It's on. It takes a while."

"Why is everybody's heat slow in this town? I froze my butt off this morning at Flint's."

"Winter gets the best of us sometimes." Mindy zipped up her sweater. "Let's get started. I noticed a few places need work."

"Only a few?" Cassie cocked an eyebrow. Her cell rang. It was her mother.

"Hey, Mom. I'm in rehearsal. Can this wait?"

"No, this cannot wait. You've been brushing me off for weeks now."

"Okay, okay. What's up?"

"We have to talk about contracts. You've got some opportunities I don't think you want to miss."

"Mom, I'm at the theatre. The director is waiting for me. I can't possibly talk about contracts now. The theatre is dark tomorrow. Can we talk in the afternoon?"

Silence.

"Tomorrow afternoon? Okay. You got it. You doing Scrooge again tonight?"

"Yes."

"I read a review online. Way to go, sweetheart. You got a rave."

"I did? Where? Send me the link."

"I thought you had to rehearse."

"The director will stop to read a good review."

"Okay. Talk to you tomorrow."

Cassie ended the conversation and went up on the stage. As she was about to start, her phone dinged. She checked. There it was, a review from the Times Herald Record.

"Mindy, our first review!"

The two women huddled together over the phone. Cassie read aloud.

They say necessity is the mother of invention. When emergencies ruled at the Pine Grove Playhouse, sidelining her lead and understudy, theatre director, Mindy Winslow, became inventive. Instead of canceling the performances of Dickens' A Christmas Carol, the Musical, Ms. Winslow turned the tables on us.

She offered up a female Ebenezer Scrooge. And who could play such a part? None other than the beautiful and talented Cassandra Wells!

What a stroke of genius. Instead of being deprived of this inspiring holiday play, we were witness to an incredibly professional performance on the fly of this Christmas classic. Switching a few other roles and providing support to Ms. Wells enabled the actress to put on a first-rate performance as Eleanor Scrooge. The entire cast rose to the occasion, but none rose so high as Ms. Wells. In makeup which almost made her look old and ugly, Ms. Wells delivered an emotional, gut-wrenching perfor-

*mance as the repentant skinflint. We were so pleasantly surprised as to
be almost speechless.*

*Way to go, Ms. Winslow and Ms. Wells, for out-of-the-box thinking
which worked beautifully. Don't miss this performance. You're unlikely
to be able to partake of this Christmas treat ever again.*

"Fantastic!" Cassie's heart swelled with pride.

"Amazing! Your mother must be thrilled."

Cassie nodded. Of all the good reviews she'd gotten thus far in
her career, none could quite compete with the emotion of this one.

"Back to work. Now we have a reputation to live up to!" Mindy
clapped her hands and the actors opened their scripts.

MONDAY NIGHT'S PERFORMANCE had bested the one on
Sunday. Again, she and Flint had stayed up late celebrating and making love. The barrier between them had crumbled to dust. They had
become inseparable. With the work finished on the store, Cassie
agreed to signing the papers finalizing the sale of the place.

Tuesday morning, they met at Drew's office.

"I'm sorry it's so cold in here. They turn down the heat over the
weekend." He flipped on a space heater.

Cassie rubbed her hands together. "That's okay. I'm getting used
to Pine Grove being part of the polar ice cap."

Drew explained everything and laid out papers and pens. Cassie
handed over a check for thirty-five-thousand dollars, the same price
Flint had paid. The deal was concluded quickly.

"Where are you heading now?" Drew scooped up the paperwork
and put it in a folder.

Cassie tucked the deed into her purse. "Back to the theatre."

"More rehearsing?"

She nodded. Flint took her hand as they walked to the truck.
During the ride to the Playhouse, Cassie wondered how the conver-

sation with her mother was going to go. Caroline had something up her sleeve, and it set Cassie on edge.

Flint parked close to the entrance.

"Should be reasonably warm in there, since there was a show yesterday." Flint closed the truck door.

"I don't know. Mindy likes to turn down the heat to save money."

Flint stopped her at the entrance to the theatre. "What are you going to do now the store is legally yours?"

Her gaze connected with his. "I don't know."

He shook his head. "At least that's honest."

They went inside. Cassie strode up the aisle to join Mindy and the rehearsal in progress.

"Cassie, wait!" Mindy called.

But she was interrupted by a familiar voice.

"Cassie. Nice to see you."

The young actress whirled around to face her mother rising from a seat in the back of the auditorium.

"Mother!" Cassie's eyes grew wide, and her jaw fell open.

"Yep."

"What are you doing here?"

"You agreed to talk to me this afternoon. I thought it best we speak in person."

"Oh my God. Mom." Cassie sank to the floor and crossed her legs. "Your timing couldn't be worse."

"And if you'd talked to me any of the ten thousand times I called, left messages, and texted you, this wouldn't be necessary."

"How did you get here? When?"

"I flew in last night and rented a car. I'm staying at The Inn."

Dread filled Cassie. No way could this be good.

Caroline looked around. "Would you mind if I had an hour or two alone with my daughter?"

Mindy shrugged. "Of course. Go ahead."

Cassie got up and joined her mother in the aisle. "Flint, this is my mom, Caroline. Mom, this is Flint McKay."

He extended his hand and she took it, but the frown never left her face.

"I'm sure you two are having a wonderful time, but Cassie has a career, commitments. I hope you realize this before you make plans to bury her in this hamlet."

Flint stiffened at Caroline's tone. "I think what Cassie does with her life is up to her, don't you?"

"Not necessarily."

"I guess we'll have to agree to disagree." Flint faced his lover. "If you don't need me to give you a ride, I'll head to the office."

"Mom's got a car. But thank you. We'll go to the Inn. I'll see you back here?"

"Of course. Nice to meet you." Flint's face impassive, he nodded once at Caroline and made his way to the parking lot.

"Let's go. I have GPS. I'm guessing you don't know your way around this burg."

"You're wrong. I do. I can direct you."

They drove in silence. Once inside, Cassie headed for a sofa in the lobby facing the enormous fireplace.

"I've got a suite. Let's talk upstairs."

Cassie followed her mother. Once inside, she was pleased to see a fire had been laid in the sitting room area. There were French doors leading to a terrace facing the Catskills iced with snow. She stood by the window.

"I'll call downstairs for some food. Do you know how to light this thing?" Caroline gestured to the fireplace and picked up the phone.

Cassie got the fire started while her mother ordered. "No, Mom. Not salad. I'll have a cheese steak sandwich and a cup of soup. Oh, and an iced tea, too."

Caroline raised her eyebrows. "Really? So fattening." But she ordered as her daughter wished. Grateful not to battle with her mother over food, Cassie suspected Caroline was behaving well to soften her up for something. Cassie sat close to the fire, warming her hands.

Within fifteen minutes, there was a knock on the door. The waiter laid the food out on the small dining table near the window. The women sat down.

CAROLINE PREPARED A cup of coffee then dug into her salad. She was rail thin, an example for her daughter, maybe? Cassie cut the cheese steak sandwich into quarters and chowed down.

"I need this to keep up my strength for performing."

"Congratulations, by the way. On another outstanding performance."

"Thanks. Why don't we cut to the chase? What do you want, Mom?"

"I want you home for Christmas."

"Not happening."

"Why not? Don't you want to be with your family for Christmas?"

Cassie narrowed her eyes. "You have something besides a baked ham and gingerbread cookies cooked up, Mom. What is it? I don't want to be rehearsing on Christmas. Or attending dance classes or singing lessons. I want to be right here, with my new friends, singing carols, drinking hot chocolate, and exchanging presents." Cassie took a bite of her sandwich.

"Oh, an old-fashioned Christmas? Ah, to be with the country folk, how mundane. You know we don't do Christmas that way."

With a piece of her sandwich in hand, Cassie rose from her seat and went to the window. "We don't do Christmas at all. Let's see, what have Christmases been like in the past? Hmm. Attending A-list parties to make new connections? Check. Sending gifts to influential people who might sign me for a new movie or play? Check. Hosting a fancy dinner at a tony restaurant for the 'right' people? Check. No thanks. Been there. Done that."

"You wanted this life. You wanted to be an actress. And to be the best. I only did everything I could to make sure you had the training and opportunities to make your dream come true. Now I'm a monster?"

Cassie finished the sandwich in her hand before speaking.

"You're right. That's what I wanted at sixteen. And twenty-five. But not at thirty."

"You could have had a lovely life if you'd simply agreed to tag along with Basil for a bit. You could have lounged your butt off in London as the wife of the famous actor. Taken time off. But you turned your back on him. Why?"

"Basil only had eyes for himself. I wanted more. It wasn't love, Mom. It was convenience, it was good for his career, and, he assumed, he was for mine as well."

"Why didn't you say something? The way you acted, I assumed you were head over heels for him. Did he do something to you?" Caroline started to rise, but Cassie gently pushed her back down.

"No, he didn't. Basil's in love with Basil and there's nothing left over for anyone else. I wanted more. I need more."

"And you have it with this local yokel, Flint?"

"Don't call him that."

"Okay. Sorry."

"I do. He's a wonderful man and takes good care of me."

"You're a meal ticket."

"Mother! What a horrible thing to say! You don't even know him."

Caroline narrowed her eyes. "How much has he borrowed from you?"

"Nothing. Not a penny. In fact, I live in his house—yes, rent-free!"

Caroline made a face.

"And I bought the store back from him."

"I'll bet he made a tidy profit from you. What'd you pay?"

"You're wrong. I paid not one penny more than he did. And the lawyer backed him up on that."

"How much?"

"Thirty-five thousand, if that's any of your business."

"The lumberjack isn't very bright, is he? He probably could have gotten three times as much from you."

"Don't call him that. He's not a lumberjack, and he's not stupid. It's not about the money for Flint." Anger curled in her chest.

"Look, I've already accepted a half-dozen invitations on your behalf. You have to come home."

Cassie shook her head.

"And then there's the little matter of shooting the movie version of *Shooting Star.*"

"I don't want to do it."

"You promised. And you signed the contract. When you signed to do the Broadway play, the movie deal was part of it. You've already received the bonus for doing that. You have to do it."

"And if I don't?"

"I'll lose a lot of money, and so will you."

"But you have a lot of money."

"And you'll never make another movie again."

"So?"

"And they'll take you to court. And I'll take you to court for breach of contract, too."

Silence.

Cassie's eyes widened. "You wouldn't."

"Try me." Caroline's face became a cold, impassive mask.

"I'm your daughter."

"This is business, Cassie."

Pain seared through her chest. Her voice softened until it was barely audible. "You'd take me to court? Your own daughter?"

"If I have to. This is business. I'll not have my reputation go up in flames because you've got the hots for some country stud."

"It's not like that."

"Isn't it?" Caroline cocked an eyebrow. "Come back with me for Christmas and do the movie, or hire a lawyer. The choice is yours." Caroline picked at her salad.

Cassie shivered at her mother's icy tone. "You win."

"Good."

"I have two conditions, Mom."

"Doesn't look like you're in much of a position to slap conditions on this agreement."

"Do you want to go to court? The media will have a field day."

"Okay. Shoot. What do you want?" Caroline frowned, the lines in her face deepening. She shifted in her seat.

"I want to stay to do the play. I promised. I will return the day before Christmas, period. And, after the movie is done, we tear up my contract with you."

"You're firing me?" Her brows shot up.

"Yes. I'll no longer need an agent. I'll be taking back my life."

"We'll see. I'm not agreeing to anything now. You might change your mind when the movie wraps. I'll come and get you."

"I'm not a child, Mom. I'm thirty. I can fly to California alone. I don't need you to bring me home."

"I don't mind, dear. I'll take care of all the arrangements, like I always do."

Cassie sighed. The decision was made. "Are we done?"

"You haven't finished your sandwich."

"I'll wrap it up and take it with me."

"If you insist. I must call your father. He'll be so happy to know you'll be home for the holiday."

"Will he?"

"Oh yes. He's looking forward to the party at The Beverly. The old hotel is newly refurbished and it's the 'in' place to have events. We've been invited and he's buying a new tux for it."

"Well, whoop-de-do."

"I've bought a few new dresses for you, too. But seeing how you're eating these days, I might have to exchange them for larger sizes."

"You do that, Mom. I wear a size eight now. Knock yourself out."

"An eight? Well, hell, what am I going to do with all the size fours?"

"Give them away. I don't care." Cassie checked her watch. "I've gotta go. Don't tell anyone about our deal, okay?"

"Are you kidding? Tell anyone I had to threaten my daughter with a lawsuit to get her to come home for Christmas? Not on your life. Not even your father."

"Oh, he'd understand."

"Cassie, I hope you know I love you and I'm doing this for you." Caroline clasped her hands together. Her softening expression almost convinced Cassie. Perhaps her mother was an actress, too?

"Mom, you stopped doing things for me a long time ago."

"I'm sorry you feel that way."

"So am I. Goodbye." Cassie headed for the door.

"Need a ride?" Caroline walked her to the door.

"I'll get a taxi or Jess will give me a lift."

"Okay. See you on the twenty-fourth." Caroline returned to the table to finish her coffee.

Cassie walked out, slamming the door behind her. Her eyes filled. What had she done? Given in to extortion. She'd be gone for months, filming. And miss Christmas with Flint, Mindy, everybody in Pine Grove. She sighed.

Trapped in a life she'd accepted long ago, she saw no way out. Not until after the movie. Did she really want to cut her mother loose? The woman had done an amazing job running her career. But Cassie didn't want her old life anymore, did she? Her head ached. Things had been so simple. She thought she had the answers. But now? She wasn't so sure.

Chapter Nineteen

Flint watched Cassie drive away in her mother's rented Mercedes. A fancy car made quite a splash in Pine Grove. So did Caroline Wells, casually clad in a mink coat. Flint's brows furrowed. On instinct alone, he didn't trust her.

He stopped by the office but couldn't concentrate, so he headed home. Hunger gnawed at his belly. He checked the clock. Yep, it was one, past lunchtime. He heated up soup and slapped together a peanut butter and jelly sandwich.

After making a fresh pot of coffee, he poured a mug and, disregarding the cold, stood outside on the veranda, watching the road, waiting for her return. After fifteen minutes, he figured he'd freeze his nuts off, so he returned inside.

He wolfed down the food then cleaned up. A car pulled up. He spotted Jess Lennox at the wheel. Cassie got out and ran up the steps. Flint stood in the front hallway. She stopped, stared into his eyes, burst into tears, and threw herself in his arms.

As she sobbed against his chest, he folded his arms around her and kissed her hair.

"What is it? What happened? What's wrong?"

But Cassie didn't stop. Pain and confusion mixed in his brain.

"Did someone hit you? Assault you? Did you have a car wreck?"

She shook her head, pushed off him, and stood back. He reached into his pocket, pulled out a handkerchief, and offered it. She mopped her face.

His brows knitted. "Are you all right?"

Pain clouded her eyes. "I can't. I can't talk about it." She ran up the stairs into their room and slammed the door. A million questions occurred to him, but he knew better than to bother her when she was this upset.

Half an hour later, curiosity got the better of him. He crept up the stairs and into their room, only to spy her tucked under the comforter, sleeping peacefully.

As much as he wanted to know what was going on, he didn't have the heart to wake her. Instead, he put up a fire in the living room, picked up the local paper, reheated coffee, and made himself comfortable on the sofa.

"Patience, Flint. When dealing with women, ya gotta be patient." A nugget of wisdom from his father, and though Flint had presumed it referred to sex, it also applied to the present situation.

A call came in from Marty.

"I've got an emergency print job. Can you do dinner?"

"No problem."

"There's ground beef and veggies in the fridge. Figure it out. Gotta go."

The phone went dead. Flint finished his drink and ambled into the kitchen. Maybe he was ready to improvise with food? If he failed, there was always pizza. He took the ingredients out of the fridge and turned on the radio. "Mistletoe and Holly" played, lifting his spirits. Cooking was a good way to avoid the inevitable. If the meeting had gone well between Cassie and her mother, there was no way his girl would have ended up sobbing.

As he chopped and sang along, a telltale creak alerted him. A barefoot woman, snuggled into his robe like a big sleeping bag, came down the stairs. She padded into the kitchen and stared through puffy eyes. Her red nose reminded him of Rudolph, but he kept his observation to himself.

"We have to talk," she said.

The four most dreaded words in the English language to any man. He put down the knife.

"NOT HERE. I WANT TO go to the store. Now it's mine."

"But there's nothing there."

"Right. And we need to fix that."

"You're going to stock up the store now?"

She nodded. "Why not? No better time. Gives me something to do."

"Is this what you wanted to talk about?"

"Wait until we get there. I'll be right back."

Flint continued cooking. In fifteen minutes, Cassie returned. Wearing leggings and his flannel shirt but no makeup, she looked adorable, real, and totally vulnerable.

"Let's go." She grabbed the truck keys.

Flint shoved the casserole dish in the oven and put it on warm then he washed his hands and joined her. Apprehension settled in the pit of his stomach. He wanted to believe this was going to be a good conversation, but his head wouldn't let his heart go there. They rode to the store in silence. Once inside, Cassie ran for the thermostat and cranked up the heat.

"It's freezing in here." Flint left his coat on.

"There should be chairs in the back."

He looked around. The contractors had done a wonderful job. The place looked great—fresh, clean, like an empty slate waiting for someone to write something. He got Cassie's desire to fill it full of stuff. But if she did, who would run it? He followed her.

She plugged in the new coffeemaker, added water and grounds.

"Our first cups of coffee."

"What did you want to talk about?" The anticipation ate away at his gut.

"I'm getting to that."

Flint stood up. "Look, Cassie. You're killing me here. Whatever it is, it can't be good. So blurt it out. Let's get this finished."

She turned to look at him and placed her hand on his forearm. "I'm sorry. I didn't mean to make you worry."

"Well, you are. So spit it out." He returned to his seat.

Cassie put out mugs. "I had a talk with my mother today."

"I know." Tension rose from his stomach to his shoulders. "Get to the point."

"Seems I didn't remember when I signed the contract to do *Shooting Star* on Broadway, I also agreed to do the movie. In writing."

"What?"

"Yeah. They'll start shooting in January. I have to be available for costume fittings and rehearsals right after Christmas."

He rose from his seat. "You're leaving right after Christmas."

Wiping a tear from her cheek, Cassie looked away. "Before Christmas."

He must have heard wrong. She'd promised to stay for Christmas, they had plans, he had plans, lots and lots of plans. "You're kidding, right?"

She faced him. "Look at my face. Does it look like I'm kidding?"

He sank down, almost missing the chair.

"Mother is forcing me to go back before Christmas. Said she wanted me there with the family. But that's a big lie. She could care less about that. She wants me there to do the movie. So the producer doesn't sue her."

"She'd get sued?"

Cassie nodded. "Yep. Her and me, too."

"Shit." Sweat coated his brow. "Doubt shit. Shit. Shit. Shit."

"I know. I want to have Christmas here with you."

"What about *A Christmas Carol*?"

"I'm staying until the twenty-fourth, the end of the show."

He put his head in his hands. The news was worse than he'd imagined. He looked up. Fuck. How long would she be gone? "How long is the shoot?"

"I don't know. They can't predict these things. Something always goes wrong and shoots usually last longer than planned."

"But we can spend weekends together? I can fly out to see you?"

"We're shooting in Brazil. It's summer down there. It's cheap, and we can shoot outside."

"Fuck. Double fuck. Sorry." Tears pricked his eyes, but he forced them back. No way would he cry, especially not in front of her. Pain pierced his heart. It was bad enough when he thought she wanted to leave, but he suspected she'd changed her mind. The sadness of her expression, the knitted brows and damp eyes confirmed his feeling she didn't want this.

"I had to tell you. At first, I wasn't going to."

"You were just going to up and leave?" He pushed to his feet.

"Uh, yeah. But I changed my mind. Besides, it's too big a secret to keep. Please don't tell anyone else."

"I have to tell Marty."

"Okay, Marty, then. But no one else. Please?"

"Promise."

"Thank you. We'll have to make the most of the time we have left."

"Three weeks?"

"Less."

When he took a deep breath, his chest hurt.

"Let's start with stocking the store. Will you help?"

He sat down. "Where do you want to start?"

"I think we could find some really cool catalogs online. I left the laptop in the truck."

"I'll get it." Flint pushed to his feet.

The pink-and-orange sunset mocked him with its news of a bright, sunny day on the morrow. From now on, he'd not have many sunny days, and he shot angry eyes at Nature's perversity. After retrieving the computer, he slammed the truck door. Stopping, he rested his forehead on the cold passenger window. A few tears refused to be held back and splashed on the frigid ground. What was he going to do? No time to think. He had to play along, do whatever she wanted while she was still with him.

But what about him? Flint sucked his lower lip over his teeth. He'd get along. He'd figure it out, man up. When he straightened up, he resolved to make the most of every day they had left. Live two lifetimes in the space of weeks. He rubbed his sleeve across his face, let out a breath, and strode toward the front door. These weeks must be unforgettable. He had no idea who she might meet after she left Pine Grove, so he'd make the most of every minute now.

He opened the computer. "I'll set it up on the desk."

"Perfect." She stood behind him, resting her hand on his shoulder. Her sweet perfume danced beneath his nose. He closed his eyes and inhaled then took her hand and kissed it. He'd remember her scent forever.

WHILE FLINT WENT OUT to warm up the truck, Cassie closed the laptop. She two-stepped around the store, briefly, singing a song from the Dickens show. She envisioned the space filled up with colorful goods, tall glass jars of nickel candy on the counter, bolt after bolt of brilliant reds and soft pastel cottons and wools, standing side by side. She pictured a freezer full of the best flavors from local ice cream makers, two shelves of books, their spines advertising intriguing mysteries and romances, boxes of rice and pasta, cans of fruit and vegetables, and jars of spaghetti sauce, filling out the shelf space.

Even though it was still chilly—she'd turned the heat down since they'd be leaving—a gust of warm air surrounded her. Could it be the spirit of Gram? Wouldn't her grandmother be pleased at how she and Flint saved the store?

But what now? Cassie would leave soon, and the beautiful place would once again stand empty. Cassie chewed her lip. Flint held her coat.

"This is gonna be great. But I need someone to run it." She pushed her arms into the sleeves.

"Don't look at me. I've already got a job."

"I know, I know. But if you have any ideas, let me know."

He nodded. "Let's go, truck's warm and dinner's ready."

She slid in next to him and looked out the window. It was five and already dark. As they headed home, lights large and small, twinkling and steady, glowed in windows. House after house had a Christmas tree visible from the street. Some homes had swag with blinking lights outlining windows and doors, while others had a simple candle in each window. She sighed. The best season of the year had arrived, and she'd be leaving too soon.

At home, Flint went to the kitchen, Cassie lit a fire, then headed for the liquor cabinet.

"Want a drink?"

"Yeah. A double."

She nodded. After filling a glass with red wine, she poured him two fingers of scotch before making her way to the kitchen.

"Rocks?" She peered at him. He nodded, so she opened the freezer and plunked a couple of ice cubes into his drink.

He took the glass and leaned in for a hard kiss. "And don't you forget it."

She snaked her arms around him, then Marty walked in.

"I gotta get my own place," Flint mumbled, breaking from her to pull a dish from the oven.

"Nice greeting! I've been working my ass off, covering for you. Is dinner ready?" Marty hung up his coat.

"Yeah, yeah. Keep your pants on." Flint put the hot food on the table.

"Looks like it's you who's got trouble keeping his pants on." Marty snickered as he sat down.

During dinner, Flint relayed the news about Cassie. The trio quieted. When they finished, Cassie and Flint cuddled up by the fire. Marty went to his room.

"No fires in the fireplace in California at Christmas. And it'll be summer in Brazil." She sighed.

"You'll miss this?"

"I'll miss everything about Pine Grove."

"There's time for you to join in on some stuff. Next Tuesday is the carol sing. The theatre'll be dark."

"Do you go?"

"Every year. And I can't carry a tune."

She laughed.

"There's more." Flint rattled off a list of activities.

"Christmas in the country. Nice." After finishing her wine, Cassie brewed a mug of hot tea to warm her. "It's still cold in here."

"I'm not going to make it tropical. Get used to it. It gets cold in Pine Grove."

"Okay, okay. Don't bite my head off."

He put an arm around her and drew her close. "I'm sorry. Still pissed you're leaving."

"That makes two of us."

"You can still do stuff, even if you're performing at night, right?"

"Sure."

"Good. Let's get the calendar updated with events you can go to. Okay?"

She grinned. "Okay."

Flint played Christmas music on his phone and covered the two of them with a blanket. Before long, they were asleep. At two, Marty shook Flint.

"Go up to bed."

"Hmm? Hah?"

"Up to bed."

Flint, barely awake, nodded and yawned. He slung a laughing Cassie over his shoulder and marched upstairs. Once tucked under the thick quilt, they fell back to sleep.

THREE DAYS LATER, FLINT dropped Cassie at the theatre for rehearsal and went to his office.

"I'm going to be taking a few days off." He hung up his coat and faced his brother.

"And that's new?"

"All right, all right. I haven't been doing my share. I admit it. But there are reasons."

"I know the reason. One cute blonde. Period." Marty scowled.

"Are you jealous? Aren't you the one who told me I should get it on with her and stop trying to find a substitute?"

"I didn't mean for life to grind to a halt, Flint. We have a business to run. And now an extra mouth to feed."

"Oh? It's about money? You want to charge her rent? Because I'm sure she can pay whatever you want. What's the matter with you, Marty?" Flint sank onto a chair next to his brother's desk. Marty picked up a pen and twirled it.

"I don't know. I don't like this. She's gonna leave, and you're gonna be in pieces."

"I hope not."

Marty's head shot up. "Didn't she tell you yesterday?"

"What I mean is, well, I'm hoping she'll come back."

"Is it realistic? And if she does, for how long? Are you going to spend your life seesawing between being together and being apart?"

"I hope not."

"I wanted you to have a few nights with her and get her out of your system so you could find a local girl and have a life." Marty put the pen down.

"Doesn't look like that's going to happen. What about you?"

"Leave me outta this. We're talking about you." Marty stood up.

"I'm done talking. No reason to beat this thing to death. We don't know what the future will be, so there's no sense speculating. I'm trying to take it one day at a time."

"Good luck with that."

"Yeah. I know. Bring me up to date." Flint checked his watch. "First delivery for the store is due in three hours. I need to be there."

"Guess you're out of the office until she leaves." Marty sighed.

"I'll try to be here as much as I can."

Marty nodded. He opened his desk drawer and pulled out a folder. "Here are the accounts."

Flint sat down and turned on his desktop. "Gimme."

Marty handed the folder to his brother.

"Boy, this stuff has backed up."

"Why don't you take the laptop to the store. You can work on some of this stuff while you're waiting for deliveries."

"Good idea."

"We can't let this pile up."

"I know, I know. I have this." Flint tucked the folder under his arm and headed for his desk.

He looked back. "Thanks."

After two hours of doing paperwork, he rose and stretched. Shrugging his coat over his shoulders, he headed for his truck. "See you tonight."

With the cell phone at his ear, Marty nodded. "I'll get right back to you with a timeline, Mr. Samson."

The glacial air slapped Flint across the face. He hurried to his vehicle and blasted the heat. The store was cold enough to keep meat. Flint turned up the thermostat then shoved several pieces of wood in the woodstove.

He loved the old stove. Remembering winter days when he'd stop in to get warm and end up buying a comic book or a piece of candy. By slipping him an extra piece, Gram made him feel special. He'd warm his hands at the ancient potbelly before braving wind chills near zero to return home.

Flint had had the stove refurbished, cleaned out, and made ready to use. It gave an old-fashioned, country flavor to the place. A truck pulled up outside. Two men got out and opened up the back.

As the logs in the stove caught, the air warmed. Flint opened the door for the men who unloaded five giant boxes. He signed their manifests and they left. He took a deep breath and stared at the cardboard.

"Effing boxes aren't going to unload themselves." He reached behind the counter, found his pocketknife, and slit the tops. He unloaded boxes of cereal and canned goods. After wiping down the shelves, he arranged the food then broke down the boxes.

Twisting open a bottle of Coke, he leaned back and took a long drink. Yep. This was going to be his life for the next few weeks. And then there was the paperwork for the store, a bank account to open, credit card companies to contact. Frowning, he carted the boxes out to the curb for trash pickup. Flint was going to be busy, too busy to fuss about Cassie leaving. He sighed. Why didn't anything in his life go as planned?

Chapter Twenty

Tuesday morning, her day off, Cassie woke up with the sun, smiling. She threw down the covers and climbed over Flint. "Let's go! Get up!"

"Huh? Wha...?"

"It's Tuesday. Let's go to the store." She grabbed her robe and skipped to the bathroom.

"Why? What's the rush?"

"You said stuff arrived. I want to unpack and put it away."

He laughed. "I already did. Most of it anyway. Well, maybe some. Go right ahead. You don't need me." He rolled over.

Cassie jumped on him, straddling his hips. "Come on, lazy. Get up!"

"No!" He pulled the covers over his head. But she tugged them down then bent, kissing his neck.

"Stop. You're tickling me!"

"Not until you get up."

"Oh yeah?" He grabbed her and rolled around. She shrieked in delight. He tickled her waist and blew raspberries on her neck. Cassie screamed with laughter until she couldn't breathe. He stopped, looming over her, and kissed her. She softened, winding her arms around his neck.

"You're crazy, you know that?"

She nodded.

"I love every crazy inch of you." He kissed her again. Flint lifted his knees, one at a time, and wedged them between her legs.

"Oh? I see."

"There are lots of ways to wake up."

"And you choose this one?"

He nodded.

"Good choice."

Cassie slid her feet up, raising her knees. Her skimpy gown slid down to her hips. Flint's eyes glowed with passion as he sat on his haunches. He lowered himself until his tongue touched her flesh.

She arched her back and moaned. Before the heat ignited inside her grew unbearable, he filled her. They rocked in their own rhythm. Her eyes drifted shut. She gripped his strong shoulders, digging her fingertips into his muscle. One leg wrapped around his waist as he plunged into her.

The brush of his chest hair against her nipples hardened them and sent chills down her spine. Her heart swelled. She wanted him, needed him with every fiber of her being. Desire spiraled, coiling tighter and tighter until it burst forth. Her muscles contracted, tightening around him. She muttered his name as her hips bucked.

"Oh, baby. Oh, baby," he replied.

She raked her fingernails down his sweaty back as he dipped his forehead to hers. Perspiration gathered between their chests. Sliding her hands down, she gripped the powerful muscles of his butt as he stopped to thrust hard one last time. A loud groan from him vibrated against her chest and neck. Damn, she loved it when her sexy man came.

"Oh God. You're, you're..." He stopped and took a breath.

"I'm what?"

"I love you." He pushed up on his hands, his gaze connected with hers. His lopsided grin looked tentative.

"And I love you, too. Good morning." She cupped his cheek.

"Best way to wake up." He pulled out and rolled off the bed. She watched his adorable butt as he padded to the bathroom.

After a quick shower together, actually anything but quick, they dressed. She dried her hair while Flint fried up eggs.

"Marty left a note. He went to the office early. He's got a job due today."

"He works hard." Cassie fluffed her hair.

"He's working a lot harder than I am these days."

"I'm sorry." Cassie placed her hand on his arm. "It's my fault. You can stop doing stuff for the store."

"I like helping out at the store. Besides, we're getting closer to being fully stocked. The bank account is open, and the bank said after two weeks, they'll issue a credit card merchant account number. DBA and state tax forms are filed."

"Drew is a sweetheart."

"You sure bailed out his wife." Flint chuckled.

"I love the show. It's fun."

"And it's sold out through the last day."

She smiled—she still had some star power.

Flint jingled the truck keys. "Let's get to the store. Tonight's the carol sing."

"Oh, right."

"You're coming?"

"Wouldn't miss it."

CASSIE UNLOCKED THE store door. Flint lifted two of the four boxes piled up outside.

"Guess we should have been here earlier." She pushed inside.

He put them down and returned for the others. Cassie cracked a window and turned up the heat.

"Heat and window open?" He cocked an eyebrow while easing the large carton to the floor.

"We need fresh air."

Ripping open the first container, Cassie pulled out thick wool socks in grays and beiges, glassware, bright-red and solemn black umbrellas, boxes of oatmeal, and tiny fishing lures. Chewing on a nail, her gaze swept the room, looking for spots for the new merchandise.

"Fishing lures might go with the three rods, over there? And the socks with the jackets?" Flint pointed.

"What about the other stuff?"

Flint shrugged. "Miscellaneous."

"And where's that?" She laughed.

"Anywhere you want it to be."

They worked until lunchtime then headed to The Cozy Café.

"Turkey salad on rye's on special today. With a cup of my green pea soup." Laura Dailey greeted them.

"Sounds good to me," Cassie said, stopping at the bulletin board. Someone had posted a schedule of holiday activities. When her eyes got to the ones she wouldn't be around for, her lips compressed into a frown. Leaving Pine Grove behind grew harder each day.

Flint corralled a table. The delicate, lacy decoration of frost on the window bespoke of winter's beauty. Soup warmed their insides. Before they finished eating, the town fire alarm went off. Flint rose, kissed Cassie, and hustled out the door.

"Back as soon as I can."

After she finished her sandwich, Cassie ordered a piece of homemade apple pie and a cup of tea. It was three, and the place had emptied out. Laura Dailey brought a cup of coffee to Cassie's table.

"May I join you?"

"Please do." Cassie gestured to the empty chair.

"I saw you in *A Christmas Carol*. You were terrific."

"Thank you."

"You sure picked it up fast."

"It's my job."

"I heard you're leaving soon."

"Are there no secrets in this town?" Cassie feigned surprise.

"Nope. Never have been. Never will be. Who's gonna run the store?"

"You interested?" Cassie cocked an eyebrow.

"I've got my hands full working here with Amy. Besides, cookin's my thing."

"Got someone else in mind?"

"I was thinkin'. I mean. Well, just a nosy old woman's opinion."

"No, seriously. Tell me." Cassie slipped her hand over the older woman's.

They talked for an hour before Flint returned. He smelled of smoke and grease.

"Grease fire at the Roberts' house. Not much damage."

She wrinkled her nose at the acrid scents wafting off him. "Let's go home. You need a bath."

"Ya think?" He laughed.

"Thanks, Laura."

"You'll think about it?" The older woman followed them.

"I will." Cassie opened the door, and Flint raced her to the truck.

Back at the house, Flint showered while she reheated leftovers. They ate quickly and left to join Marty and the other carolers at the firehouse. They started there and wandered through the town, stopping at churches.

"Cassie, will you lead us in 'Silent Night'?" Pastor Thomas of the Methodist Church stepped aside.

Her voice started it off, then the others joined in. Her spirits rose as her voice rang out. It had been so long since she'd sung for sheer pleasure. She caught a gleam of pride in Flint's eye.

After an hour, the carolers finished up at Homer's, where the proprietor treated them to free hot chocolate. When Flint finished his drink, he took Cassie's hand. "Let's go home."

The heat in the truck didn't do much to warm her up on the short ride back to Flint's house. She changed and jumped into bed.

"Hurry up. I'm freezing."

A salacious grin spread across his face. "I might be able to warm you up."

"You're a heat machine."

He laughed and slid between the sheets.

"No fooling around until I warm up."

Flint wrapped his arms around her and pulled her tight against his chest.

"Have you decided what to do about the store?"

"I think so. Laura Dailey had a good suggestion."

"Oh?"

"I don't want to jinx it. I'll see if I can set it up tomorrow."

"Ah, I love a mysterious woman."

"You love a willing woman."

"That, too."

Then he leaned over and made love to her.

WHEN FLINT WOKE UP, Cassie was already downstairs. He smelled the sweet aroma of butter melting and the rich scent of coffee. Throwing on sweats, he bounded down the stairs.

"You started breakfast?"

"Today's the day."

He quirked an eyebrow.

"The day?"

"To settle the store."

"What have you decided?"

"Let's eat first."

After breakfast, they bundled into Flint's truck and drove over. Cassie opened the door, turned on the heat, and fiddled with her new high-tech cash register.

"Expecting company?" Flint leaned against the doorjamb.

She nodded.

"Is this private?"

"Please stay."

"You sure?"

She nodded.

When the bell over the door jingled, in walked Winnie Briggs.

"Well, I'll be a gopher's uncle! Look at this place!" She wandered around, staring.

"Hi, Winnie."

The older woman approached. "You did this?"

"Yep. Fixed it up. With Will Lennox's help."

"Open for business yet?"

"Nope. I'm leaving in a few days, and I need someone to run it."

"You hiring?"

"Yes. I want to hire you."

"Me?" Winnie pointed to her own chest.

She nodded. "You."

"I have a job."

"Do you like it there?"

"No. But I need to work. I can't work here for nothing."

She struggled to keep her excitement in check but found it terribly difficult. "Oh, you'd be paid more than you're making now."

"Really?"

"Yes." She gestured toward the newly stocked shelves as well as the store in general. "I'd like to make you co-owner of the shop."

Winnie's eyes rounded. "Co-owner?"

Cassie nodded, her excitement finally pushing through in the form of a huge grin.

"Why me?"

"Because you and I were robbed of being family for so many years. We can't fix that, can't get the past back. But we could work together and share this little store. What do you say?"

Winnie's mouth hung open. "I don't know what to say."

"Then say yes."

"Is that why the sign says Charlie's General Store?"

Cassie's eyes filled. "He was my father, and I never even got to meet him."

Silence blanketed the room. Flint stayed motionless.

"I still miss him." Winnie stepped up to Cassie and took her in her arms. "Thank you. Thank you so much."

The women clung together. Tears cascaded down Cassie's cheeks. She broke first, taking a deep shuddering breath before speaking.

"You'll take the job?"

Winnie nodded.

"Good."

A knock and the tinkle of the bell interrupted them. All eyes turned to the door. Drew Armstrong hesitated in the doorway. "Cassie?"

"Come in, come in. We're ready."

Drew put his briefcase on the counter and pulled out a handful of papers. "I've got the paperwork right here."

While Drew and Winnie put their heads together, Cassie caught Flint's eye. She raised her eyebrows and he nodded in return. Whew! Not sure what his reaction would be, she'd withheld her plans. Deep down inside, she knew his approval would make this crazy idea solid. She let out a breath.

"Cassie, will you sign here, please?" Drew offered her a pen.

After affixing her signature in three separate places, she moseyed over to Flint.

"So? What do you think? Crazy idea?"

"Brilliant. And, yes, crazy."

"The right thing to do?"

"Absolutely." Flint smiled.

"She probably doesn't realize if the shop's doing okay, in two years, I'm transferring total ownership to her."

"Is Drew going to tell her?"

Cassie shook her head. "I don't want her to see it as a test. I'll have him do it when the time comes."

"I'm proud of you. It's huge."

"Thank you."

Flint snaked his arm around her shoulders and pulled her in for a hug.

"Okay. That's it." Drew returned the papers to his case and closed the latch. "I'll file these, but you can consider yourselves official co-owners now. Ready to open for business?"

Winnie shook her head, a wry smile on her lips. "I gotta give notice."

"Of course." Cassie walked Drew out. "Thank you so much. Send me your bill."

"Will do. Thanks."

Cassie turned to Winnie. "I can't wait for two weeks to open the shop. Can you start right away?"

"I'll talk to the manager. I'd sure love to get this place going."

"Great." She hooked her grandmother's elbow with her own. "Let me show you where everything is."

After the grand tour, Flint buttoned his coat. "I'm going to go to the office. Call me when you're done."

Cassie kissed him then returned to her grandmother. "I've finally figured out how the cash register works. Let me show you."

"I don't know anything about running a store. Just so you know that. I'm not pretendin' I do."

"I know. Neither do I. But Flint, Marty, and Drew said they'd pitch in. You can call them and they'll help you with the tax stuff, and online stuff."

"Whew. Thank God." Winnie grinned. "This is going to be fun."

"And a lot of hard work."

"Ain't hard work when it's yours." Her smile gleamed.

Cassie opened a laptop lying on the counter. "Here's the inventory sheet on Excel. Flint said he'd show you how to work this. And the price list." Cassie hit another button. "And the contacts for all the vendors."

"Where are you going? Why can't you do this with me?" Winnie lifted her gaze from the screen to connect with Cassie's.

"I'm going to be doing a movie in South America. Besides, I don't know crap about this stuff."

"Really? Makes me feel better. South America, huh? Sounds exciting. Are you coming back? What about Flint?"

"Oh, I'm planning to come back." Cassie bit her lip. "I hope Flint will wait for me."

"I hope so, too. Now here." Winnie pointed to something on the laptop screen. "What does this mean?"

Chapter Twenty-One

Flint frowned as he drove. Secretly, he'd hoped Cassie wouldn't find anyone to run the store and she'd have to stay and do it herself—lawsuits be damned. But it wasn't going to happen. If she wasn't going to run it, he approved of her decision to hand it over to Winnie. It was a decent thing to do. Whether the woman could run the store or not remained to be seen. He and Marty would help.

His brows knitted. Cassie was actually, really, seriously leaving. And sooner rather than later. Christmas lights in windows mocked his gloomy mood. What was there to be happy about? The love of his life would be going into the jaws of the unknown, perhaps never to return. Powerless to stop her departure, he battled frustration. Banging his fist on the steering wheel caused a minor skid.

"Shit!" He hit the brake and pounded the wheel one more time. He roared into the parking lot and pulled into the first available spot. Griping to himself about winter, he headed for the office. Once inside, he ripped his coat off and jammed it on a hook.

"Well, good morning to you, too," said Jane, their part-time secretary.

"Sorry."

"Coffee? I made a fresh pot a few minutes ago."

Coffee wouldn't fix what was wrong with him. He shook his head and went into his office. Unintentionally, he slammed the door and plopped down in his chair. The creak of old hinges drew his attention.

"Ah. Hurricane Flint has blown into town." Marty lounged against the doorway.

"Shut up, Marty."

"Ooooh. Angry words."

"I'm in no mood."

"Duh. I get it, I'm sympathetic. I get it. You're heartbroken. But what the hell did you expect? Did you think Cassandra Wells would give up the theatre and movies to become a housewife?"

"No."

"Good. Because if you did, I'd have to have you committed."

"I just didn't think. I went with...things."

"Listened to your dick instead of your brain? That's not surprising. And not the first time. But if she leaves you at the altar, it will be turnabout is fair play, won't it?"

"There is no altar."

"You haven't asked her? Isn't the ring burning a hole in your pocket?"

His fingers stole over the small box tucked in his jeans pocket. "None of your damn business."

"There are people in this town who would say you got exactly what you deserved, but I'm not one of them."

Flint shot his brother a look. "And why not?"

"Because I knew all along you were in love with Cassie. Before even you knew it. Didn't I try to talk you out of getting engaged, what? Three times?"

"And I didn't listen."

"No, you didn't. And now? Well, as the songs say, it's your turn to cry."

"Your sympathy is overwhelming."

"What do you want me to say? How many times did I tell you not to get involved? A hundred? A thousand? Did you listen? No."

"I can't help it. My brain agreed with you every time. But my heart? Went its own way."

"And look at you. Angry, sad, pissed off, and no damn good to me or our business."

"That's all you think about." He threw his hands into the air. "What about my life?"

"You've messed it up. You'll have to fix it yourself. I can't help you."

"And would you, if you could?"

Marty patted his brother on the shoulder. "Of course, I would. You're my big brother. I'd do anything for you."

Flint's lips twitched. "Wish I believed you."

"Look, I get you're angry, but don't take it out on me. Be mad at yourself." Marty left the room and closed the door behind him.

Flint stared out the window. As usual, his little brother had hit the nail on the head. He had no one to blame but himself. Still, he couldn't stop loving her. Maybe Marty was wrong. Maybe Cassie would come back. Sure, she'd never be the docile little housewife, but he didn't want that anyway. Never had, never would. He had to believe. She'd said it and he'd have to trust her heart.

He shuffled a stack of papers but couldn't focus. Pushing to his feet, he ambled over to the window. Pine Grove, a peaceful place to live, had captured Cassie's heart. She'd said so, more than once. If he couldn't rely on her feelings for him, could he count on her love for the town?

Then he remembered the crowd outside the stage door. The eager faces of people shoving paper and pens in front of her. Autograph hounds, people yearning to take a small piece of her home. And she'd obliged each and every one.

His brows creased. What did he want? He wanted a piece of her heart. Would he get it? Unlikely. Back at his desk, he forced himself to open the folder there and read the first document, a brochure of houses for sale.

"New listing. Fixer-upper."

Yeah. New listing. His heart. Broken, a fixer-upper. He looked at the picture and wiped a tear from his cheek.

DECEMBER 23

Cassie took the cake layers for their Christmas celebration out of the oven. Since she would be leaving on the morrow, they had tonight to exchange gifts. Next, she shoved a roast beef in and closed the door.

The meal would be memorable. Marty offered to create his famous mac-and-cheese. Flint opted for handling the salad. And Cassie was in charge of the meat and dessert.

She turned on the radio and switched to Christmas music. The carols and upbeat melodies did nothing to lighten her mood. Pulling the ingredients for frosting down from the cabinet, she forced herself to sing along. Damn it! She'd do everything to give Flint a heart-stopping Christmas.

He'd become so quiet, solemn, and distant. Uncertainty about their future clouded her heart. It's not like he'd proposed or even talked about getting engaged. Did he want her to come back?

Her love for Pine Grove covered even the icy winter. But she longed to return in the summer, the season she'd loved at Gram's. Why come back? If Flint didn't want her, she had no place to go and no reason to be in Pine Grove. She might as well knuckle under to her mother and continue chasing success around the world.

Spreading the white frosting on the dark-chocolate cake set her mind to thinking about colorful cake decorations. She opened the cabinet doors, poking around, but didn't find any sprinkles or even food coloring. So much for a holiday theme for the cake.

As she added icing around the sides, she faced a big question. What does the future hold? The time to live was now. She shut her mind to negative thoughts and hummed along with the radio.

When the cake was done, she yawned and climbed the stairs to take a nap. Snuggled down under the warm comforter, Cassie daydreamed of happiness with Flint, until her eyes closed.

"Hey, sleepyhead. Time to get up." A hand shook her shoulder. She spied Flint, smiling as he sat on the bed.

"Come on, honey. Dinnertime."

Cassie sat up. Covering her yawn, she studied his face. Was the old Flint back? Maybe.

"Let me wash up and I'll be right down."

He pushed to his feet and kissed her head. "See you downstairs."

Cassie brushed her teeth and slipped on flannel lounging pajamas. She skipped down the steps. The small tree she'd decorated had presents beneath it. Christmas music played and something smelled wonderful—must be the aroma of the roast mixed with the lingering scent of the cake.

Flint popped a bottle of champagne. In the kitchen, Marty carved the roast. Cassie carried a dish of creamy mac-and-cheese, and then the salad bowl to the table.

As they ate, Cassie stole furtive glances at the tree. Her gaze searched for a small box, in vain. She'd hoped to leave Pine Grove engaged. Forcing a smile, she tried to cover up her disappointment. Looked like this would be her last day in Pine Grove, maybe forever.

Her stomach churned. She turned down a slice of cake.

"Really? You made this work of art and now you don't want to eat it? Come on, Cassie. It's Christmas." Marty pushed a plate toward her.

"Let's do the presents." Flint got up.

"I'll make coffee." Cassie headed for the kitchen.

Flint, Marty, and Cassie sat cross-legged on the carpet and opened their gifts. Laughs from gag gifts like a tie with a bull on it joined sincere thank-you's for warm slippers, books, chocolates, and whiskey.

By nine, all the gifts had been opened. Marty poured a glass of brandy. Cassie's heart sank as emotion closed her throat. She forced a smile and ignored the sting of tears behind her eyes. As she went up on her knees to leave, Flint grabbed her arm.

"I wasn't going to do this. But the damn thing's been burning a hole in my pocket."

She met his gaze.

"I know we agreed while we're separated, we'd date other people or at least be free to date other people."

"Right."

Flint still held her in place. Marty stopped at the edge of the rug.

"But I don't want to. Date other people. So, even if you turn this down, even if you never wear it, I have to give it to you."

He pulled the small dark-blue velvet box from his bathrobe pocket. Cassie gasped. Tears she'd managed to hold at bay ran down her cheeks. Her pulse kicked up.

Flint opened it, revealing a gorgeous, round diamond ring. "It's not the fanciest or most expensive. But well..."

"Shut up and ask her!" Marty yelled from across the room.

"Marry me, Cassie."

"Isn't it supposed to be a question?" Marty cocked an eyebrow.

"Shut up, Marty." He focused on the woman who owned his heart—who'd always owned his heart. He pushed up on one knee. "Will you marry me? When you get back?"

Cassie launched herself at him, taking him off guard, knocking him to the ground, and falling on top of him. "Yes! Yes, I will!"

Flint laughed, closing his arms around her waist.

MARTY PRODUCED AN ICE-cold bottle of champagne he'd hidden in the back of the fridge. He popped the cork, poured, then made a toast. "The fourth time's the charm. May this one stick!"

"Won't be me taking off." Flint gave a laugh before taking a mouthful of the bubbly.

The three finished the bottle. A bit wobbly, Flint managed to carry Cassie up the stairs and make love to her. With her hand closed over his shoulder, she kept an eye on the stunning ring on her finger as he pumped into her. As usual, Flint's body pushed all other thoughts from her mind.

The strange presence of a ring on her finger woke her several times during the night. She held it up to the gentle moonlight tiptoeing in her window. The diamond caught the light, throwing it back with a brilliance mirroring her feelings.

Was she dreaming? She couldn't wait to call her mother, and when she spied seven o'clock on the clock radio, she threw down the covers, grabbed her cell, and headed downstairs.

"Mom? Did I wake you?"

"It's four o'clock in the morning."

"Oh. Sorry. Guess what?" Her voice bubbled up like fine champagne in a crystal flute. "I'm engaged!"

"What?"

"I'm engaged. Flint and I are getting married."

"Cassie, this is not a good time for jokes. Really. You're leaving for home today, right?" Her mother's voice didn't hold the excitement it had when she'd told her about Basil's proposal.

"Yeah. So? I'm coming back. And we can do the deed then."

Her mother snickered. "I assume you've already done the deed."

"I mean, tie the knot. Whatever. You know what I mean."

"Honestly. You have the worst timing."

"Aren't you happy for me?"

"Is this what you want? Are you going to give up a huge career I've killed myself to make happen for you over this...this...man?"

"I'm happy, Mom. Can't you share my joy, just for a minute? Can't you put career stuff on the back burner and share this with me?"

"If you're happy, I'm happy. Of course. It goes without saying."

"It doesn't go without saying."

"Okay. You're right. If you're sure he's the right man for you, I'm happy. There. Satisfied?"

Cassie frowned. It wouldn't get any better. "Okay, Mom."

"Did you get a ring?"

"It's beautiful!" she all but squealed.

"You can't wear it."

"What do you mean?" Cassie raised her eyebrows.

"You're filming next week. No rings during shooting. Remember? No jewelry at all. I told you not to pack any. There's no place to keep a diamond safe while you're filming. It is a diamond, isn't it?"

"Yes, it is." Disappointment swirled in her chest. "Damn. You're right."

"Leave it with him."

"I guess."

"Well, congratulations, darling. I've got to run. See you later." The line went dead.

"Gives me a reason to come back," she said, turning her engagement ring round and round.

Returning to the bedroom, she poked Flint. "Will you hang on to this for me?"

"Wha...? Huh?" He rubbed sleep from his eyes.

"Mom reminded me. No jewelry. I can't wear it while filming, and I don't want to lose it or have it stolen. Will you keep it for me? I'll be back to get it."

He sat up. "That's crazy. What do married movie stars do?"

"I don't know"—she grinned at him—"but I'll find out."

"Okay, okay. Give it to me." He shoved the blankets down and swung his legs over the side. Naked, he strode to the dresser and plucked out the tiny box. "Here. Gimme. We'll keep it right here. In the box. In my top drawer. Okay?"

She sighed. Reluctantly, she slid the beautiful ring off her finger and returned it to its resting place. Flint pulled her hand to his lips. "It'll be right here, waiting for you."

"Three months." She sighed.

"Seems like forever." He tucked the box into the corner of the drawer.

"It'll pass quickly."

"Yeah? I hope so."

Cassie pulled her suitcase out of the closet. "Time to pack."

"I'll make coffee." Flint shrugged his bathrobe over his wide shoulders and padded down the stairs.

After dressing quickly, she tucked her makeup bag into a corner of the valise. Sadness closed over her heart like a heavy coat. She wanted to cuddle up in front of the fire with Flint, not hop on a plane for California, followed by a grueling trip to Rio. Sure, Rio de Janeiro sounded exciting but not without Flint. She'd start working on the plane, going over her lines again. She closed the luggage and slipped her feet into sneakers.

"Ready?" Flint lounged against the doorframe. Words failed her so she simply stared at him, committing every line and whisker on his face to memory. The sound of a car horn broke the silence. Marty stepped up and hugged her. She kissed his cheek.

"Guess it's time." He grabbed the luggage handle and headed for the door. Cassie followed. Pain in her gut made her double over for a moment. Never had leaving been this hard.

"Flint, I..."

"I know, baby. I know. I don't want you to go, either. Only three months."

"Then together forever," she whispered, matching her palm to his.

"Together forever," he echoed.

Marty opened the front door and toted the suitcase to the limousine's trunk.

"I love you." Cassie looked up into Flint's eyes. "And I always will."

"I love you, too, Cass. Text. Email, Message, Instagram, whatever. Let's not lose touch."

"I'll do whatever I can. But I can't promise when or even every day. I don't know where we'll be or if I'll have Internet. But I'll tell you as soon as I know."

Flint opened his arms and she flew into his embrace. Tears coursed down her cheeks; emotion stole her voice. She sobbed against him. He hugged so tight she could hardly breathe.

"I'll love you forever, Cassie. Come back. Come back to me." His voice was soft and raspy.

Marty opened the door. Flint unlocked his arms and took her hand. They kissed once, again, and a third time.

"Miss, we have a plane to catch."

"Of course." Cassie cupped Flint's cheek and eased down on the seat. She swung her legs inside. Flint closed the door. She opened the window and reached out. They clasped hands until the driver put the car in reverse.

The cold stung her face. Cassie closed the window but flattened her hand against the glass. Marty waved then went inside. Flint stood still, his hand raised. She watched until they were too far to distinguish his facial features. But he stood on the stoop, like a statue, frozen in the icy wind. Cassie's heart thumped. When the car turned onto the highway, she couldn't see even the house.

The size of the adventure, the challenge awaiting loomed large. She knew this part so well, she had little worries about the character or the lines, but being in a foreign country on her own, away from her mother and Flint—missing him and everything familiar, scared her.

She'd figure it out, like she'd learned to do. Sitting back against the seat, she rubbed the place on her finger where the engagement ring had rested and wondered what lay ahead.

Chapter Twenty-Two

C assie awoke with the sun. Snuggled into a big bed in a rustic room, like a log cabin, she blinked in the bright light. After throwing on sweats, she padded to the windows and gazed upon a majestic view and a sign that read *Pousada Tankamana*. Must be the name of the hotel? She knew she was in Petropolis, in Brazil. Yawning, she scanned the room, finally spotting a coffeemaker. She put up a small pot and picked up an envelope with her name on it on the desk in the corner. The message inside read.

Welcome to scenic Petropolis, Cassandra. Please meet me in my suite #200 on the second floor for breakfast at 8.

Lucas Santiago

Luke was the director. Cassie checked her watch. On Brazil time, she only had twenty minutes before the meeting. She jumped in the shower and thought of Flint as she scrubbed her body. Leaving her hair to air-dry, she donned black leggings and a long-sleeved turquoise tunic. It was chilly in the air-conditioning.

"Welcome, Cassie! How great to see you. Isn't it beautiful here?" Luke pulled her into a brief hug, interrupted by a knock.

"Ah, food's here. I ordered for you. I hope you don't mind. Come in!" Luke headed for the table. A waiter brought in a large tray and set it down. Each plate was covered with a metal dome to keep the food hot. Both plates had the same food, scrambled eggs, bacon, and potatoes. The sweet pungent aroma of coffee drew Cassie's eye to a large pot.

"Brazilian coffee?" Her mouth watered.

"Absolutely. Here," he said, pulling out a chair.

Hunger gripped her belly. "This looks great." She picked up a piece of bacon. "What did you want to talk about?"

He gave her a smile she'd seen before. Having worked with Luke previously, Cassie read him like a book. He wanted something—something she probably didn't want to give or do or see or hear. She swallowed. He poured her coffee first. She narrowed her eyes and put her fork down.

"What is it, Luke?"

"The script has changed a little. I mean from the play."

"Okay. I'm sure I can learn new lines quickly."

"It isn't just new lines." He glanced down at his plate before making eye contact with her.

"Then what?"

"We've added a nude scene."

Cassie's eyes grew. "What?"

"A nude scene. A couple in fact." He lifted a forkful of food to his mouth.

"You've added nude scenes? I didn't agree to that."

"Actually, you did. See? Right here. You initialed. Where it says if nude scenes are called for, you agree to do them." He pulled a folded wad of papers from his back pocket. "See, right here. Lemme find it."

While he riffled through the pages of her contract, Cassie struggled to keep from throwing up. She'd had a big discussion with her mother about nude scenes. They'd argued about it, but Cassie had dug her heels in and refused to budge.

"You're closing a lot of doors over a couple of minutes being a little bit embarrassed."

"What would Dad say if he could hear you?" Anger had flamed in Cassie's breast.

"He'd say you're passing over big bucks."

"Fine. I have enough money."

"It's your funeral."

"It's my body, and my right to keep it private."

Her mother had shrugged. Now here she was, with famous Lucas Santiago hunting through paragraphs looking for her initials. She'd signed and initialed everything on the contract her mother had circled. Cassie hadn't read it. She'd simply trusted her mother. Mistake number one.

"Here it is. See. Your initials. You get a bonus. Extra hundred grand."

"Great. Just great."

"I thought we should go over those scenes here, in private. I'll tell you how I envision them unfolding."

Tears pricked at the backs of her eyes. Sold down the river by her own mother. And Flint didn't know about this. Wait until he found out. Shit. Damn. The last thing she wanted was to go over those scenes.

"You've got a nice rack. Time to expose it to your fans." He put down the contract and the roll he munched and retrieved a script from the sofa. "Here. Let's go over the scenes."

"Scenes? How many?"

"Two? Three? Not sure. We can add some, if you want."

"No! No. Two, okay. If I agreed. Okay. One would be better."

"Here." He thumbed through and stopped. "It's a scene here with Tom. Remember this from the play?"

"Of course. But I was dressed in the play."

"In the movie, you won't be. It was only a nightgown anyway."

"And Tom?"

"He'll be shirtless."

"That's all?"

"Do you want to be skin to skin with Tom Reynolds?"

"No, I don't."

"Okay, then. He keeps his boxers on."

Luke got into it, describing the emotion and actions of the scene. Cassie moved the food around her plate with her fork. She barely heard him. A shiver stole up her spine. Here she was, a million miles from home, on her own. Lucas Santiago didn't give a damn about her or her feelings. All he wanted to do was get the movie shot as fast as possible.

The only person who cared about Cassie was thousands of miles away. Her thoughts turned to Flint. As she pretended to listen and nodded in appropriate places, she envisioned what Flint would be doing.

Maybe he'd be getting up and putting on coffee. Or he'd stop off at the store to check on things before heading to his office. The air would be cold, but the sun might be shining in Pine Grove. Damn, why wasn't she there with him, instead of here, getting ready to be humiliated?

"NOT HUNGRY?"

"Nope."

"You're not upset about a little nudity, are you?"

"Of course I am. I don't do nude scenes."

"Then why did you sign off on it?"

"My mother." She sighed. "I trusted her."

"Always read anything before you sign it." Luke took the last bite of his food.

"You're right."

"I'm going to hold you to this. I have every right to. It's too late to rewrite the movie because of your childish modesty. I hope you understand."

"I do." Tears clouded her eyes.

"Oh, please. Waterworks? You know tears never work on me."

She shook her head. "It's not a manipulation. I don't want to do it."

"We'll make it a closed set. The scene is brief. I'll make it as easy on you as I can."

"Why are you doing this? This was a hit on Broadway without nudity."

"Because the titillation, the interviews with you about how it felt to do a nude scene, will bring viewers. People who already saw the show will come to see the movie."

"Just to see me naked?" Flabbergasted didn't begin to describe how she felt.

He shrugged. "Probably."

Another shiver shook her body. "You're putting me on display."

"Cassie, you're beautiful. Show it off. Haven't you ever been to a nude beach?"

"No."

"Worn a tiny bikini?"

"Not tiny."

"Yeah, but not big, either, I bet."

She wrung her hands in her lap. "But not naked. In front of strangers."

"Come on. Be a big girl. This movie is going to gross a fortune. And you get a nice bonus for the nude scenes. I'd planned on three, but we can cut it down to two. Better?"

"Better." Her stomach lurched. Cassie jumped to her feet and raced to the bathroom. She threw up. Tears cascaded down her face as she sank down on the floor, resting her hot forehead on the cool porcelain bowl.

A knock on the door and Luke's voice startled her.

"Hey, you okay in there?"

"Yeah. Be right out." She pushed to her feet, washed her face, and rinsed her mouth out. She returned to the table.

"A waste of an expensive breakfast."

"I'm sorry. I wasn't expecting this."

"Your nude scenes will take your career to a new level." He put an arm around her and squeezed her shoulder.

"Yeah, like a porn star."

Luke laughed.

"It's not funny."

"Come on. It'll show you're willing to do whatever it takes to make the best movie possible. You're an adult and not afraid to show a little skin."

She nodded. He was the director, she'd signed the contract, there was nowhere to go. "I get it." Her pulse jumped into high gear.

"Good girl. Take the day off. Swim, get a little sun, no burn though. Be careful. Enjoy yourself. Get to know Tom Reynolds. The scenes will go a lot easier if you two are friends."

"You mean if we're sleeping together?"

Luke laughed. "I didn't. But now that you mention it. Couldn't hurt."

"I'm engaged. I have a fiancé back home."

"Oh, really? I didn't know. Congratulations. Too bad for Tom." He rose and strolled over to the window. "Costume fittings begin tomorrow at nine sharp. Eva has everything ready, she only needs to check for adjustments. We begin shooting at the end of the week. Brush up on your lines. There are some changes from the play."

"Thanks." Cassie headed for the door with Luke trailing.

He hugged her. "Welcome, Cassie. This is going to be a great film."

She nodded and opened the door. Escape into the warm Brazilian air helped. Cassie returned to her room. She changed and headed for the pool. Staking out a lounge chair in the shade, she texted Flint.

Cassie: *We're staying at a nice resort. It's warm and sunny. Miss you loads. Wish you were here.*

"Miss, can I get you anything?"

A rumble in her belly reminded Cassie she needed food. "Can I get breakfast?"

"Of course, miss. You are with the production company?"

She nodded.

"Ah, then there will be no charge. What would you like?"

The attractive waiter with the wonderful accent took her order and flashed a stunning smile.

"Can I join you?" a deep voice said. Cassie looked up into the sea-green eyes of Tom Reynolds.

"Sure, Tom. Grab a chair."

"Thanks for agreeing to the nude scenes."

She cocked an eyebrow. "Oh? You want to see me nude?"

He blushed a deep red. "No, no. Sorry. That's not what I meant. I mean it'll boost the picture. You have so many fans. I'm sure they'll turn out in huge numbers to see you."

"To see my naked body? Great. Thanks." Sarcasm rolled off her tongue. "But it doesn't make me feel any better."

"I'll do everything I can to make you comfortable. Honest."

She noted the sincere look on his face. Yeah. Sure. Tom Reynolds was an accomplished actor and this might be an academy award performance.

FLINT PUT HIS COFFEE mug down and picked up his phone. The text from Cassie made him smile.

Flint: *Nothing exciting here. Take pics and send them. Missing you.*

He clicked on a new tab on his computer and searched for Tom Reynolds. He clicked on the man's Wikipedia post. He read and sipped until the mug was empty. Damn, the man had serious acting credentials. But he'd been married three times, was thirty-eight years old, and not dating anyone currently. Sweat broke out on Flint's brow.

"Have you signed those contracts yet?" Marty inquired from the office doorway.

"Huh?"

He approached his brother. "What are you doing?"

"Checking out the competition."

Marty stopped and read the screen. "He's not the competition. He's an actor. They're making a movie together. Get over it. At this rate, you're going to make yourself insane in a week. Please read and sign the contracts. We have to get going on those projects."

"Okay, okay." Flint clicked on "sleep" and turned his gaze to the pile of papers on his desk.

"Bring 'em in when you're done."

"Will do."

Flint leaned forward in his chair and picked up the first contract. He needed to put Cassie on the back burner. Who knew where this film would lead her? He had to trust her. Still, her being so far away and doing love scenes with another guy rattled him.

Trust was easy even when you lived together or at least in the same town, same state, same country? If he could see her every day, there wouldn't be a problem. But, wait—hey, wasn't the definition of trust being something to be extended without proof? He sighed.

Forcing himself to concentrate, he read through the contracts, made revisions on some, signed others, and trotted over to his brother's desk. "Here. Done."

"Thanks. How are you doing?"

Flint frowned. "Okay. I guess."

Marty made eye contact. "It's hard, huh?"

"You could say that."

"It's only for three months." Marty patted his brother's shoulder.

"Three months in Hell," Flint muttered.

He returned to his office, deleted the screen with Tom Reynolds smiling face, and grabbed his truck keys. His stomach told him it was lunchtime. He'd pick up something at The Cozy Café, drop in on Winnie, and check on the store. At least it would give him something to say to Cassie after her next text.

Bright sunshine filtered through his windshield, but it did nothing to lift his mood. As he drove, the drabness of his life flashed before him. There she was in exotic Rio de Janeiro with a handsome leading man. Here he was, skidding on slick, icy streets, going to and from the office and the grocery store. Why would she choose him? He had no clue.

And what if Tom decided to make Cassie the fourth Mrs. Reynolds? Flint was powerless to fight it. What could he do from so far away? As he drove, he wracked his brain to think of some way he could still be in her life.

He parked in The Cozy Café lot and went inside. Laura Dailey greeted him.

"Hi, Flint. What do you hear from Cassie?"

"Hey, Laura. Not much. She got there okay. What's on special today?"

After Flint ordered, he took a table overlooking Cedar Lake. Cold sunlight danced off ripples in the lake kicked up by the wind. The dock stood solid, despite the weather. His mind dialed back to lazy summer days, jumping off and racing to the float, of dunking each other, and lying in the sun with Cassie. He didn't notice Mrs. Dailey approach.

Carrying two mugs of coffee, Laura joined him. "You seem kinda down in the dumps."

"Missing Cassie, I guess."

"She's off shooting a movie, right?"

He nodded, taking a sip.

"I hear Tom Reynolds is her co-star."

"That's right."

"He's single, too."

"Yep." Sweat broke out on Flint's upper lip.

"Whatcha gonna do about it?" Her mouth set in a firm line.

"Me? What can I do about it? I'm a million miles away. It's all about trust, Laura."

"Oh, cow patties! Trust, my foot."

Flint's gaze connected with hers.

"You know the old saying, 'faint heart never won fair maiden', right?"

"So?"

"I had a couple of ideas."

His eyebrows rose. "You did?"

"Yep. Romance still runs deep in this old frame."

He laughed. "Bring it on, Laura." He listened in silence, drinking his coffee and nodding from time to time. When she finished, he smiled.

"Thank you. You've given me a lot to think about."

He paid his bill and steered toward town. Talking to himself out loud helped.

"Hell, I'm not dead. Not helpless. I can do stuff. Right? Right."

He pulled into a spot in front of the store and parked.

"Damn right." His step lightened as he made his way to the front door. The bell jangled when he went in. Winnie looked up.

CASSIE PEELED OFF HER sweats and shrugged a terry robe over her bare shoulders. After sliding her feet into flip-flops, she padded over to the makeup tent.

"Take off your robe, dear. Let's see what we have to do to your body." Tessa Allan rubbed her chin and narrowed her eyes. Cassie cringed as she shucked the garment.

"Here. They call it a 'modesty patch' or some such nonsense. Stick it over your private place." The woman stuffed something into Cassie's hand.

The tent flap opened, and Lucas Santiago appeared, script in hand. Fear spiked through her.

"Here. Go over your lines. It'll take your mind off things. The set is closed and ready. Thanks for doing this, Cassie." He shoved the document into her hands and left.

Cassie brushed up on her lines, ignoring the patter from the makeup lady.

"Been on a lot of sets with nude scenes. You'll be fine. It'll be over before you know it."

"From your mouth to God's ears." Cassie put the tiny patch in place, pulled on her robe, then strolled to the set. The lights were on.

"Tom, you come to her from behind. Grab her shoulders, gently. Will, get a shot in front."

The cameraman nodded. *Yeah, get a good shot of my boobs. Close up. Don't miss a nipple.*

Her body stiffened.

"Keep your robe on while we block the scene."

"Nervous?" Tom took her hand and kissed it. "Don't be. Think of it as only you and me."

Strong lights glared down, making her look away.

"You can't see beyond the lights. Like it's just us, you know?"

"Thanks, Tom." She gave him a small smile. But being naked in front of him wasn't any better. Half an hour later, Lucas called out. "Ready?"

Cassie swallowed and nodded.

"Okay, then. Let's go."

The assistant cameraman stepped between her and the camera and held up the electronic slate. "Scene 32, shot A, take 1."

After the guy clapped the slate together and stepped out of the shot, Lucas said, "Action."

She opened the robe, let it slide down, and tossed it to a chair off camera. The set grew quiet. She blew out a breath, grateful for the silence. She could pretend there was no one on the other side of the lights. Tom gave the cue.

"Tori, don't think about Cal. It's you and me now. Just you and me." He approached her from behind and curled his fingers around her shoulders. "Love me, honey. Love me as I love you." He spoke clearly, with passion.

An image of Flint flashed through her mind. She spoke as if directly to him.

"I do love you. I do. Yes, it's just us now. You and me. Forever. They can't stop us now."

"No, sweetheart, they can't." Tom spun her around and kissed her.

Then she was in his embrace, her face turned toward his neck. Cassie pretended he was Flint. Tom stepped back, slipped one arm under her waist and the other under her knees. He lifted her effortlessly.

"Time for bed." He carried her to the bed and laid her down.

"I'll love you forever, Derek." Cassie looked up into his eyes and saw Flint's.

Tom bent down to kiss her shoulder and work his way to her mouth. They stretched out on the mattress, and she kissed him with all the passion she felt for Flint.

"Cut! Fantastic!"

Tom rolled off her. Cassie clutched the sheet, covering her body.

"Wow. Whoever you were thinking of, he's a lucky guy." Tom's eyes glowed.

Cassie chuckled. "I hope he feels the same when he sees this movie."

"You two were great. Take fifteen."

A gofer handed the actors bottles of water. Makeup people touched them up, and they were ready to go.

"One down, one more to go." Cassie took a deep breath.

"That wasn't so bad, was it?" Tom's eyes pleaded with her.

"You were great. Still don't know why I have to be naked for this. I mean, I could wear a nightgown or a slip or lingerie, or something."

"It's all about the marketing for this one." Tom smiled. "You in the raw will draw people to the theatre."

"I know some people think that's a compliment. I don't. It creeps me out. People coming to peep at my body. Ugh." She shivered.

Tom put an arm around her. "Don't think of it like that. Think of all the guys out there who are madly in love with you and will see the movie two or three times, even buy the DVD, just to have the image of you."

"You make it sound nice, decent. Maybe if the guy was someone I was in love with, yeah. But total strangers? Too creepy. No thank you."

"I get it."

"Have you ever done a nude scene?"

"Full frontal? Nope. Guys don't have to."

"That's sexist."

"I suppose. But it's the way it is."

She sighed. "Yeah. I know."

"You were great. The next one will be a piece of cake."

"Are we doing the other one today?"

"I think so. Luke said it was easier to do those at the same time, even if they're out of order. He said it was a giant pain to clear the set."

"Okay. Let's do this and get it over with."

Tom patted her hand. She padded to the bedroom set and dropped her robe. *Flint. I hope you understand.*

Chapter Twenty-Three

When Cassie got back to her dressing room, there was a big package on the table. She plucked a card from the thin paper.

Happy first day.
All my love,
Flint

Grinning, she ripped the paper off, revealing a sumptuous bouquet of twelve...no, fourteen...no, eighteen roses. Pinks, whites, and reds mixed together provided vivid, velvety color.

She plopped down on a little bench and stared at the blooms then went about sniffing each one, inhaling the sweet scent of a flower at its peak. A knock took her by surprise.

"Cassie? You left your watch..." Tom entered. "Wow!"

She turned. "Huh?"

"Your watch?" He handed her the timepiece.

"Oh yeah. Thanks."

"Who sent those?"

"My fiancé. Isn't he sweet?"

"Fiancé? You're engaged?"

"Yep." She took the watch. "Thanks, Tom. Was there something else?"

"Nope." He frowned. "By the way. You were great today."

"So were you. See you tomorrow."

Tom raised his palm, his lips pulled up into a half smile as he left her dressing room. When the door closed, Cassie laughed, quietly, before turning back to the flowers. Not knowing exactly what time it was in Pine Grove, she grabbed her phone and tapped out a text to Flint.

Cassie: *Flowers are beautiful. Thank you. I love you so much!*

Cassie hung up her robe and got dressed. It was seven in Brazil, and her stomach protested.

A gofer stuck her head in Cassie's room. "Dinner's on in the dining room."

"Thank you." Cassie joined the cast and crew. Tom had saved her a seat next to him.

Day-after-day passed uneventfully. Cassie knew her lines, hit her marks, and got along fine with Tom Reynolds. In the evening, she crossed the day off her calendar and texted Flint good night.

Each week, something new arrived. He sent chocolates, more flowers, and even a new book, *Break My Heart*, the second one in the series she was reading.

Then it happened. When she hit the set, crew members buzzed about, taking furtive glances at her and then at a newspaper.

"What? What is it?" She reached for the paper.

Tom intercepted. "Nothing. Really. Don't bother."

"It's not nothing. Come on, Tom." She held out her hand. "Give."

He blocked her with his left shoulder, but she outfoxed him by reaching around his right and snatched the paper away. It was a copy of *Celebs 'R Us,* the rag that masqueraded as a newspaper.

The headline read, *Cassandra Wells and Tom Reynolds. Is it Love or Just an Affair?*

Horrified, she quickly flipped to the page where the story continued. There it was, a photo of her, nude, with Tom standing behind her, clutching her shoulders. Although it wasn't full frontal, her breasts were exposed except for two black bars obliterating her nipples. Her stomach knotted, and her pulse went into overdrive. She swallowed.

"This is untrue! It's a lie! Where did they get this?"

"Must've been some stupid bastard on set with a camera." Tom frowned.

"How could he get on the set? I thought it was closed!" Her throat was so dry she could barely speak.

"It was." Tom shook his head. "I have no idea."

The crew stared at Cassie with knowing looks. They didn't believe her.

"This is a shot from a scene. This photo was taken here, on the set. Not in my hotel room or Tom's."

"When are you two going to get engaged?" someone from the back piped up.

"Who said that?" Her face flooded with color and her voice with fury. Silence.

"What Cassie said is true." Tom spoke up. "We're not having an affair. That's taken from a scene from the movie."

"Where's Lucas? How could this happen?" Cassie shoved the paper under her arm and stormed up to the director's room.

When he opened the door, she pushed in, raving. Lucas glanced at the publication.

"That?"

"Yes, that! Who took that? How could you allow that? I thought it was a closed set?"

He shrugged. "I have no idea. People do things. Rags like this pay big bucks for sexy pictures. Who knows what lies the person who took the photo told the magazine?"

"But this is terrible!" Powerless to stop the spread of the magazine, Cassie panicked. "It's a violation. A personal violation." She took a deep breath.

"Is it?" He cocked an eyebrow. "I'd say it's great publicity. People will flock to see this movie. They'll be salivating to see the love scenes between two people they think are having an affair in real life."

"Oh yeah? Great. Just great." She popped her fists on her hips. "What about my fiancé? What's he gonna think?"

Again, Lucas shrugged. "That's life when you're engaged to a star. Let me finish my breakfast. I'll see you on the set. Don't worry, darling. This will blow over. You'll see. He'll forget. Especially when you tell him about the big bonus you got for doing the scenes."

Before she knew it, Cassie was in the hall. Fear spiked through her. Flint! She had to get to him before he saw the paper. She rushed to her dressing room and picked up the phone. It didn't matter how much the call cost, she had to talk to him.

RESTLESS, FLINT DECIDED not to make his own breakfast. He drove to The Cozy Café. Inside, the smell of fresh coffee soothed his spirits. Cassie had been gone for two months with one or maybe two more left to go. Every day he questioned his decision to let her go and still be engaged. At night, before he got into bed, he opened his top drawer, took out the ring, and stared at it. The twinkling diamond bolstered his confidence.

Th sizzle of bacon frying drew his eye. He took a table.

"Bacon and scrambled eggs, please, Laura."

"Coming up." She cleared the empty coffee mug from his table and returned quickly with a fresh one filled to the brim. On a neighboring table, he saw the local newspaper and a copy of *Celebs 'R Us*. When Laura put his plate down, Flint reached for the newspaper. Laura snatched the gossip rag.

"Oh, you don't want to read this." She shoved it under her arm but not before he peered at the front page.

"Not usually. But did I see Cassie's name there."

"No, no. Must be some other Cassandra." Laura turned to walked away.

Flint stared hard at the older woman as he closed his hand over her forearm. "Let me see that, please."

"Nope. I haven't read it yet. I'll give it to you when I'm done."

Flint raised his eyebrows. "What?"

"You heard me. I'll be finished with it in a week or two. Maybe three. You can have it then."

"What the hell is going on? Give me the paper, Laura."

She backed away. He rose to his full height, towering over her. "Laura..."

"Don't believe everything you read!" Her voice pierced the quiet in the café as she released her grip on the paper. Flint grabbed it and returned to his seat.

His eyes went immediately to Cassie's name big and red in the headline splashed across the top. *Affair?* He frowned. Shoveling in a forkful of eggs, he put the paper down on the table and thumbed through to the page with her story. Fortunately, he swallowed before he got there. When he spied the nude picture, his jaw fell open. He sensed the red in his face and put down his coffee cup.

Laura frowned. "Everyone's entitled to a trial before they're found guilty," she mumbled returning to the kitchen.

He read the short article. If a stare could start a blaze, the paper would already be ashes. The picture showed Tom's head bent over her neck. He was topless and so was she. He was kissing her, and she had her eyes closed in utter ecstasy. It didn't look good. Pictures don't usually lie, but they don't always tell the whole story.

"Must be a scene from the movie."

But Cassie had sworn to him she'd never do a nude scene in a movie. Hmm, then what could it be? Maybe, exactly what it looked like? The food he'd eaten sat like a block of cement in his belly. He pushed his plate away.

"Can I have this?" He looked at Laura. She nodded.

"There has to be a good explanation." Laura wrung her hands.

"I hope you're right." He pushed his plate away, dropped a ten on the table, and left.

Although he usually stopped by the store after breakfast, not today. He placed the paper on the front seat next to him and headed for Route 97. What he needed was a long drive in the mountains then a walk on the riverbank to clear his head.

Pain gripped his heart. They'd agreed to date others but fall in love? Not part of the bargain. Flint had divided his time between movies at the local theatre and television. Used to going out on Friday night, he strong-armed Marty into joining him for dinner at Homer's every Friday. Otherwise, he'd led the life of a monk.

But it appeared Cassie wasn't doing the same. In his mind, he brought up the image of her sad, tear-stained face peering at him from the window of the limousine as it took her away. Hell, that was the face of a woman who did not want to leave. Everything about her had reassured him she loved him and would return.

But now? With this evidence—if that's what it was—did he even want her? It crushed his heart to think she'd go off with Tom Reynolds, maybe even marry him, and not return, First, he had to give her a chance to explain.

His phone, sitting on top of the paper buzzed. He glanced at it. It was Cassie. Flint was too angry, too confused to talk to her. He let it ring and take a message. Damn, always a man to pursue the truth, did he want it this time? Or did he prefer to hide behind a convenient lie to get her back? This was insane. Living like this would never work. Something had to change, if they were going to be together. And that was a big "if."

DURING A BREAK, CASSIE grabbed her phone. She texted Flint.

Cassie: *We have to talk.*

She waited, but no response came. Tom came up behind her.

"Give him time. Guys need time to sort shit like this out." He gave her a brief hug.

"But I haven't had a chance to explain anything. I don't want to do it in a text or email. But he won't answer my calls or respond to my texts."

"Back off. Give him some space. If he knows you well enough to marry you, he won't jump to any conclusions. Not without talking to you first."

"He's mad. I can tell."

"By his silence?"

She nodded. "Flint talks. Hollers sometimes but always talks. If he's shut down, it's not a good sign."

"Give him space."

"He's probably jumping to all the wrong conclusions. I could kill Luke." Her hand balled into a fist.

"He didn't do it."

"He said it's good publicity. I wouldn't be surprised if he didn't get someone to do it."

"That rag pays a lot of money for a picture like that. Ten grand, maybe more."

Her eyebrows shot up. "Really?"

He nodded. "Makes it worth it for the rats of the world."

"It's no biggie for you."

Tom smiled. "Being sexually linked to the hottest actress today? It'll give my career a big boost, too."

At the end of the day, right before bed, her phone dinged. At last a text.

Flint: *Yes. We do. Not on text, or email or phone. Face-to-face.*

Relieved he was still speaking to her, she replied quickly.

Cassie: *Okay. I'll be finished here at the end of April.*

The reply came quickly.

Flint: *Will you return to Pine Grove?*

Cassie: *Yes. Where do you want to meet?*

She scrubbed her face and brushed her teeth with one eye on her phone. When she slid into bed, the response came.

Flint: *Meet me at my house. Let me know what time you'll arrive, and I'll be there.*

Cassie: *Okay. I love you.*

But the phone fell silent. No answer. No returning "I love you." Tears filled her eyes. How could this be happening? He was the best thing to happen to her, and now she was losing him? And where was trust? Didn't he trust her? She'd thought about texting, "It's not what it seems." But she changed her mind. It would simply raise questions she didn't want to answer in a text. He was right. They had to meet face-to-face.

She wanted him, wanted him to believe her, to love her, to be there for her while she lived through this shit storm. She'd had calls from all sorts of news media but refused to speak to anyone. Marty texted her:

Marty: *Don't give any interviews. Don't talk to anyone. Don't do anything. Give Flint time.*

Cassie: *Thank you.*

It was the best advice. At least she couldn't make things worse by keeping her mouth shut, right? But she missed Flint, missed talking to him. There were no more deliveries of flowers or candy. The gossip going around the set said he'd dumped her. As tough as it was, she maintained her silence. There was too much riding on this to mess it up with a stupid, offhand remark.

Nobody had the right to know anything except Cassie and Flint. Thank God for Marty. At least she'd have time with Flint, time to explain what happened. She prayed he'd believe her. Meeting would give him a chance to see she was telling the truth. A good actress on stage or screen, Cassie Wells was a lousy liar and he knew it.

She wiped her eyes and took a deep breath. Flint would see the truth and things would be okay again. She had to believe that.

IT WAS A SUNNY SPRING day in Pine Grove. As the mountain snow melted, it made the roads muddy but nourished flowers. There were daffodils blooming everywhere. The bitter cold of early March had kept the flowers from bursting forth, but they were in full force now and spreading dazzling color everywhere.

Cassie took a limousine from the airport right to Flint's house. She left her bags on the front stoop and went for a walk. His house abutted the woods but wasn't far from Cedar Lake, either. She did an eeny, meeny, miny, moe to decide which path to take.

After texting Flint her arrival time, he'd responded he had a meeting and would join her as soon as he could. She wandered down the street, among the quiet houses hugged by bushes and tucked away on perfectly mowed lawns.

Begging and pleading with Lucas resulted in her getting an unedited DVD of the first half of the movie, which included her two nude scenes. She'd overnighted it to Flint. She hoped he'd seen it. Then he'd know the truth.

Of course, if he objected strenuously to her doing nude scenes, then they were finished anyway. If he really loved her, then he'd be okay with everything. And it would be her last movie for a very long time.

She stopped to watch a hungry squirrel dig up some of his buried treasure. The song of a chickadee drew her ear. The sun beat down. She unbuttoned her jacket. Nothing bad could happen on such a perfect spring day, could it? The chickadee answered her silent query. Her phone dinged.

Flint: *I'm here. Where are you?*

Fear fluttered through her. The moment of reckoning was at hand. She took off, running toward the house. Once she was in his arms, everything would be okay, wouldn't it?

Spying him by the front door, she called his name and waved. He raised his hand but didn't move. A bad sign? As she got closer, Flint came down the steps, moving toward her.

"Flint!"

As she sped up, he opened his arms. Tears of joy gathered behind her eyes. She hit him full speed, knocking him back a few steps. He laughed. Snuggling her face into his shirt, she clasped his middle tight.

"Can't breathe."

She loosened her grip, grateful to hear his voice. "Sorry."

"Let's go inside. Coffee?"

"Sure."

He opened the door and picked up her luggage. After depositing it by the stairs, he entered the kitchen. The aroma of fresh coffee wafted toward her. The familiar smell of the old house soothed her. To be home again felt so damn good!

Flint prepared two mugs then carted them outside. They sat on chairs on the deck, facing the backyard. The bird feeders were up and filled, providing them with feathered company.

"I don't know where to start." she said, then took a sip.

"How about at the beginning? I thought you weren't going to do nude scenes?" His eyebrows rose.

Cassie mustered all the strength she could to keep from kissing him. He'd greeted her like an old friend, not a fiancée.

"Well, I guess I messed up by not reading the contract myself. I kinda trusted Mom..." she began then ran through the whole story.

Cassie made eye contact with him. As she related the details, she noted his response. He seemed sympathetic but only as a friend.

"So you were naked with Tom Reynolds only on the set?"

She nodded. "He was very nice about it, too."

Flint laughed. "I'll bet he was."

"No. Really. He didn't make me feel uncomfortable or stare at my privates or anything."

"I bet that was hard to do."

"I didn't ask, and he didn't say."

"I hope you understand I don't like that you spent a lot of time naked with this guy." Flint shifted in his seat.

"I do. I get it. And if things were reversed, I wouldn't, either. But nothing happened."

His eyebrows rose again. "Did you want something to happen?"

Tears choked her. She took a deep breath. "I only want you, Flint. Then, and now."

He handed her back the DVD.

"Did you watch it?"

"I did."

"What did you think?"

"I'm impressed how much better a movie is when it's edited."

"Come on. You're stalling." She rested her hand on his.

"Okay, yeah. Sure. I saw the nude scenes. Was I happy? No. Was I totally appalled? No. It's business. I suppose it's naïve to think you could skirt it forever. I wasn't prepared. Didn't expect it. I almost choked to death when you dropped your robe."

"I figured seeing it was better than any explanation."

"I did get that the picture in the newspaper had been taken on the set and not in a hotel room."

"And were you satisfied?"

"You mean, was I convinced you weren't sleeping with Tom Reynolds? Maybe. I mean, even if the picture was bogus, did you have a relationship with him?"

Her mouth fell open. She hadn't expected that. Facing him, she spoke. "No. I did not sleep with Tom. We became friends. Platonic friends. Only friends."

"Any plans to see him again?"

"Maybe at the premiere?" Cassie crossed her legs.

"Oh. Yeah. Forgot about that."

"Are you okay with everything?" She willed it to be so.

"I guess."

"That's not very positive, Flint. Didn't you miss me?" Her heart sank. Even after this was cleared up, he hadn't expressed his love or said he'd missed her or wanted to continue. Nothing. Was she wrong about what they'd had?

He pushed to his feet and walked to the edge of the deck. He cleared his throat several times. "Are you kidding? How can you ask me that?"

"How can I *not* ask you?"

Still facing away, he spoke. "I missed you every minute of every hour, every morning when I woke up and you weren't there. Every night when I fell into bed exhausted, running around like a lunatic so I could sleep through the night without you there. I crossed off every day. I can produce the calendar if you don't believe me. Every time I took down my coffee mug, I couldn't stop staring at yours, sitting on the shelf." He turned toward her, his face flushed, eyes full. "I couldn't stop wondering if I'd ever fill your cup again. If I'd ever see you again. Or if you'd disappear."

Cassie sucked in air. "Flint..."

"Did I miss you? Yeah. I missed you. Every God damn day." He nodded, turning his back to her. She saw his arm move up as he wiped his eyes with his hand.

Emotion rushed through her, robbing her of speech. She pushed up from her chair and came up behind him, winding her arms around his middle, resting her face on his broad back.

"Oh my God. Flint. I'm so sorry. So very sorry. I love you so much."

He turned, taking her in his arms. His mouth came down on hers in a hungry kiss. Cassie stepped back.

"You didn't trust me?"

"Of course I did. But the picture was pretty convincing. And I know Reynolds' rep."

"Maybe that's all gossip, too. He seemed like a pretty decent guy." Tom never made a pass.

"Glad to hear that, and glad it's over."

"So you did trust me?"

"I wasn't going to leave without giving you a chance to explain."

At long last, the tightness in her chest eased.

"I love you, Cassie. I have for years. Marty was right. You messed up those engagements. Because it was always you I wanted."

She smiled at him. "And now you have me."

He reached into his pants pocket and pulled out the small blue velvet box. "Can you put this back on now? And keep it on?"

She nodded. Flint slipped the ring on her finger. Cassie stared at it and beamed.

"Mrs. Flint McKay." He smiled.

"Mrs. Cassie McKay."

He chuckled. "I stand corrected."

She pushed up on tiptoe to kiss him. He held her against his chest, sliding his hands down to her hips.

"Wanna go upstairs?" he whispered.

"Thought you'd never ask."

Epilogue

It was hot, even for July. Cassie and Flint padded down to the dock at Cedar Lake at midnight.

They jumped in and swam to the float. Pulling up on the ladder, she stretched out and stared at the moon.

"Have you decided on a date yet?" Flint took her hand in his.

"Uh-huh."

"When?"

"January."

He squeezed her hand. "Why wait so long?"

"Because I have a new job."

He cocked his head. "A job?"

"Yep. Starring in a play."

"Uh-oh. Broadway?"

"Nope."

He sat up. "Where?"

She rolled over. "Right here. In Pine Grove."

His eyebrows rose.

"Mindy Winslow offered me the lead in her fall play. So we have to put the wedding off until after it closes. You okay with that?"

He grinned then kissed her forehead. "Absolutely."

"Good."

He kissed her nose. "January it is."

"Yep. A small wedding. Honeymoon somewhere warm?"

"I'll get on it." He kissed her chin. "Anything for you, my leading lady forever."

Wrapped in each other's arms, they kissed in the moonlight.

THE END

If you enjoyed this story, would you please leave a short review?

Books by Jean C. Joachim

HARLEY BRENNAN, RUNNING BACK
OVERTIME, THE FINAL TOUCHDOWN
A KING'S CHRISTMAS
THE MANHATTAN DINNER CLUB
RESCUE MY HEART
SEDUCING HIS HEART
SHINE YOUR LOVE ON ME
TO LOVE OR NOT TO LOVE
HOLLYWOOD HEARTS SERIES
IF I LOVED YOU
RED CARPET ROMANCE
MEMORIES OF LOVE
MOVIE LOVERS
LOVE'S LAST CHANCE
LOVERS & LIARS
His Leading Lady (Series Starter)
NOW AND FOREVER SERIES
NOW AND FOREVER 1, A LOVE STORY
NOW AND FOREVER 2, THE BOOK OF DANNY
NOW AND FOREVER 3, BLIND LOVE
NOW AND FOREVER 4, THE RENOVATED HEART
NOW AND FOREVER 5, LOVE'S JOURNEY
NOW AND FOREVER, CALLIE'S STORY (prequel)
MOONLIGHT SERIES
SUNNY DAYS, MOONLIT NIGHTS
APRIL'S KISS IN THE MOONLIGHT
UNDER THE MIDNIGHT MOON
MOONLIGHT & ROSES (prequel)
LOST & FOUND SERIES
LOVE, LOST AND FOUND
DANGEROUS LOVE, LOST AND FOUND
NEW YORK NIGHTS NOVELS

THE MARRIAGE LIST
THE LOVE LIST
THE DATING LIST
PINE GROVE SERIES
UNPREDICTABLE LOVE
BREAK MY HEART
RENOVATING THE BILLIONAIRE
YOU BELONG TO ME
JUST ONE KISS
REWRITE THE STARS
SHORT STORIES
SWEET LOVE REMEMBERED
HOLIDAY HEARTS
CHAMPAGNE FOR CHRISTMAS
CHRISTMAS DUET
HANUKKAH HEARTS
SANTA'S SURPRISE
THE FINAL SLAPSHOT
THE HOUSE-SITTER'S CHRISTMAS
THE HOUSE-SITTER'S COUNTRY CHRISTMAS
TUFFER'S CHRISTMAS WISH
HANUKKAH HEARTS

About the Author

Jean Joachim is a USA Today best-selling, award-winning, international romance fiction author, with books hitting the Amazon Top 100 list since 2012. She writes contemporary romance, which includes sports romance and romantic suspense.

Liz & Nick: One Fine Day won second place in the erotic romance category of the Oklahoma Romance Writers of America's 2018 International Digital Awards.

Dangerous Love Lost & Found, First Place winner in the 2015 Oklahoma Romance Writers of America, International Digital Award contest. *The Renovated Heart* won Best Novel of the Year from Love Romances Café. *Lovers & Liars* was a RomCon finalist in 2013. And *The Marriage List* tied for third place as Best Contemporary Romance from the Gulf Coast RWA.

To Love or Not to Love tied for second place in the 2014 New England Chapter of Romance Writers of America Reader's Choice contest.

She was chosen Author of the Year in 2012 by the New York City chapter of RWA.

Married and the mother of two sons, Jean lives in New York City. Early in the morning, you'll find her at her computer, writing, with a cup of tea, and a secret stash of black licorice.

Jean has 57 books, novellas and short stories published. Find them here:

JEAN C. JOACHIM

http://www.jeanjoachimbooks.com. Chat with Jean in her Facebook group, JJ's Book Buddies. Join here: https://www.facebook.com/groups/489790604419710/

Made in the USA
Middletown, DE
28 December 2020

30184496R00184